Praise for
Cassie Edwards's Indian Romances

"*Silver Wing* presents readers with a meaningful portrait of the proud Nez Perce and their love and respect for the land—an adoration that translates itself through a lovely story."
—*Romantic Times*

"Cassie Edwards pens simply satisfying Indian romances." —*Affaire de Coeur*, for *Lone Eagle*

"Heartwarming, very descriptive, the story will make you think. Clearly essential for your fall reading list." —*Rendezvous*, for *Rolling Thunder*

"A fine writer . . . accurate. . . . Indian history and language keep readers interested."
—*Tribune* (Greeley, CO), for *Wild Bliss*

"Edwards moves readers with love and compassion."
—*Bell, Book, and Candle*, for *Flaming Arrow*

"Edwards puts an emphasis on placing authentic customs and language in each book. Her Indian books have generated much interest throughout the country, and elsewhere."
—*Journal Gazette* (Mattoon, IL), for *Wild Abandon*

Sun Hawk

Cassie Edwards

A SIGNET BOOK

SIGNET
Published by New American Library, a division of
Penguin Putnam Inc., 375 Hudson Street,
New York, New York 10014, U.S.A.
Penguin Books Ltd, 27 Wrights Lane,
London W8 5TZ, England
Penguin Books Australia Ltd, Ringwood,
Victoria, Australia
Penguin Books Canada Ltd, 10 Alcorn Avenue,
Toronto, Ontario, Canada M4V 3B2
Penguin Books (N.Z.) Ltd, 182–190 Wairau Road,
Auckland 10, New Zealand

Penguin Books Ltd, Registered Offices:
Harmondsworth, Middlesex, England

First published by Signet, an imprint of New American Library,
a division of Penguin Putnam Inc.

First Printing, May 2000
10 9 8 7 6 5 4 3 2 1

PUBLISHER'S NOTE
This is a work of fiction. Names, characters, places and incidents are
either the product of the author's imagination or are used fictitiously,
and any resemblance to actual persons, living or dead, business
establishments, events, or locales is entirely coincidental.

With much love and pride I dedicate *Sun Hawk*
to my beloved niece and nephew—
Aimee Decker and Brian Decker.
For always,
Aunt Cassie

Forever, my love,
Forever my life,
Forever my heart belongs to you.
The paths we walk,
The talks we talk,
The love only we can have,
The heartaches we share,
Shall always make us strong.
Everything that we endure,
Makes our love
. . . . Forever stronger . . . .
Forever our hearts,
Forever our minds,
Forever our love will last through time,
Everything life can bring,
Makes our love,
. . . . Forever stronger . . . .

—Donna C. Bradshaw Keeton
(For Gary, her husband)

1

My life, as spider's web's cut off,
Thus fainting have I said,
And living man no more shall see,
But be in silence laid.
—Anna Bradstreet

The Minnesota Wilderness—1840
September, Bina-kwa-gisis, *"Leaves Falling Moon"*

Wa-wassimo, lightning, was flashing in lurid streaks across the darkening sky. Like summer rain, autumn leaves were falling from the trees as the wind became brisk and began to howl.

Suddenly it was a world of black, rolling clouds. Lightning leaped from one cloud to the other. The thunder sounded like the distant rolling of many drums.

Chief Summer Hope of the Northern Lights band of Ojibwa knelt on a high bluff, her eyes fearfully watching the play in the heavens, the suddenly much colder wind sending goosebumps up and down her flesh.

She was dressed in a beaded buckskin dress and knee-high moccasins, her hair hanging in long, thick braids down her slim, straight back. She had left her village alone not only to collect herbs and roots for medicinal purposes, and wild greens for her meals, but also to take this time to pray for her people and for strength to do the job assigned her.

When her chieftain father had died, Summer Hope had been named chief, and now she had the full responsibility of seeing that things were right for her people.

Since it was a rare thing for a woman to be chief, she felt this responsibility even more deeply inside her heart than most men might.

Ay-uh, yes, an *ee-quay*, a woman, had much to prove, yet so many said that she had already proven enough to her people. On the fateful day of her parents' deaths during a snowslide in Northern Canada, she had saved others, even knowing that she had just lost the two most precious people in her life.

Realizing that no one could get to her parents in time, since they had been covered by tons of snow, she had hurried to help dig out those who were close enough to the surface to be saved.

That day had changed everything in Summer Hope's life. She had lost her parents, but because her people saw her as *nush-ska-wee-zee*, strong and capable, a woman of much courage, she had been given the honor of leading them as chief.

Shortly after that tragic snowslide, and hating the snow and mountains where her parents still lay buried, Summer Hope had decided that her people would be better off leaving the icy northern country of Canada and moving south into the land of many lakes.

On their search for the perfect place to build their wigwams, Summer Hope had discovered a new fort just inside the border between Canada and America, not that far north of the Minnesota Territory. She had decided that she would take her people onward out of Canada, yet stay close enough to the fort to be able to purchase provisions.

Her people were proud of their new home. It was *mee-kah-wah-diz-ee*, beautiful, a place beside the mighty waters of Lake Superior.

Summer Hope had since learned enough about the Englishmen at the fort to know that it was a Northwest Company that had completed its move to Fort William in 1805 after abandoning the Grand Portage fort in 1803.

Since she and her people had only been in the area for a short time, they had not made acquaintance yet with those who resided at the fort. They had been busy establishing their village.

Most of their homes were built now, but there were still those who had to get ready for the onslaught of the long winter months . . . months that should be much more tolerable than they had been in Canada.

One thing was for certain—she was glad to have discovered that America's Secretary of War did not think that treaties alone were enough to keep peace among whites and Indians. Since he thought that dishonest traders and land-hungry settlers were the cause of Indian unrest, he had seen to it that laws were enacted to control the activities of white traders and settlers in the Minnesota Territory.

Congress had passed a series of laws called the "Indian Trade and Intercourse Act," which required the licensing of traders, forbade the purchase of Indian lands by individuals, and punished whites who committed crimes against the red man.

It had become a crime for non-Indians to hunt or destroy game on this land of beautiful lakes.

Passports were even required for travel in Indian country!

That made this land even more desirable to Summer Hope. Her Ojibwa people felt blessed to find their new home beside a beautiful lake with its shimmering crystal water surrounded by forest land. From the forest came many things that made life good for them. From the waters of Lake Superior came wonderful fish.

Another crash of thunder and several drops of rain on her face brought Summer Hope from her deep thoughts. She gazed heavenward again and knew that rain would soon fall in blinding sheets.

But she could not leave just yet. She had not prayed.

She smiled as she thought about how the *Anishinabe* spiritual philosophy, culture, and traditions were blended together as though woven into a fine piece of cloth. Each part was like a different color or fiber, and together they made a beautiful piece, representing the lives of the Ojibwa people.

Long, long ago, *Gitchie Manido* sent them a being who was both physical and spiritual in makeup. This being's name was *Way-na-boo-zhoo* and had been sent to teach the Ojibwa about the mysteries of life and proper moral behavior. *Way-na-boo-zhoo* could change itself into any animal, mineral, or plant. It could also take human form. It showed them how foolish their people sometimes were.

Lifting her eyes, Summer Hope prayed to *Gitchie Manido* to give her the wisdom that her chieftain father had been blessed with. "Help me make wise decisions that will keep my people safe," she said aloud.

Caught up in the moment, she did not even wince when a bolt of lightning struck near her, splintering a tree in half.

"In the face of *nah-nee-zah-ni-zee*, danger, give me the strength to meet it with a brave *gee-day*, heart!" she cried.

A movement down below in the thrashing waters of the lake silenced Summer Hope's prayers.

She gazed down at a large canoe carrying four white men. Two of those men were wrestling with their paddles as they struggled to keep their water vessel afloat. The wind and waves threatened to topple it sideways.

Summer Hope was in awe of the canoe. It was much larger than those her people made.

And the men!

They were burly, whiskered, and . . .

Her heart stopped dead when one man suddenly looked up and saw her where she still knelt on the edge of the bluff.

For a moment their eyes met and held, until his attention was drawn back to the water. He gripped the sides of the canoe as it careened from side to side, then bounced high over a wave.

Still reeling from the piercing fear that had grabbed at her insides when the white man had noticed her, Summer Hope scrambled to her feet and rushed over to where she had left her basket of herbs and greens.

"*Gah-ween*, no," she groaned when she found the basket gone, along with it her half day's work of gathering the precious herbs and greens.

Hoping the wind had not carried it far, she looked from side to side.

When she saw no signs of it, and again remembering the evil-looking men, she forged her way down the side of the steep hill.

She now realized the foolishness of leaving the village alone, especially on land that was unfamiliar to her, where it was known that voyagers and bush rangers often passed by in the water.

Yet she had been told that, for the most part, the voyagers weren't a threat to the red man. They were not there to take her people's land, although she had discovered that some voyagers did leave the water when they reached Grand Portage. There they portaged across the land, carrying their big boats instead of riding in them, to get where the water could not take them.

Summer Hope had made certain her people's village was not established too near the portaged land for it to be a threat to their tranquility.

But as for the bush rangers? As though there were no laws, they came and went as they pleased, and took, and killed, and threatened anyone who met them.

She hoped that the men she had seen in the canoe were not bush rangers!

Finally on flat land, she made a sharp right and rushed into the dense forest, then took a shortcut to her village.

The rain only fell in drops here and there.

The worst was yet to come. She hoped to be home before then, in the safe shelter of her wigwam.

Again she thought of the white men. By now they should be far away.

But having seen them, and having felt threatened when the one man looked up and saw her, had taught her a valuable lesson today. She should never allow herself to feel totally safe while alone.

A noise at her left side made Summer Hope stop suddenly. But when the wind sent a spattering of leaves down from the limbs of a huge oak tree, she smiled in relief.

She took only one more step before her heart sank. The burly, whiskered man whose eyes had met hers stepped out into her path, a rifle leveled at her.

"Mademoiselle, squaw, where do you think you're goin'?" Pierre DuSault asked, his dark, beady eyes gleaming.

"*Koo-gah-bo-win*, get out of my way," Summer Hope said. She lifted her chin defiantly. "Let me pass."

"I'll let you pass, all right," Pierre said, chuckling as three more heavily whiskered, filthily clothed men stepped out and stood with him. "Right into our boat."

The Frenchman snickered as he glanced over at his friends. "Ain't that so, monsieur?" he said. "We bush rangers welcome a female ridin' companion, now don't we?"

"Pierre, you've hit the nail directly on its head this time," one of the men said, wiping drool from his beard with the back of his hand.

Pierre lowered his rifle. He spat over his left shoulder, then stepped up to Summer Hope. "Mademoiselle, we're only fooling with you," he said. It was obvious to her that he was forcing kindness, and she was sick at heart to now know that these men were bush rangers.

"*Ma chérie*," the bush ranger continued, "we're sorry if we gave you a fright or two. What we want of you is to talk trade. We have many trade goods for your Indian people. Would you like to see them? They're in our canoe."

"*Gah-ween*, no, I do not wish to see what you have," Summer Hope said, trying to keep her voice steady. She was afraid, for she didn't trust what they were saying. She could read people well and knew that these men had no good intentions in mind today.

"*Gee-mah-gi-on-ah-shig-wah*, I've got to go now," Summer Hope said guardedly. "I wish to go on to my village. I would like to get there before it begins pouring."

"Aw, now, squaw, surely you want to at least see the beads," Pierre said.

As he stepped closer to Summer Hope, her senses reeled with disgust at his stench, a mixture of sweat and old tobacco.

"Squaw, we have beads of many colors," Pierre continued. "They've been brought from Europe. We even have fine lace from Brussels!"

Were it true—so badly wishing it were—Summer Hope would love to see such fine lace and beads. But she knew that they were using this as a ploy to lure her to their canoe. She would not play along with them.

Seeing that she would probably be taken by

force at any minute now, she had to make a break for it. Only by doing that could she feel pride in herself—that is, if she came out of this alive.

Sucking in a deep breath of courage, Summer Hope took a sudden sharp step left and started to run. Her breath was knocked out of her when one of the other men grabbed her and wrestled her to the ground.

In the fall, her head hit a rock, momentarily disorienting her.

But she was conscious enough to know that she was being lifted into a man's arms.

She was very aware of being placed on the floor of the canoe next to trade goods that were protectively covered by a large piece of leather.

When the canoe shoved off again and rode the thrashing waves, the men laughing and talking about their latest catch, the squaw, Summer Hope found the strength to push herself up from the floor of the canoe.

She sat on a seat in the center of the vessel, her chin held high as the men jeered at her, sometimes even poking at her with their paddles.

She prayed that a large wave would come and topple the canoe.

Only then could she possibly escape these lunatics!

Until then, she made certain that she behaved in a chiefly way by displaying dignity in the face of humiliation and danger.

2

As the storm became more threatening by the minute, Sun Hawk, chief of the Enchanted Lake band of Ojibwa, gazed up at the rolling black clouds. He winced when he saw flashes of lightning streaking down from the sky.

Fear was not the cause of his reaction. It was memories of another time, another place, when another storm was brewing.

Even then it was not the storm that had made him afraid, but the band of renegade Indians that had grabbed his father from the pulpit inside his small church in Kentucky. As one of them slung Sun Hawk, who was then called Jeffrey, across his shoulder and carried him as if he were a sack of potatoes, another renegade dragged his father outside.

When Jeffrey got outside, he was devastated to find his mother, Eugenia, stretched out on the ground, dead.

Today, dressed in only a breechclout and

moccasins, his muscled chest bare, Sun Hawk circled his hands into tight fists at his sides. He couldn't help but remember what had happened on that fateful day, when his life as a white boy changed into something entirely different.

After his Baptist preacher father was slain by a blow to his head by the blunt end of a hatchet, Jeffrey had been taken away on horseback by the murdering renegades.

He remembered now how he had looked back at the scene of the massacre and how his mother and father lay so quietly in the shadow of his father's tall church steeple. His eyes had moved then to a bell that was to be installed inside the belfry of the church on that day, a bell inscribed with his family's names . . . Herschel, Eugenia, and Jeffrey Davidson.

Tears came to his eyes even now as he recalled how proud his father was of the new church bell, which would have been rung on Sunday mornings to bring his father's flock to church for his special, heartfelt sermons.

On that day not only had his father been silenced, but also that *go-to-tah-gun*, bell, before it had even had the chance to ring out across the hills and valleys and streams of Kentucky.

The silence that day had quickly been broken by the war yelps of the renegades, who had ransacked his family's home, taking the meager valuables his parents had possessed. Most of the money his father received on Sunday mornings when the collection plate was passed had been spent to better his church so that more people would be lured into its pews.

As raindrops began to fall, Sun Hawk was brought back to the present and reminded of why he was beside Lake Superior this early afternoon. He had gone downstream from his village where hunting was good. His *gee-mah-nays*, canoe, was piled high even now with rich pelts.

Not wanting them to get wet before he had the chance to get home, he grabbed a thick buckskin and secured it over the pelts. His canoe was safely anchored onto the rocks.

As *ah-nah-mee-kee-kah*, thunder, echoed all around him and the waters of the lake crashed in great waves along the shore, Sun Hawk's thoughts returned again to that day when thunder and lightning and great winds added to his fear of being taken away by renegade Indians.

Their faces had been luridly painted. Their eyes had revealed a strange sort of *nee-shkah-dee-zin*, madness, in their depths. Their words were unfamiliar to him as they shouted to one another in their strange language.

But it had mainly been the knife secured at the waist of the Indian who held him hostage on horseback that had truly frightened Sun Hawk. He was not sure how long the renegades would want to fool with a young boy. One swipe of the knife across his throat would end his uncertainty quickly.

But the way they kept looking at him gave him hope. He had heard tell of Indians taking young boys and raising them as warriors. *Wah-bi-shkah*, *Ah-nee-shee-nah-bay*, white Indians, he had heard them called.

He had often wondered about how it would be to live among Indians in their tepees.

But he had never wanted to actually live with them.

It was just the curiosity of a small boy, sparked by the stories his father had read to him at his bedside before the evening prayer was said along with final good-night kisses and hugs.

Yet fate had led Sun Hawk into that sort of life, after all. After the renegades arrived in the Minnesota Territory, everyone but Jeffrey had grown ill with a strange spotted disease.

The men being too sick to stop him, Sun Hawk had escaped and traveled weaponless and on foot until he had passed out from exhaustion.

When he awakened, he was in a wigwam, an Indian's lodge with a conical roof, and was told in plain enough English by a friendly, soft-spoken Indian maiden that he had been found unconscious and brought to her village.

She had explained that her people were of the Enchanted Lake band of Ojibwa, who, even though they did not trade with whites, were not their enemy.

Jeffrey had broken down in tears and told her everything that had happened.

Understanding that he had no family left in

Kentucky, and that he was too far from his home to be taken back, anyway, the sympathetic Indian woman and her husband, who were childless, had adopted him. He became as one with their people, an integral part of their lives, even after whites came and established forts in the vicinity of their village.

By then Jeffrey was grown up and called by the name Sun Hawk, more Indian than white.

His skin was sun-tanned bronze.

His eyes were a deep brown.

His black hair grew to waist length, and throughout the year, except in the blustery months of winter, he wore only a breechclout and moccasins.

So trusted and loved by his Ojibwa people, at his age of twenty-five winters, when his adoptive chieftain father had died, they had named him chief. A powerful, noble man, Sun Hawk soon proved that he was the leader they had known that he would be.

But not long after he had become chief, he was orphaned. Brokenhearted over her husband's death, Sun Hawk's Indian mother died shortly thereafter.

Suddenly Sun Hawk's thoughts of his past were stilled when he caught sight of a large canoe racing by in the water in the middle of the lake. It was being whipped by waves and wind.

But that was not why Sun Hawk felt a sudden concern inside his heart. In this canoe was an Indian *ee-quay*, woman. Those with her were white bush rangers, two of whom were fighting the waves with their paddles to keep the canoe from capsizing.

It was the way the woman sat so stone-faced and straight-backed, not even wincing when the canoe threatened to spill her into the thrashing waters, and the look of rage in her eyes, that convinced Sun Hawk that she was not with the white men of her own choosing.

And he knew that no Indian maiden would ally herself with loathsome bush rangers. Since there were so many trappers and traders who wanted to come to the Minnesota Territory to deplete its land of game, a license to trade was required. Those who refused to purchase a license were called bush rangers, and most made their permanent homes in Canada. They came into the United States and hunted, then traded and sold their pelts away from the Minnesota Territory, where a license wasn't required.

The bush rangers that Sun Hawk had become acquainted with were all devious, scheming, heartless killers.

He had heard much about one bush ranger, especially, named Pierre DuSault. He was of French descent, yet he seemed more English than French since he had mingled so often with Englishmen.

Thus far Sun Hawk and his people had been fortunate not to have had a run-in with this Frenchman. They made certain to try to avoid contact with all bush rangers.

Sun Hawk didn't take any more time to think about who was with the woman. Nor did he stop to consider the size of the waves compared to the size of his canoe and that he could lose his whole morning's catch.

He could think of nothing but the safety of the woman.

The farther away from him she got with the bush rangers, his chances of being able to rescue her became less and less.

His jaw tight, Sun Hawk fought against the slapping of the waves as he pushed his canoe into the water.

After jumping aboard and getting seated, he grabbed his paddle and forced his muscled arms to take the canoe out away from shore.

He could no longer see the other canoe.

Rain was now falling in blinding sheets. The wind was howling. The waves were fierce and threatening.

But nothing would deter Sun Hawk's determination to save the Indian maiden from the white men.

He squinted through the rain for any signs of the bush rangers' canoe.

His muscles ached as he kept rhythmically pulling his paddle through the thrashing waves.

Sun Hawk jumped with alarm and looked quickly to his right when a great, quick bolt of lightning crashed from the clouds and struck a huge Norway pine, sending it down to the ground in a deafening thud.

When Sun Hawk looked back over the water, he was glad to see that the rain miraculously had all but stopped, as had the wind. There was even a break in the clouds overhead, and a rainbow with its vivid arch of color took shape along the far horizon.

And then he saw something else—pelts floating in the water, as well as paddles, and pieces of birchbark that had broken away from a canoe.

Sun Hawk's heart hammered inside his chest. The canoe that he had been following had surely capsized, but what of its occupants?

Had they drowned in the frenzy of waves?

Would he soon see the lovely, proud maiden floating lifelessly in the water?

And what of her abductors? Had they lived?

Sun Hawk hurried along, his eyes frantically scanning the water and then the shoreline for the woman.

He yanked his paddle from the water and his heart stopped for a moment when he saw her lifeless form stretched out on the embankment, her legs still dangling in the water.

As he turned his canoe in her direction, and he desperately paddled toward her, his eyes looked cautiously along the rest of the shore for the men.

When he was only a few feet from the woman and still had not seen the others, he hopped overboard. He dragged the canoe the rest of the way and beached it safely onto rocks.

His pulse racing, his eyes never leaving the

woman, Sun Hawk went to her and knelt beside her.

She was lying on her side, her long braids soaking wet and twisted beneath her head. Sun Hawk quickly saw how *mee-kah-wah-diz-ee*, beautiful, she was. Her skin was the same soft copper color of his Ojibwa people.

Her face was beautifully shaped.

Her lashes were long and dark against her cheeks.

Her perfect lips were softly parted, revealing smooth, white teeth.

Her buckskin dress was wet and clung to her body, accenting her shapely curves and the movement of her breasts as she breathed heavily in and out.

"And she is *bee-mah-dee-zee*, alive," Sun Hawk whispered to himself.

He bent down even closer to see if she was visibly injured. She was unconscious, but he hoped that was only because of the traumatic experience and her exhaustion from having saved herself from drowning.

A movement beside him in the tall grass made Sun Hawk flinch. He reached to his right and grabbed his knife from its sheath. Foolishly, he had momentarily forgotten about the bush rangers. Seeing the woman, being taken in by her loveliness, and being so relieved that she had survived, had made him think of nothing but her.

Ready to pounce on whoever might be lurking in the brush, he crept away from the woman and searched around him.

But when he discovered only a doe leaping past, he went back to the woman and lifted her into his arms and carried her to his canoe. He had no idea where she was from, or which tribe, so he had no way of knowing where to take her. Surely she had been abducted from somewhere way north.

He would have to wait for her to awaken before he could know how to return her to her people.

But what was important now was to get her far away from where the bush rangers' canoe had capsized, for if any of them *had* survived, they would certainly come looking for her.

Ay-uh, yes, now he would take her to a safe place until she awakened and told him where she lived. Then he would take her home, but hopefully their good-byes would not be final. He hoped to get to know her better . . . possibly even establish a more lasting relationship with her, if she did not have a husband, and if she wanted him to pursue her.

Sun Hawk laid her gently in the canoe. He reached beneath the buckskin covering and pulled out a dry pelt to warm her.

As he started to lay it over her, he noticed a cut at the back of her head and a slight lump protruding from it.

Now he understood why she was still unconscious. She had apparently hit her head when she had fallen from the canoe.

Somehow she had stayed conscious long enough to swim to shore and drag herself to safety.

He studied the contusion. It was not all that bad.

Soon she should awaken, but he would proceed until they were far enough away so that he could safely stop and build a fire to warm her. He would doctor her head wound with herbs that he would gather from the forest floor.

Carefully he wrapped her in the pelt, then glided off into the lake. As he rode the gentler waves, he kept watching over his shoulder for any signs of the bush rangers. Had they survived, they wouldn't have gotten far.

Sun Hawk knew not to let down his guard, knew that bush rangers would as soon kill a man as look at him, especially one whose skin color seemed to differ from theirs. He shivered at the thought of what they might have had planned for this lovely woman. Surely they would have taken turns raping her, and then would have killed her and left her to the wolves.

"Gah-ween-wee-kab, never!" he growled, his eyes filled with an angry rage. He would never allow anything to happen to this beautiful woman whose courage matched that of a man's!

3

Hither, my love!
Here I am! Here!
With this just sustained note,
I announce myself to you,
This gentle call is for you, my love, for you.
—WALT WHITMAN

Feeling as though they had finally traveled far enough, Sun Hawk paddled his canoe toward shore. He hoped the woman would regain consciousness soon and could tell him who she was, and where her village was located. He suspected that by now she was missed by her people. Surely warriors from her village were looking for her.

He hoped that after she was reunited with her people, she would want to become better acquainted with him. He had not taken a wife. Now at his age of twenty-eight winters, it was time for him to look more seriously at women and find the one he wanted to live out the rest of his life with. Although his duties as chief kept him satisfyingly occupied, there was an emptiness inside his soul that could only be erased by a woman sharing his bed each night.

He gazed over his shoulder and down at the woman, who was still in a deep sleep. Never had he seen such a face of perfection. It was hard not to keep looking at her. He knew that she was a woman of much strength and conviction, the sort that would shine like the sun itself next to a chieftain husband in council.

He smiled recalling the defiance in her eyes when she had been with the bush rangers. He would never forget that stubborn, proud lift to her chin. She had shown no signs of being afraid.

And she almost seemed as noble in bearing as a chief might be in the face of danger. Ah, if only he could have met her under different circumstances.

He wondered why she was so alone that the bush rangers had been able to abduct her.

Feeling the underside of his canoe scraping over rocks, he put down his paddle, rushed over the side of the canoe, and soon had it secure on the embankment.

The afternoon sun was now bright in the sky with only a few traces of puffy white clouds along the horizon. The wind had shifted to the south and was pleasantly warm.

Only after Sun Hawk had a fire going and had the woman snuggled in pelts close to it did he leave long enough to find the herbs required to treat her slight head wound.

He was gone for just a brief time, but when he returned, he was disappointed to discover that the woman was still in a deep sleep. At least the fire and the sun's warmth had dried her hair. And beneath the pelts, her buckskin dress was now only barely damp.

At least she was no longer chilled.

Needing to unbraid her hair to better get at the wound, Sun Hawk lay his small buckskin pouch of dried herbs aside and untied the thong from the end of one of her braids.

As he unwound her hair, his eyes returned to the woman's face. The more he looked at her, the more he was entranced by her.

But what if she was married?

What if she had children?

Even so, it would be hard for him to get her off his mind, for each moment he was with her, he felt more for her.

And it was not empathy over her having been wronged.

It was an attraction a man feels for a woman when he is taken, heart and soul, by her loveliness!

Knowing that he must concentrate on her welfare, Sun Hawk quickly unwound the second braid. He combed his long, lean fingers through her waist-length hair to straighten it. Its texture was like pure silk against his flesh.

A smell similar to jasmine wafted up from her hair, as though she might have recently washed it in rain water that had been perfumed with wild flowers.

"What am I doing?" he whispered harshly, dropping his hands. He knew that he should fight against his feelings for her, feelings that were new to him. He had never paid such attention to any other woman, but none had ever been as captivating as this one.

He firmed his jaw and focused only on helping her. He separated strands of her hair so that the contusion was readily accessible for medicating. He sprinkled some of the dry herbal mixture from his bag into the palm of one hand, then smoothed the medicine into the open wound.

When she winced and groaned, Sun Hawk jerked his fingers away.

Thinking that she was awakening, Sun Hawk's heart pounded as he watched her eyes. He soon realized that she had only been reacting unconsciously to the sting of the medicine.

Believing that he had placed enough of the mixture on her wound, and not wanting to cause her any more pain, Sun Hawk spilled the remaining herbs from the palm of his hand onto the ground, closed his small buckskin bag, and tied it onto the waistband of his breechclout.

Frowning, he again studied the woman at length. It just didn't seem right that she was still unconscious. He had sustained worse blows to the head and had not lost consciousness. Perhaps she had suffered before the spill into the water. If the bush rangers had already defiled her body . . . !

The sound of footsteps approaching behind him made Sun Hawk turn his head with a start.

His rifle was too far from his hand for him to grab it for protection.

He had no chance to even attempt to reach for it. Several warriors dressed in full buckskin outfits had rushed from the brush and surrounded him, their bows notched with arrows aimed directly at him.

One of the warriors laid his bow and arrow on the ground and hurried past Sun Hawk to kneel beside the woman.

As Sun Hawk pushed himself up slowly from the ground, he scarcely breathed. He watched the warrior unwrap the pelts from around the woman, then study her from head to toe, his fingers deftly parting her hair when he saw the head wound.

He turned and glowered at Sun Hawk, but said nothing. He turned again and just as he began to lift the woman into his arms, her eyes fluttered open.

She seemed disoriented as she looked past the warrior and stared questionably at Sun Hawk, then looked at the other warriors, who still stood with their arrows notched to their bows.

"Black Bear, what happened?" Summer Hope managed to say. "Where am I? How did I get here?"

She gazed again at Sun Hawk. "Who is that *ah-way-nish-ah-ow,* man?" she asked warily, then winced and closed her eyes when a sharp pain shot through her.

"You do not recall why you are here, or why

you are with this warrior?" Black Bear asked, giving Sun Hawk a quick frown. "You do not know this man?"

Summer Hope slowly opened her eyes again. "I remember a storm and much water, but nothing else," she said softly.

"Chief Summer Hope, when the storm came and you did not return from collecting herbs and greens, your people became frightened for you," Black Bear said thickly. "Your warriors have been searching for you. We only now found you."

He placed a gentle hand on her cheek. "My *chee-o-gee-mah*, chief, you are far from your home," he said. "Did this man abduct you? Did he bring you here? Did he . . . *wee-suh-gan-dum*, harm, you?"

"My head hurts, but I do not know why, or what happened," Summer Hope replied. Her eyes wavered when she gazed more intensely at Sun Hawk.

Sun Hawk, in awe that this woman was a chief, felt his insides tighten as her eyes moved slowly over him. He knew that she could tell he was not truly a red skin. His only hope was that she had heard about him and why he dressed and behaved as an Indian. A man who was even an Ojibwa chief!

News such as that did have a way of spreading far and wide. He was too proud of who he was and his part in the Ojibwa's lives ever to be concerned about what others, especially whites, thought about it.

But even though news spread from tribe to tribe, and band to band, he had not heard about this woman chief, which meant that she must be far from her home. He hoped to know everything about her soon, but for now, he must think about protecting himself.

Summer Hope's eyes suddenly narrowed angrily. "I do not remember anything, yet I see no reason for me to have been found with this man unless he had abducted me."

She eagerly wished to question the stranger about why a white man would choose to dress like a red man. But she did not want to give him any cause to believe that she cared an iota about him. She especially did not want him to know that she saw him as perhaps the most attractive man she had ever encountered.

As a woman, she knew that this man was special in some way, and she wanted to find out everything about him.

But as a noble chief, she must act insulted over being found in his company, surely forced to be there with him.

Sun Hawk realized that the woman had no idea who he was. Hoping that if he explained that he was a chief as well, and a person who would never harm a woman, they would believe him and allow him to be on his way, he started to speak up in his own behalf. He only got a few words out before he was stopped.

"I am—" he began, but Black Bear reached back and grabbed his hair and gave it a hard yank.

"If you want to see another *mo-kah-un*, sunrise, it is best that you keep your words to yourself," Black Bear hissed. "You will speak only when spoken to. You will especially not address our Ojibwa chief unless given permission."

Knowing that they were Ojibwa gave Sun Hawk his first glimmer of hope. Perhaps once their tempers cooled, he could explain everything to them. They would surely believe him and release him to his own people.

He saw much softness in how Summer Hope sometimes looked at him. By witnessing how she was treated so gently by the warriors, he knew that she was a woman who deserved gentleness, which meant that she was a woman with a good heart who would listen to reason when the time came for him to explain himself.

For now he would cooperate and stay quiet, for he had no other choice. He was only one man against a group of ten warriors. A confrontation with them could make them enemies forever. But since they were all Ojibwa, he imagined the possibility of them becoming allies against white interlopers on this beautiful land of lakes. The more Ojibwa warriors that could be combined as one large force, the better.

He smiled at the thought of what Summer Hope's reaction might be when she discovered that he, too, was an Ojibwa chief, even though his skin color did not match hers or that of her warriors. He would enjoy explaining how he had become chief of his proud band of Enchanted Lake Ojibwa!

He watched Summer Hope being carried into the forest by a large warrior. Although she was a chief, there was so much about her that was delicate and vulnerable, or else how could she have allowed herself to be taken by whites?

The way she laid her head on the warrior's chest ate at Sun Hawk, desiring her head to be on his chest instead.

He hoped that in time, once the air was cleared between them, she would see him as someone who could protect her, who would go to the ends of the earth for her!

He knew that he was letting his imagination run too wild, for although he at least knew now which tribe she was from, he still did not know if she had a husband, or children, or even ever desired to have either. Her career as chief could be her life . . . could fulfill her so much that she needed no man, nor children.

Those thoughts were stilled inside his heart when he was shoved into the shadows of the forest, toward the shine of the lake.

He looked over his shoulder to where he had been forced to leave his pelts and canoe behind.

His heart sank when he saw two warriors carrying his morning's catch and his weapon.

Through a break in the trees he saw his canoe

floating away in the lake, empty, and lost to him forever.

"Wee-wee-bee-tahn, hurry up! Move onward!" Black Bear growled at Sun Hawk. "You will soon see what happens to those who wrong Ojibwa women, especially those who wrong a chief!"

Again, Sun Hawk was tempted to speak up, but he realized they were all too intent on vengeance to believe anything he might say in his defense at this time.

They would probably even laugh at him if he told them that he, too, was a chief. They would probably mock him and say that he was lying, that he would use anything to try and get out of the trouble that he was in.

And he doubted they would believe him when he told them that he no longer saw himself as a white man, that he was Indian in all respects, that his thoughts, feelings, deeds, and desires were Indian. Inside his heart, too, he was Indian.

Ay-uh, yes, it was best to keep quiet until they were not as angry. Then he would tell them that he was a powerful chief, that he was a man of peace . . . that he was also Ojibwa!

He would tell them that if they did not set him free, his warriors would come and find him just as they had gone after their own chief. He would warn them that should his loyal, devoted warriors find him being held prisoner, they might not wait for an explanation before doing what they saw was right.

He hated thinking that the lovely chieftain woman might suffer in the end, after all, and at the hand of Ojibwa, instead of white bush rangers.

Somehow he had to find a way to make sure that did not happen!

When he reached the lake, he saw several beached canoes. He was forced into one, while the woman got into the one next to him.

She turned to him as she sat down on the seat, her arms wrapped in blankets, and their eyes met and held. Sun Hawk found it hard to read her expression. She was trained well as a chief, for she knew how to control her emotions and disguise all feelings that might betray her.

Sun Hawk had the same skills. He forced himself to look as blankly back at her as she looked at him.

The canoes were sent out into the water and they began traveling, single file, farther and farther away from land and the forest he always passed through to get to his village. This morning, when he had left for the hunt, he had not even thought of facing danger before night fell!

4

Diverge, fine spokes of light, from
the shape of my head, or anyone's
head, in the sunlit water!
                    —WALT WHITMAN

Glad to be alive after the traumatic spill into the
lake during the worst of the thunder storm,
Pierre DuSault stumbled through the forest, his
eyes intent on the glow of a fire in a clearing
ahead.

He found it hard to put one foot ahead of the
other. When he had fallen into the water, he had
been sucked beneath the surface over and over
again, his strength weakening more each time
he struggled to get back to air.

And when he had finally reached the shore,
he had fallen asleep from exhaustion.

On awakening, he realized that he might be
the sole survivor from the canoe. There hadn't
been any sign of the others.

His thoughts went quickly to the woman. If
she survived, he needed to find her and silence
her before she had a chance to tell her warriors
about him. They would come searching for him
and would not hesitate to kill him.

But first he needed food, dry clothes, warmth, and rest. When he heard laughter coming from the campsite ahead, he had hopes of finding someone who would befriend him and help him. Perhaps if he told them about the expensive pelts that had gotten lost in the storm, they might help him search and rescue what they could.

They might even be intrigued at the thought of finding an Indian squaw that he would offer to share with them.

Finally at the break in the trees, Pierre's weak knees would not hold him up any longer. They buckled. He fell out into the open, his eyes pleading with the two white trappers as they turned and gave him a look of bewilderment.

When he saw their own stack of hides, which must have been acquired illegally in this area, he smiled, for he knew that he had found more bush rangers. All bush rangers looked out for each other, and these men would take him in.

"Bonjour! Bonjour! Help me," he cried, crawling toward the two men. His throat was scratchy and sore from having swallowed so much water while trying to save himself from the waves. He reached a trembling hand out to the men as they rushed to their feet and ran toward him. "Help me!"

One of them helped him from the ground, flung one of Pierre's arms around his shoulder, then eased him to the campfire.

In a rush of words Pierre explained to the

men, who thankfully were of French descent like him, what had happened.

When he mentioned the woman, he saw their eyes light up with interest and knew that he had found more allies in crime after having lost his other companions.

He smiled as a steaming hot cup of coffee was placed into his hands. One of the men helped him down onto soft blankets beside the fire.

"You've got yourself a deal," Jacques Cadoux chuckled as he leaned his whiskered face into Pierre's. "We've always wondered how it would feel to have an Injun squaw."

"Monsieur, it's better'n you'd ever imagine," Pierre said, pretending to have already been with the woman sexually. "It's exquisite. *Merveilleux*. Why, you'll all find yourself fightin' over who'll bed her next."

Their eyes gleamed as they glanced from one to the other, then Jacques responded, "We'll do what we can to help you."

"*Merci beaucoup*," Pierre said. He offered a handshake. "Pierre's my name." He grinned. "If you help me find the squaw, I guarantee you that pleasure's my game."

Laughing, the men took turns shaking Pierre's hand.

5

O flames that glowed!
O hearts that yearned!
They were indeed too much akin.
The drift-wood fire without that burned,
The thoughts that burned and glowed within.
—HENRY WADSWORTH LONGFELLOW

Now that he was at Summer Hope's Ojibwa
camp, Sun Hawk understood why he hadn't
known about it. It sat farther north from where
his people usually went to hunt or fish, just
barely south of the Canadian border, not that
far from Fort William.

Sun Hawk and his band avoided most white
people. He never traded with them. He had
kept his people cut off from the troubles that
came with dealing with whites, especially the
British.

And if Summer Hope and her people had
moved this close to the fort for the convenience
of trading with them, they were soon to be disappointed. News had spread to Sun Hawk's
camp that, as the Grand Portage fort had been
abandoned, so would this fort in the near future.

As he was shoved roughly up the embankment toward the village, Sun Hawk saw that
although many wigwams were erected, these

Ojibwa were still in the process of building more, an indication of the newness of the camp.

He could even hear the sound of trees being felled a short distance away, and he soon saw which kind of trees. Birch. They were being used to construct more birchbark canoes.

His gaze shifted and stopped on great red slabs of meat drying on racks in the shade. The warriors must be skilled hunters, he thought.

The fragrance of food cooking over fire pits wafted toward Sun Hawk. He felt an immediate hunger, for it had been many hours since he had eaten.

But even so, food was not important at this time. Proving his innocence was.

Thus far, every time he had opened his mouth to speak, he had been ordered to keep quiet. Him being white and dressed as an Indian had not even peaked the warriors' interest enough to ask about it, although he had seen many quizzical stares on the canoe journey to their camp.

"*Wee-wee-bee-tahn*, hurry up. Move faster," Black Bear growled as he gave Sun Hawk another shove. "Do not look with such interest at my village and our people. As you see, none are interested in you. You to them are like the wind, invisible."

Understanding why, since Sun Hawk himself had been taught as a child never to stare at newcomers in the village, whether friends or foe, he focused only on the wigwam he was being directed toward. It had no windows. Nor did it have a buckskin covering for the door. The door was made of long strips of cane, on which was a large latch, which meant that these people had prepared themselves for the possibility of prisoners.

His jaw tightened when he thought of the disgrace of he, a great chief, being locked up like a criminal. He had wondered just how far these people would go before finally giving him permission to speak, to prove how wrong they were to have brought him among their people as a captive enemy.

That was not the way it should be. They should be thanking him for saving their chief! If not for him, Summer Hope might have been taken prisoner again. Even though there had been no signs of the bush rangers anywhere, there was always the possibility that they might return to abduct her.

Although maybe Summer Hope would be the last thing on their minds once they realized they had lost their wealth of pelts in the lake.

Just before being shoved into the wigwam, Sun Hawk looked over his shoulder in time to see Summer Hope going into a larger dwelling nearby. He watched as several women, and then a man who he assumed was this band's medicine man, went into the lodge. It was obvious that Summer Hope would get the best of care, for he could tell that she was revered by everyone.

And why wouldn't she be? he thought to himself

as he walked inside the small, dark dwelling, cringing when he heard the lock latched behind him. It was rare in the Ojibwa tribe for a woman to be named chief, so he knew that she had to have done something awesome to have achieved such a high standing among her people.

Gee-nah-ta, alone, Sun Hawk looked slowly around him as his eyes adjusted to the darkness. The smoke hole overhead his only means of light, he saw that bulrush mats covered the floor, but that was the only convenience in the dwelling.

He went to the fire pit and knelt beside it. He saw no ashes, which meant that this lodge had not yet been used. His village had a prisoner lodge, also, but it had rarely been occupied. He was filled with anger to know that he, who was revered by his own band of Ojibwa, was being shamed in such a way.

"That will soon be remedied," he whispered, settling down on the mats. He crossed his legs and straightened his back, his eyes steady on the closed door. When someone came, he would let no one silence his words again. This had gone far enough.

He smiled at why he had even allowed it, for he knew that he could have stopped this insulting treatment long before now.

But he had wanted to first test the waters with this band of Ojibwa before befriending them. If they were the sort who saw too much importance in allying themselves with the British, he, upon his release, would advise his people to avoid them at all cost. His own village was at an isolated place, where no strangers were allowed to go.

Before telling anyone, even another band of Ojibwa, where it was located, he had to know they were trustworthy enough. The worst scenario would be to make friends with this band, only to have them tell the British where his village was hidden.

From that point on, Sun Hawk's people would lose their freedom, their ability to live without interference.

Ay-uh, telling them who he was might be risky.

He glanced again toward the closed door. Getting free depended solely on himself. His warriors would have no real reason to be worrying about him. When he had left for the hunt, it had been clear to everyone that this was something he wanted to do alone. He did his best thinking while alone with the forest animals, birds, flowing streams, and trees.

And it was ordinary for him to stay away from his home for more than one night as he hunted and then communed with the Great Spirit.

No one but these Ojibwa knew where he was. And they had no idea whom they had wronged. Soon, though, they would know. As soon as someone came to see him, he would tell them.

He would then demand release and warn

them to be more careful in the future whom they took as their prisoner!

They were lucky that Sun Hawk was the chief of a peace-loving band of Ojibwa. If not, Summer Hope would soon learn how wrong it was to judge someone as quickly as Sun Hawk had been judged!

Wondering just how long he was going to have to wait for someone to arrive, Sun Hawk became restless. He rose to his feet and went to the door and tried it.

His jaw tightened when he found that it was, indeed, still bolted shut.

He sighed heavily and began to pace. Soon after, he heard the bolt lock slide aside and felt the rush of sunshine on his body as the door swung open.

The sun silhouetted the person standing in the doorway, and Sun Hawk knew immediately that it was not a man. He saw a slender yet shapely body, and long hair that fell unbraided to a woman's waist.

He became aware of a faint smell of flowers, and recalled how Summer Hope's hair had smelled during those moments when they were alone. Rainwater scented with wild flowers.

His heart thudded inside his chest as she came into the wigwam, then reached a hand out for him. *"Mah-bee-zhon,* come with me," she said softly. "Come to my lodge where it is more comfortable. We must talk."

Nodding, and feeling hopeful of making a

lasting peace with the beautiful woman chief, Sun Hawk stepped around her and left the lodge.

Having grown too used to the dark wigwam, Sun Hawk winced when the sun poured into his eyes, stinging them, but he kept his composure and walked on ahead of Summer Hope.

His pulse raced as he felt her eyes on him, studying his every movement. He straightened his back and squared his shoulders and held his chin high, also very aware of being watched by villagers standing in the doorways of their wigwams.

He glanced sideways and saw many children following alongside him, their dark eyes looking at him. Now that he had been in the village long enough, it was apparent that people no longer saw the need to ignore his presence.

It seemed that everyone wanted to see this white man who posed as an Indian, not realizing that in his heart he was as Ojibwa as they!

Summer Hope quickly stepped around him.

With a hand she gestured toward her wigwam. "Go inside," she said. "This is my lodge. We will speak in private."

Realizing that she truly trusted him, as there were no guards visible anywhere, Sun Hawk stopped and gave her a lingering look. When she smiled, Sun Hawk was taken aback, for there was nothing about her behavior now that made him feel uncomfortable.

He certainly no longer felt as though he was

a prisoner. In her eyes he saw sweetness, and even more than that. He saw the look of a woman who wanted to impress a man with her smile.

Things had changed between them. Her memory must have returned and she remembered that he had had no role in taking her hostage.

Although she had been unconscious when he had found her, surely instinct told her that it was he who had cared for her until her warriors had arrived.

"Go on inside," Summer Hope said, hating how this man had caused her cheeks to heat with a blush. When he had looked at her, it had not been with the eyes of an enemy. She saw gentleness, warmth, compassion, and more. She had seen a man who was interested in a woman, and not because she was a powerful chief, but because she was a woman!

She wanted to feel free to follow her own sensual feelings for this man, but there was so much about him that puzzled—no, intrigued her. He was a white man who was tanned as dark as her own skin and who dressed and behaved like an Indian. She struggled to remember what had happened . . . how it was that she came to be with this white Indian.

But no matter how hard she tried, the memories just wouldn't surface. It was all a blur, like fog impairing one's view of the lake on an early, cool autumn morning.

One thing was certain; it was time to allow

this man to speak. Only then would she truly know how it was that they came to be together.

Once inside the large wigwam, Sun Hawk became aware of the same familiar scent that would always remind him of Summer Hope. It hung in the air like a sweet caress.

Summer Hope nodded toward a thick pallet of pelts beside a slow-burning fire in the fire pit.

"We will sit by the fire and have private council," she murmured, gathering the skirt of her buckskin dress into her arms as she sat down opposite him.

In a quick glance, Sun Hawk saw the neatness of her dwelling, the plushness of the pelts and blankets hanging from the walls. Clean bulrush mats covered the floor. A wicker chest sat at the foot of her bed made of blankets.

In an open basket beside one wall were beaded necklaces, bracelets, and earrings. In another basket were feathered fans.

A row of moccasins, beaded with different designs, was placed neatly just to the right side of the entranceway.

He also saw a wooden tray upon which were various vials of both soft and brilliant colors of paint to use to decorate her face for celebrations.

He saw so many other things, all feminine. He could feel her in everything that he saw and was relieved to know that there were no visible signs in her lodge of a husband or children.

But something did puzzle him. Although she was a woman, he saw no cooking utensils.

"Tell me what happened," Summer Hope said, interrupting Sun Hawk's thoughts. "Tell me how you found me, and where."

"Then you do believe that I am not your enemy," Sun Hawk said, his eyes watching her long, slender fingers weaving her hair into braids.

Sun Hawk was taken even more by her, for she did everything with such grace.

Even the way she sat, so poised, so proud, made his pulse race as it had never raced before when in the presence of a lady.

He saw a threat in this.

If for some reason they could not see eye to eye about things, he would feel the loss twofold, for he would not only lose her as an ally to his people, but he would lose her as the woman his heart could not help but desire.

"I never did see you as an enemy," Summer Hope said, now twining her hair into a second braid. "I saw no choice but to bring you to my village so that we could be alone, to talk, to delve into the mystery of what did happen to me. I hope you have answers, for it tears at my very soul to know that for a while I lost total control of my destiny, which is also my people's."

"I will tell you all that I know," Sun Hawk said, forcing his eyes away from her fingers, from the fantasy of those fingers on his face instead of her hair. He could even now feel them explore his lips, her fingertips soft against them.

He cleared his throat nervously, then started from the beginning, when the storm had come in its fury of wind, lightning, and rain.

He explained how he had seen her in the larger canoe with the white bush rangers, and how he had determined that she was there as a hostage, and had decided to follow and rescue her.

He told her how he had found her lying unconscious on the shore and how he had taken her quickly from the area so the bush rangers could not find her, if they had survived.

He explained how he had medicated her wound, how it seemed to have pained her by how she had winced even while she was unconscious.

"And then my warriors arrived," she said, finishing it for him.

"*Ay-uh*, and then your warriors arrived," he repeated.

"I apologize for not trusting you sooner," Summer Hope said, certain that how he had described things were true. There was too much honesty about this man to mistrust him ever again. "And I *mee-gway-chee-wahn-dum*, thank you, for helping me."

"You were an *ee-guay*, a woman in distress," he said, drawing his legs up before him, hugging them to his chest. "I am glad that I was able to rescue you."

"Explain to me how it is that you are dressed differently than your white brethren," Summer

Hope said, resting her hands on her lap now that her braids hung long down her back. "Tell me why you would want to behave as a red man, instead of white." Her gaze went to his hair. "You even wear your hair long, as do my warriors. It is also as shiny. Do you use bear's grease in your hair to give it the shine?"

"*Ay-uh,* it is my practice to do so," Sun Hawk said, smiling.

"You even use some words of my people," Summer Hope said, forking an eyebrow. "*Ay-uh* means yes. How do you know this?"

"Only by birth am I white. Deep in my soul I am Ojibwa," Sun Hawk said, pride in his voice and eyes. "I breathe, eat, and live Ojibwa. I am a proud Ojibwa chief."

Her eyes widened. She gasped.

"You, who are white by birth, are a chief of a band of Ojibwa?" she asked, her voice low. "How can that be?"

"It began so long ago," Sun Hawk replied, in his mind's eye again reliving that dreadful day when he had been abducted after his parents' massacre. "I was a very young man when the renegades came that day in Kentucky. . . ."

He gave her only a brief description of what had happened. He didn't see any reason to go into detail about his parents, and about his father being a minister of the Lord.

It hurt too much to talk about his mother and father, for even still he missed them with every beat of his heart.

And he saw no reason to tell her his birth name was Jeffrey. When he had chosen to walk the road of the red man, he had chosen to leave his true name in the past, to avoid having to explain how he came to own two names.

One was enough.

Sun Hawk. Yes, Sun Hawk suited him well!

"I was named Sun Hawk by those who took me in," he said proudly. "And when my adoptive chieftain father died, I had proven worthy, and was named chief of the Enchanted Lake band of Ojibwa."

"The story is so intriguing," Summer Hope said, touched deeply by how, as a child, he had become as one with the Ojibwa. "Where do you make your home? I am new in the area. I have yet to have council with any other bands of Ojibwa. Can I come soon to your village with my warriors? I wish to have council with you and your people. It will be good to make friends so soon with people of my own tribe."

Sun Hawk's spine stiffened. His eyes narrowed.

He had not anticipated her asking to come for council at his village, yet he should have known that once she saw him as a friend, she would.

But no one, absolutely no one except his own people, knew where their village was located. That was the only way to assure them a continued, peaceful existence. Once their village was opened up to others of his own skin coloring, would not those whose skin was white soon follow?

"I will bring my people to you for council," he offered.

"*Gah-ween*, no," she said, a coolness in her voice that was not there moments ago. "We shall come to your village for our first council."

Sun Hawk suddenly felt trapped. He was afraid that no matter what he said now, it would not take away the tension that his refusal to allow her to come to his village had created.

But until he knew that he could trust this band of Ojibwa, there was no way he would invite them to his village. His people had cherished their privacy. He would not be the one to take it away from them, not even if it meant losing friendship with this woman who stirred his very soul with want.

"You have positioned your village close to the British fort," he said in an effort to steer the conversation elsewhere, and to see how she felt about the British. "Is that because you are going to ally yourselves with them?"

"*Ay-uh*, yes, it was my intention to open trade talks with them," Summer Hope said, hating it that things were no longer as friendly between her and Sun Hawk.

But it was how he seemed to want to keep the location of his village a secret that unnerved her.

That meant he did not trust her!

Yes, she knew that trust had to be earned, yet she had hoped that their instant attraction toward one another, and the fact that she had proven her trust of him, would change things between them.

She could not deny being attracted to him.

To be near him made her heart flutter strangely . . . a first for her while in the presence of a man!

But as always, she had to put her feelings second to those of her people, even if it meant turning away from this man who had stolen her heart the very instant their eyes had met.

"My band of Ojibwa avoid the British at all cost," Sun Hawk said, his voice tight. "If you ally yourself with them, then you cannot ally yourselves with my people."

Enraged by his implications, Summer Hope jumped to her feet. She placed her hands on her hips as she glared down at Sun Hawk. "Are you saying that you do not trust me?" she said. "That you do not trust my people? That we cannot meet in council after all?"

Sun Hawk rose slowly. "It is not that I do not trust you," he said evenly. "It is the British—I have never trusted them. That is why I keep the location of my village a secret."

"Anyone can find a village, should they try hard enough," Summer Hope said, laughing sarcastically.

"I would not try," Sun Hawk warned, his hands in tight fists at his sides.

Furious, Summer Hope rushed from the lodge, then hurried back inside with a hefty guard at her side. "Take him and lock him up again!" she screamed, her eyes flaring angrily.

"What?" Sun Hawk gasped, his eyes wide as he stared disbelievingly at her. "Just because I do not agree to tell you where my village is, you will lock me up as though I am your enemy?"

"How do I know that you are not?" she said, close to his face. "Anyone who is as secretive about his village's location as you are surely has many secrets."

Sun Hawk glared at her as the guard grabbed his arm and forced him outside.

He jerked himself free then walked nobly to the smaller wigwam and went inside. He heard the lock slide into place again.

"That she would do this to me again . . ." he whispered, kicking a bulrush mat out of place.

He sighed heavily and sat down on another mat.

It was all because he had refused to allow her to come to his village for council.

If I had it to do over, I would do the same, he thought to himself, knowing that now was not the time to become careless about his village's whereabouts. Especially if this Northern Lights band of Ojibwa befriended the British!

He gazed toward the door, then up at the smoke hole. The sun was setting. Soon it would be dark.

When he had awakened this morning at sunrise, anxious for the hunt, never would he have imagined in his wildest dreams that when the sun set on this day, he would be imprisoned like a hardened criminal. Worse yet, by a band of Ojibwa with a female chief!

He must escape at the first opportunity.

He must show Chief Summer Hope that she had no true control over his destiny . . . or his people's.

He gazed at the closed door. "I shall be gone from here *soon*," he said aloud, his voice low, yet filled with fire.

6

The foe long since in silence slept,
Alike the conqueror silent sleeps.
—RALPH WALDO EMERSON

Unable to get Sun Hawk off her mind, and feeling guilty as she ate a nourishing meal of rabbit stew knowing that Sun Hawk must be hungry, Summer Hope shoved her wooden platter aside.

Again she went over in her mind all that Sun Hawk had told her. None of it sounded fabricated, and he didn't have the look in his eyes of a man who would lie.

But she remembered how he refused to trust her enough to tell her where his village was. In her whole lifetime, she had never known an Ojibwa band to be so secretive.

She could not help but be suspicious of it.

And the fact that he had such little trust in her, even after she had trusted him, still made her blood boil.

"I must get him to open up to me fully," she said aloud, hurrying to her feet, deciding to go see him.

A sensual thrill ran through her as she thought of how handsome he was. When she envisioned him reaching out and grabbing her and kissing her, she felt the heat of a blush rush to her cheeks.

She couldn't believe where her thoughts had taken her. She never thought of men in such a way.

And blushing!

But she was very attracted to Sun Hawk. It was something she could not shake. She certainly knew now that she wanted more than friendship with him. She wanted . . .

She tried to force herself to quit thinking such ridiculous things, but even while trying, without realizing what she was doing, she grabbed a cloth and wrapped it around the handle of the pot that hung over the fire. She lifted the pot away from the fire pit and smiled wickedly. "I have heard it said that the way to a man's heart is *mee-gim*, food," she whispered. "Well, I shall see about that."

Carrying the pot, in which a ladle stood half immersed in the delicious stew, Summer Hope went to the entranceway of her lodge and used her shoulder to shove the buckskin flap aside.

Beneath the light of the moon, serenaded by a loon singing over water in the distance, she hurried her steps. She gazed at the small wigwam where Sun Hawk was being held captive, then glanced around at the wigwams that sat in a semicircle around the center of the village. She could see smoke spiraling from the smoke holes. She could see the glimmer of fires.

She could hear laughter, singing, and distant wolves howling at the full moon.

In the evening breeze came a slight chill, a reminder of the colder winds of winter that would soon be upon her people.

But the snows would not come as early as they had at their previous village.

And there were no mountains where landslides could suddenly rob you of your entire family!

Ay-uh, yes, this place did seem perfect, especially now that she had found a man whose voice and face made her senses reel.

She had to do everything within her power to make things right with Sun Hawk. She had to give him reason to trust her enough to take her to his village.

Enchanted Lake, she thought to herself.

The name made her envision a place of serenity and loveliness.

She must see it, firsthand. And she would!

When she got to the small wigwam, Summer Hope set the pot of food on the ground long enough to slide the bolt lock aside.

She stopped, though, before opening the door. She could just imagine how angry Sun Hawk was about being kept so long as a captive. He was probably ready to grab the first person that entered the lodge so that he could make his escape.

She didn't want to be crushed by a man whose powerful muscles could squeeze the very life from her.

"It is I," she said, only loud enough for him to hear. Her people must not know that she had gone to the prisoner, alone.

She didn't want them to see this weak side of her character . . . the side of her that was more woman than chief.

"Sun Hawk, it is I, Summer Hope," she said, very aware of how nervous she was over seeing him again.

"Sun Hawk, I have brought you food," Summer Hope said, scarcely breathing as she awaited his reply.

Hearing her voice, hearing her name, hearing her speak his name with such feeling, made Sun Hawk's heart skip a beat. And it was not because he thought she was there to release him. It was the very nearness of her that made his knees go strangely weak from want.

He just as quickly made himself recall why he was locked up, and by whose orders. He was foolish to allow himself to feel anything except contempt for this woman.

His jaw tight, he rose to his feet and stood in the dark shadows as he waited for her to open the door. She wouldn't be alone. Knowing his eagerness to leave this small lodge, she would know not to come alone. He could quickly overpower her. . . .

He caught himself when he realized that he

was thinking things that he knew he could not do. Even if it meant that he would still be locked away like a criminal, he could do no harm to the beautiful chief. Not only because that would bring her warriors to find him and kill him, but because he cared for her too much ever to harm her.

Ay-uh, he did admit to caring that quickly for this woman, after living twenty-eight years without finding love.

It all seemed so futile, though . . . the very thought of them being able to feel free to love one another. They belonged to two bands with two different sets of ideals. She was ready to grovel to the English in order to have trade goods she desired because she was a woman. Beads, bangles, bolts of cloth, lace!

Ay-uh, being a lady, and wanting things all ladies wanted, surely that was the reason she would allow herself and her people to be duped by the British at Fort William.

"I have brought you *mee-gim*, food," Summer Hope said, picking up the pot again. "The door is unlocked. Please open it for me."

Sun Hawk was taken aback that she had unlocked the door and had actually asked him to open it for her. She was treating this visit like a social call?

He had to laugh at the irony of it, then found more than humor in the fact that she *had* unlocked the door. Maybe she was ready to give him his freedom!

Or would she feed him only to again lock the door behind her when she left for her own wigwam?

Sighing, having no choice but to play along with her until he learned her true intentions, he went to the door. At any moment, should he tire of her games, he *could* overpower her and tie and gag her long enough to escape, knowing that wouldn't harm her in any way except for her pride. He shoved open the door.

When he saw her standing there in the moonlight, her facial features bathed with soft moonlight, he was taken anew by her absolute loveliness.

At this moment in time he saw her as a woman he desired with every ounce of his being. Not as a rival chieftain leader.

And she looked so sweet standing there holding the pot, her eyes eager as she gazed into his.

Drawing in a heavy, quavering breath, knowing he must find a way to break her spell or he might never be able to put her from his mind, Sun Hawk reached out and took the pot.

"Stew," she said, her voice breaking, the awakened passion inside her so keen she found it hard to stand there and not pour out her feelings for him, to him.

She forced herself to regain her composure. She was a powerful Ojibwa chief, not a lame-headed woman whose will was broken by the mystical gaze of a handsome man.

"I have brought you stew," she said. "It

surely has been some time since you last had nourishment."

"*Ay-uh*, since this morning just prior to leaving for the hunt," he said, setting the stew down just inside the door.

"The *gee-wee-sayn*, hunt? Was your hunt successful?" she asked, forcing small talk when she so badly wanted something else from him.

She could hardly believe how she ached for his arms around her, how she hungered for his lips.

She even wanted them to promise one another they would never allow anything to come between them, especially mistrust!

But there was mistrust, she reminded herself. He didn't trust her enough to show her his village. That was why she was with him now. Not to watch him eat, and especially not to be held and kissed by him.

She wanted him to show his trust in her enough to agree to take her to his village.

"My hunt is always successful," Sun Hawk answered, then wished he could take the words back, for he sounded like a man who enjoyed boasting, whereas in truth he was not a boastful man. He enjoyed showing his success, but not openly bragging about it.

Her face flooded with color. She lowered her eyes. "I remember your pelts now," she murmured. She looked quickly up at him. "I am sorry that my warriors claimed them as theirs. I shall see that they are returned to you."

"*Gah-ween*, no, that is not necessary," Sun Hawk said, feeling suddenly awkward to gaze down at her from his height of six foot four.

The sexual tension was strong and he had to fight it with all of his being, for he should want nothing more than to be set free and return home to his people.

"But I would like to leave this place," he said boldly. "Did you come only to give me food? Or have you come, also, to say that I could leave?"

An idea sprang to Summer Hope's mind. She couldn't believe that she hadn't thought of it earlier. She could release Sun Hawk, but as soon as he was gone, she could go to Black Bear, her best friend and favorite warrior, and together they could follow Sun Hawk. Then she would find out where his village was.

But she wouldn't allow Sun Hawk to know that she knew anytime soon. She wanted him to show his trust in her by changing his mind and telling her himself.

"I came to give you food and to also give you your freedom," she said, watching closely for his reaction.

When she saw him smile broadly and relax his muscles as he sat down, she sighed with relief and sat down beside him. But she couldn't totally relax, herself. She was afraid that he being the astute man that he was, he would see right through her ploy. And then he would never trust her again.

"Eat directly from the pot," she said, nodding

toward the ladle. "I could not carry a bowl as well as the pot. It was so heavy, it required two hands to carry it."

"You have already eaten?" Sun Hawk said, reaching for the ladle.

"*Ay-uh*, as much as I needed," she replied. "*Wee-si-nin*, eat. I know you must be famished."

"You are right about that," Sun Hawk said, laughing softly. He sank the ladle into the stew and brought out a spoonful of meat, wild carrots, and broth. It tasted so good and nourishing, he forgot his manners and ate one fast bite after another.

And when he had eaten his fill, he placed the ladle back inside the pot. "You are not only a revered chief, but also a wonderful cook," he said, wiping his mouth clean with the back of a hand.

She blushed. "I do not cook," she said, hating to admit something like this to a man whom she wanted to impress. She knew that when a man chose a woman for his wife, he would want someone who could not only cook, but also sew and clean.

She could do none of those things. She had been pampered for too long by too many to know anything but the skills of leading her people.

Now she realized that she had been wrong not to learn the things all women needed to know to please a man.

Yet this was not just any man. He was a chief

of a different band of Ojibwa. It was *gee-wah-nah-dis*, foolish, ever to imagine them coming together as a man and woman in love. She was not ready to step down from being chief of her people.

And she knew that he would never give up his title. He carried it too well . . . the dignity of being called chief.

"Do not look as though it is a sin not to be able to cook," Sun Hawk said, reaching a hand over to her cheek, gently touching it. "When one wishes to learn, it comes as easily as does the first hunt for a young brave aspiring to prove that he is a man."

"I do not even know how to sew beads on a dress," she revealed, watching his eyes, stunned that no surprise showed in their depths.

"But think of all of the things that you do know," he said. "To be a powerful chief, one must know many things."

"*Ay-uh*, that is true." Summer Hope's heart thudded as he slid his hand around to the nape of her neck and began slowly bringing her face close to his.

She had only been kissed a few times.

None of those men had caused her heart to react so violently.

She tried to remember the futility of loving this particular man.

But everything except the want, the desire, was gone. Pulling her into his arms, he guided her lips to his.

When he kissed her, her heart leapt with bliss, causing a strange sort of weakness at the pit of her stomach.

Having never felt anything so wonderful, yet so frightening, she yanked herself free and jumped to her feet.

Her pulse raced as she gazed down at Sun Hawk.

Her shoulders swayed from the passion.

Her mind shouted at her to get out of there.

She was afraid that her feelings threatened her standing as chief. She was afraid that from this moment on, she would feel weak and unable to think clearly enough to guide her people.

"Just go, *mah-szhon*, leave," she said, her voice breaking. "Please . . . please leave." She turned to run from the lodge, but turned back as he rose slowly to his feet. "And please forget we did that. Please?"

"How can I?" Sun Hawk asked, stunned by the power of their awakened feelings for one another.

"You must," she said, then fled into the moonlit night.

Sun Hawk just stood there looking at the place where she had been. Her presence was still there, so strong, he felt as though he could reach out and pull her again into his arms.

He slowly shook his head as he sorted through his thoughts and realized what had transpired.

"How did I allow it to go this far?" he whispered, raking his fingers through his long hair in frustration. "But how can I deny how I feel about her? How she feels about me?"

He tore his eyes away from the spot where she had stood, and glanced outside before running from the lodge into the dark shadows of the forest.

He knew that he was trying to run from something more than having been wrongly imprisoned.

He was running from an impossible dream, for there was no way their loving one another could work.

He must find a way to forget her!

He must direct his energies toward leading his people and keeping them safe from interlopers.

"Especially from her," he said, yet he knew that no matter how hard he tried, he could never forget her.

He was so intent on his thoughts and how to deal with his feelings, he wasn't aware of being followed.

Summer Hope and Black Bear kept far enough behind Sun Hawk to avoid detection. She was adamant about finding his village, knowing where the man she would love forever lived!

She wasn't sure she could win the battle in her heart that she was fighting against loving Sun Hawk. She wanted to believe there was a way they could work things out.

There was one thing that she was certain

about. This time she had not left her village alone or unarmed. In a pocket of her buckskin dress lay a small, pearl-handled pistol, a firearm that she had recently traded for.

Before leaving Canada, she had practiced shooting it. No one would ever abduct her again—or he would get a bullet in his gut!

7

From the cool cisterns of the midnight air,
My spirit drank repose;
The fountain of perpetual peace,
From those deep cisterns flows there.
                    —HENRY WADSWORTH LONGFELLOW

Pierre DuSault and one of his newly found
friends were making their way through the forest. They had talked further about what they
would do when they found and captured the
Indian woman. Instead of abducting her for
themselves, they had decided to take her to a
voyagers' camp. Voyagers were rich and
women-hungry men who would pay well for a
feisty, copper-skinned woman.

Tired of worrying about being caught while
illegally trapping in the Minnesota Territory, the
men had agreed to Pierre's plan. To them, Indians were nonhuman, and they had been thorns
in their sides for years. Just as the trappers
would get their traps set, the red man would
find them and destroy them.

The men had decided only a few days ago, before having met Pierre, that they were ready to
return to their homes in Indiana, but they didn't
have the means to pay their way back there.

Now with this plan and the money they would receive in exchange for the squaw, they would be able to return home to their wives and get back into farming. They had had enough of risking their lives for a meager amount of pelts. They would be far from the area before the squaw's people discovered how she had been abducted, and by whom.

One bush ranger had stayed behind to guard the pelts. The other eagerly went through the forest with Pierre in pursuit of the squaw.

Little did they know that this woman was a powerful, revered chief!

8

To him who in the love of Nature holds,
Communion with her visible forms, she speaks,
A various language; for his gayer hours,
She has a voice of gladness, and a smile.
—WILLIAM CULLEN BRYANT

Sun Hawk ran through the shadowy forest of natural beauty that he knew so well, that which was home to moose, wolf, bear, and deer. He stopped suddenly when he sensed movement behind him.

Turning quickly on a heel, he peered through the darkness. The moon gave only faint light overhead through the denseness of the trees.

But he needed no light to know that he was not alone.

And the footsteps he heard were not those of four-legged animals.

Somebody was following him.

Skilled in knowing how to elude people, having done it often enough through the years to assure his people their continued privacy, he ducked low and slipped quickly into the dense brush. He crept in a stooped fashion over to an even greater cluster of bushes.

Scarcely breathing, not wanting to make any

sounds that might lead his followers to him, he waited and watched.

When he no longer heard footsteps, and he saw no one go past, he smiled. He knew that whoever had been behind him would no longer be able to follow him.

But to make sure, he would stay where he was, at least until morning. It had been a stressful, tiring day.

More than that, it had been a day of sensual awakening.

While he stayed hidden, and before allowing himself to fall asleep, he would again try to sort out his heart and mind about this woman who stole his breath away.

Smoothing out fallen autumn leaves beneath him, he settled down on his back, sighed, and gazed through a break in the trees overhead at the twinkling stars.

Would he ever be able to lie with Summer Hope beneath those stars and count them with her?

Would he ever be able to make love to her beneath them?

Or was it all a fantasy that was not meant to be?

Then it came to him, a thought that sent him sitting quickly upright.

His jaw tightened when he realized who must have been following him tonight.

Summer Hope and some of her warriors.

Surely that was why she was so eager to allow him to leave!

It was a ploy. All along she had planned to follow him, for she was even more adamant about discovering the location of his village than the British at Fort William were!

He would like to think that she wanted to know because she wished to come from time to time just to be with him, because she could not allow many days to pass without seeing him.

Yet he could not discount other reasons that might have made her follow him. If she could pass on the information of his whereabouts to the British, would they not reward her, in turn, with valuables she desired?

He was torn with so many conflicting feelings. Today he had discovered that love at first sight was possible. He doubted that *he* could allow very many days to pass before he had to see her again.

If things were reversed, and she had a secret, wonderful hideaway for her village, wouldn't he, too, follow her, so that he could always be free to go to her whenever he needed her in his arms?

"This is so *gee-wah-nah-dis*, foolish," he growled to himself.

He turned on his side and finally drifted off.

But it was not a restful sleep. In it, he saw Summer Hope moving through the forest, lost, and suddenly she was surrounded by bush rangers.

Her screams penetrated his dream like knives being thrust into his heart!

When he awakened, with cold sweat pouring from his brow, he was relieved to know that he had only been dreaming. In reality, Summer Hope's warriors would keep her safe, if it was Summer Hope who had been following him.

Although he had slept for only a short while, he realized it was long enough to get him through the night. Along the horizon, he saw faint splashes of orange as the sun made its appearance to signal the day.

Knowing that it was safe to leave his hiding place now, Sun Hawk hurried onward until he came to a rocky path that led downward to his people's private village. It was a hard-to-reach place, where they lived as one with nature in the great circle of life, where majestic eagles nested in great number in the cliffs around Enchanted Lake.

He walked on past a shallow stream of bluish-purple water that was fed by springs from the nearby cliffs.

Soon he came to Enchanted Lake, around which sat the conical-topped lodges of his people. He saw slow spirals of smoke rising from the wigwams. He smelled the delicious fragrance of food cooking over the fires.

He smiled when he saw children sitting at the lake's edge, laughing as they watched tadpoles darting in and out and around the underwater pebbles. They waited for their mothers to call them in for their morning meals.

When a warrior stepped from one of the wigwams and saw Sun Hawk entering the village, he smiled broadly and went to meet his chief. He signaled to a woman who hurried to Sun Hawk's wigwam to prepare for his arrival. The warrior stopped suddenly and frowned when he realized that Sun Hawk was empty-handed. He had no weapon and no pelts, which meant that something must have gone wrong on his private hunt.

"My chief, what has happened?" Gray Eagle asked with concern. "Where is your bow and arrow? Where are your pelts?"

"Call our warriors into council as I go to my lodge and refresh myself," Sun Hawk said, placing a gentle hand on his favorite warrior's bare shoulder. He gazed from lodge to lodge and saw that everyone had heard Gray Eagle greet Sun Hawk and knew that their chief had returned home.

He nodded to them all in greeting as they stood in their doorways, then hurried on to his private wigwam and went inside. The women had seen to it that fresh water awaited him in a wooden basin. A clean cloth and towel were beside it.

He turned and gazed over his shoulder at his fire pit, where a large pot of food was warming over the fire. The women of his village took good care of their chief, but he now knew that was not enough.

He wanted his own woman. He wanted to

return home from the hunt and know that she was there for him.

It was easy to imagine Summer Hope in his wigwam, sitting beside the fire, her long black hair hanging loose down her perfect back.

If he closed his eyes, he could even feel her hands on his face as he bent down close to her. He could taste her lips! He could smell her hair!

Shaken by his thoughts, knowing that it was wrong to get so carried away by them, especially when he could not trust the woman enough to bring her to his village, Sun Hawk quickly bent over the basin and splashed his face with cold water.

Shivers ran up and down his spine, but at least the sting of the water had brought him to his senses.

He stepped out of his moccasins and breechclout and bathed his body well, then went to his storage of clothes beneath his bed and chose a full dress of buckskins, a beaded headband to hold his hair back from his brow, and newly beaded moccasins.

After he was dressed, and his hair was brushed and secured with the headband, he stopped and inhaled a quivering breath. He looked around his wigwam and saw the lack of anything that would prove a woman was a part of his life.

And although he tried to force thoughts of Summer Hope from his mind, she lingered, still, to torment him.

"Great Spirit, what am I to do?" he asked, gazing heavenward through the smoke hole in the center of his lodge's roof. "Make her go away!"

He knelt and dipped the breakfast stew from the pot into a wooden bowl. He grabbed a wooden spoon and fed his hunger quickly, then set his bowl aside and left the lodge.

When he reached the large council house that sat back from the center of the village, he found his warriors awaiting him, in their eyes a keen questioning.

"My warriors, I know you have many questions since you saw me arrive without pelts from my hunt," he said, going to sit on a platform before them. "My pelts are now in the hands of other Ojibwa warriors. My canoe was set loose in the lake."

An instant rage filled his warriors' eyes. "What Ojibwa warriors would do this to you who are an Ojibwa chief?" Gray Eagle asked, his voice tight. "And where do they make residence? Those we know are far away, downriver. Why would they come this far from their home to take from you?"

Always touched by his warriors' devotion, reminding him time and again how they revered him and did not look to him as white, he smiled at Gray Eagle, and then at the others.

Sun Hawk hoped that his gesture of kindness yesterday, helping a woman in distress, would not eventually bring sadness and heartache into his people's lives by leading intruders there to find them.

He proceeded to tell his warriors what had happened, how he had been successful in the hunt, and how he had placed his pelts in his canoe for safekeeping until he was ready to carry them on a travois back to his village.

He told them about the storm, and then explained how he had seen the captive woman in a canoe.

He told them everything that had happened since then, except for being followed last night after Summer Hope had allowed him to leave her village.

Sun Hawk did not want his warriors to feel threatened in any way by what might have been the biggest mistake in his life, yet he could have never lived with himself had he not gone to the innocent woman's rescue.

"We must make the woman chief pay for taking you captive, even if she did eventually set you free," Gray Eagle said fiercely. "No one wrongs our chief."

"It was a *wah-nee-chee-gay*, misunderstanding," Sun Hawk said, trying to placate them. "And it is all done and behind me. Let us think no more about it."

But no matter how much he urged them to forget that Summer Hope existed, he could not stop thinking about her. Had he not saved her, and her warriors had found her dead, and blamed whites for the deed, a bloody war could have erupted between whites and red skins. That could have spread even as far as Enchanted Lake!

Ay-uh, he had done the right thing.

"So you will ignore that she and her people live this close to us?" another warrior asked, his voice wary.

"For now we shall wait before we make any decision about the Northern Lights band of Ojibwa," Sun Hawk said. "Let us see how they interact with the British. If they are able to see the British as we have seen them, as untrustworthy cheats, and they want nothing more to do with them, then maybe we will choose to ally ourselves with these Ojibwa."

"You do not mean . . . open our lives to them so much that they will be invited to our village, do you?" Gray Eagle asked, a sudden alarm in his eyes. "We have had such peace, my *chee-o-gee-mah,* chief, but only because we have avoided close contact with others. Our lives are good. They are ours."

Torn over how to handle this situation, where he had finally found a woman that made his heart sing, yet at the same time could bring danger into his people's lives, Sun Hawk sat silent for a moment.

Then he looked from man to man. "Know this, my warriors, I will never do anything knowingly that will create unrest among our people," he said, then rose to his feet. "You are first in my heart and soul, always. Remember that. *Ah-pah-nay*, forever, I will look out for your best interests.''

The warriors looked back at him with relief, and he took the time to smile at each one individually before leaving the lodge. He went to his people's sacred spring, which sat not that far from the village. Nearby was an altar made of rock where his people came to place offerings and prayers. The spring was a place where no one bathed. It was never to be soiled by human flesh, because the clear, pristine water seeped from Mother Earth.

His heart pounding, his mind confused, Sun Hawk went to the altar and knelt before it.

While dozens of eagles perched in the nearby trees and others soared majestically overhead, Sun Hawk breathed in Father Sky's strength. He began to pray, always including in his prayers his true mother and father of long ago.

He prayed about his feelings for a woman who had touched his life as no other woman before her.

He hoped that sometime soon she would remember what had happened to her. Until then, he knew that her people would hold him responsible, which in turn threatened his own people's well-being.

He prayed for strength to trust Summer Hope, for without that trust, there could never be anything special between them.

But he couldn't forget his warriors' attitude toward allowing anyone permission to come to their village. As white villages threatened to spring up around the Minnesota Territory's many beautiful lakes, Sun Hawk knew that the time would come when those whites would discover the most lovely, serene, pristine lake of all . . . the Enchanted Lake, which now solely belonged to Sun Hawk's people and the Great Spirit.

Thus far, there were only a few white settlements, and they were far south of Ojibwa land, but Sun Hawk knew that growth would come. His land had tall, beautiful trees that wealthy lumberjacks would fight over.

Yes, that was when the true nightmare would begin, the end of life as it had always been for his people.

"Give my people strength to face such a time," he whispered. "And give me strength now, for I fear that my heartache, and what I might do to ease it, will cause me to fail my people for the first time."

When his thoughts turned back to Summer Hope, he envisioned her as she was in the dream that he had had last night. The reality of what it meant came to him like a splash of cold water on his face.

"She is in jeopardy," he said aloud, his voice breaking. "As I sit here, alone, safely praying, *she* . . . is in *nah-nee-zah-ni-zee*, danger!"

He jumped to his feet and ran from his village, a panic he had never known before urging him onward.

When he realized that he didn't have a weapon, he paused, but felt that time was too much an enemy if he were right. He ran away from Enchanted Lake, empty-handed. . . .

9

"Hope" is the thing with feathers—
That perches in the soul—
And sings the tune without the words—
And never stops—at all—
                    —EMILY DICKINSON

Daybreak was sending its gilded light across the land. Sun Hawk breathed heavily as he ran in the direction of Summer Hope's village. He hoped that he was being foolish to think she was in danger just because he had dreamed she was.

But if Summer Hope had been following him last night, couldn't something have happened to her?

He felt guilty thinking about her traveling on land that was unfamiliar to her. After she had realized that she had lost his trail, and decided to return to her village, would she and her companions have been able to find their way back?

Although beautiful, this land with its dense forests and buttes and caves could be vicious to those who were unfamiliar with it, especially at night. They easily might find themselves going in circles.

He knew this to be true, for the first time he

had gone out to hunt alone, when he had been given his first bow and quiver of arrows, he had lost his way. It had taken his adoptive chieftain father and several warriors two days and nights to find him huddled inside a cave, frightened, cold, and hungry.

After that, he had made certain to memorize landmarks whenever he traveled in this enchanted forest.

But Summer Hope, thinking she would end up at his village, might not have done this.

And if any of the bush rangers had survived their spill in the river, wouldn't they perhaps be searching for her now?

Surely they knew that she had the ability to identify them to the authorities, who would imprison them for their wrongful deeds, or that she might, instead, take them back to her own village for sentencing.

The very thought of her being at the mercy of such men again made Sun Hawk's stomach turn. He knew that if the bush rangers found her, they would have to kill her.

A shudder of dread rushed up and down Sun Hawk's spine. If anything happened to Summer Hope now, he would blame himself. Had he not so stubbornly refused to take her to his village, nothing would have happened to her. She would not have been following him in the forest.

And the more he thought about being followed last night, the more he knew it had to have been her following him.

He gazed heavenward and silently prayed that when he arrived at her village, she would be there, safe, and astonished that he would have thought otherwise.

If he did find her there, would he then tell her the location of his village to make certain his premonition would not ever come true?

He was torn.

For so long he had vowed never to allow anyone permission to come into his village.

He should not let his feelings for a lone woman change that.

Yet if it would assure her safety in the future, shouldn't he make an exception?

Sun Hawk didn't have time to think any more about it. A sight a short distance away made everything he had suspected seem real. He stopped quickly and felt a sinking feeling at the pit of his stomach.

He tasted a bitterness in his throat as he stared in utter horror at a slain warrior stretched out on his side beneath a stately oak, his eyes closed, his back bloodied from a knife wound.

It was apparent that someone had come upon him and struck him from behind as cowards do.

"*Gah-ween*, no, let it not be one of Summer Hope's warriors!" Sun Hawk cried. He crept closer, circling around the tree until he could see the face of the fallen warrior.

Although he had not been at Summer Hope's

village for long, he had been there long enough to be able to recognize several of her warriors, especially those who seemed to be her most valued and beloved.

If this fallen warrior was one of hers, who else might have died in the ambush along with him?

Sun Hawk went cold with dread when he discovered that the dead warrior was Black Bear!

Hoping this warrior still had some life in him, enough to tell Sun Hawk that Summer Hope was safe at home, he knelt down beside the fallen man.

With a trembling hand, Sun Hawk touched his fingers to Black Bear's throat.

When he felt no pulse, he jerked his hand away, then moved slowly to his feet again.

Being an astute tracker, he studied the footprints around Black Bear's body. It was apparent that more than one man had come to take the life of the Ojibwa.

His heart stopped when he discovered a set of much smaller footprints, clearly made by someone who wore moccasins.

He moaned, for he knew those prints must be Summer Hope's. He had noticed how small her feet were, smaller than any Sun Hawk had ever seen before. *Ay-uh,* surely she had been there.

Leaning down for a closer look, his breath caught in his throat when he saw a trail of blood leading away from the death scene.

What if Summer Hope had also been knifed? He despaired.

With a pounding heart, he followed the trail of blood until it stopped at a stream.

He closed his eyes and clenched his teeth to keep from crying out in remorse, for if anything had happened to Summer Hope, he would forever hold himself to blame!

He had known someone was following him last night. If he had stepped out into the open and showed himself to them, maybe death would not have come to Black Bear. Summer Hope would be safe in her village. Sun Hawk would have seen to it that she had returned home unharmed.

His thoughts were interrupted by the sudden arrival of several warriors. Sun Hawk found himself surrounded.

He quickly recognized them.

They were also Summer Hope's!

"Where is our chief?" Eagle Wing asked, his notched arrow aimed directly at Sun Hawk's heart. "What have you done with Summer Hope? When we found her and Black Bear gone from our village this morning, we came looking for them. And what do we find? You, our people's enemy, not that far from our fallen comrade. You killed him, but what did you do with our chief?"

Eagle Wing looked guardedly around him, then glared at Sun Hawk again. "Where have you hidden her?" he hissed, his eyes narrowing angrily. "Is she also dead?"

Sun Hawk was filled with despair to know

that his suspicions about Summer Hope had been confirmed.

She had been with Black Bear. It had to be her blood on the ground!

Oh, if only he had trusted her more! Nothing like this would have happened.

Again he made himself fight the guilt that was eating away at him. The important thing now was to make these warriors see that he was not the enemy, and that together they might be able to find her before something tragic happened to her, if it had not already.

"I am not responsible for what happened here," Sun Hawk said, his voice steady, his eyes looking from warrior to warrior. This time he would not be silent. There was more than his life at stake here. There was Summer Hope's.

"I was on my way to your village, to meet with Summer Hope, when I came across the slain warrior," he continued. "He was dead already. It is the work of someone who hates the Ojibwa, not the work of an Ojibwa who wants nothing but peace between our two bands."

He knew better than to tell them about his premonition.

The fact that something had happened, and that she was out there somewhere, taken by evil men, or worse yet, injured or dead, made him feel sick inside.

And it seemed that these warriors were intent on mistrusting him, which meant that while they stood there, Summer Hope's chances worsened.

"Your words are wasted here," Eagle Wing said, his eyes following the trail of blood. "You will come with us. You are again our prisoner. You will not be allowed to escape again."

Sun Hawk's eyes widened. "Again?" he gasped. He yanked his arm away when one of the warriors grabbed it. "What do you mean 'again'? Your chief set me free last night. It is my belief that she did so for one reason, so that she could follow me to see where my village was located. She and Black Bear must have been ambushed while they were following me."

"By your warriors!" Eagle Wing exclaimed. "Your warriors ambushed and killed Black Bear, then took our chief away because you did not want her to know where your village was."

"That is not so," Sun Hawk said, taken aback by the mere suggestion. "If it were, would you not see my warriors with me now? Would I be foolish enough to be caught standing on ground soiled by blood? And would your chief not be with me now, as my captive?"

Eagle Wing sighed heavily. He narrowed his eyes as he studied Sun Hawk. "You are a clever man. Who knows what you might say to avoid capture," he said. "I order you now to take me to your village where we can search for our chief."

"I cannot do that," Sun Hawk said, his spine stiffening. He knew that they might become enraged at any moment and kill him. "There is no reason to take you there. Summer Hope is not there. And while you are standing here accusing me of wrongful deeds, she is out there at the mercy of whoever did abduct her."

"If you refuse to take us to your village, that leaves us no choice but to take you to ours," Eagle Wing said, angrily grabbing Sun Hawk's arm. "When we return to our village, many warriors will be sent out to scan the land until we finally have found your camp. If our chief is there, not only will you die, but many of your people will as well. If you do not wish for this to happen, tell us now where we can find Chief Summer Hope."

"How can I tell you when I do not know myself?" Sun Hawk said, holding his chin high. Eagle Wing gave him a shove, and he was forced to walk ahead of Summer Hope's warrior. Out of the corner of his eye he saw several warriors preparing a travois for transporting Black Bear's body back to the village.

"Eagle Wing, you are wrong to waste time taking me to your village when that time should be spent searching for Summer Hope," Sun Hawk said somberly. "I know this land. I know tracking. Let us work together as friends. Let us go now and search for Summer Hope. Each moment that passes while she is with the enemy is a threat to her life."

"If anything happens to our chief, you will be

totally at fault," Eagle Wing said, his throat dry. "Say no more. Just walk."

Fearing the worst, believing he might never see Summer Hope again, Sun Hawk deeply resented these warriors who would not listen to reason.

He now saw that it was virtually impossible for their two bands of Ojibwa to come together as one unit, as allies against the injustices of whites.

Today it was the red man who was wronging a white man . . . but a man who was Ojibwa, heart and soul.

He could do nothing but say a silent prayer that Summer Hope would come out of this alive and that those who ambushed her would be damned for eternity!

If Sun Hawk were given the chance, he would make Summer Hope's abductor pay for his crimes. Sun Hawk wasn't known to be a man of violence. But with every beat of his heart, he hoped to be the one to avenge his woman!

Ay-uh, his woman, for although there was some bad blood between them, Sun Hawk now knew that he could never love anyone but Summer Hope. He would get through these next few hours by reliving those precious moments when they had allowed themselves to behave as a man and woman in love, instead of as rival chiefs who did not see eye to eye.

"Hurry onward!" Eagle Wing demanded, drawing Sun Hawk quickly from his thoughts.

He looked over his shoulder and glared at Eagle Wing. "You are so wrong to take me prisoner again," he said flatly. "You should, instead, be looking for Summer Hope."

"You should be taking us to her," Eagle Wing snapped back. "When she is found, and you are proven guilty of having abducted her and having killed our warrior, you will be sorry you ever made the acquaintance of the Northern Lights band of Ojibwa."

Realizing that it was futile to try and explain his innocence again, and feeling certain that he would be able to escape before nightfall, Sun Hawk turned away from Eagle Wing.

His heart aching for Summer Hope, he walked onward.

10

Wild nights! Wild nights!
Were I with thee,
Wild nights should be
Our luxury!
      —EMILY DICKINSON

The sound of horses awakened Summer Hope with a start. She looked quickly around her, wincing at the memory of what had happened and where she was. Alone. She was alone!

"Black Bear, oh, no, Black Bear," she whispered.

Tears spilled from her eyes as she remembered the instant two men had leaped out of the shadows, one plunging his knife into Black Bear's back, the other grabbing her around the waist and wrestling her to the ground.

She had yanked her small pistol from her dress pocket and fired it.

She closed her eyes as she thought back to what had happened then, recalling the bullet's impact as it had entered the man's gut and caused him to fall away from her.

Stunned by having just shot a man for the first time, she had stayed on the ground for a moment and watched him groaning and groveling, clutching at his belly.

The other man had yanked the knife from her fallen warrior's back and stared disbelievingly at his companion. She had known that if she didn't shoot him also, her life would be over.

She had aimed at the man, freezing momentarily when she saw his face in the moonlight and recognized him as the Frenchman who had abducted her earlier.

When he had started to move toward her, his knife in the air, she was filled with hate and pulled the trigger.

But he had seen the danger in time to step aside. The bullet had only caused a flesh wound on his left arm as it partially ripped the sleeve away. His knife no defense against her firearm, the man had turned and fled into the darkness, leaving her there with her dead warrior and the mortally wounded attacker.

Filled with sadness over Black Bear's stabbing, hoping that perhaps he might still be alive, Summer Hope had stumbled past the injured man and fallen to her knees beside her friend.

When she had placed her fingers at his throat, despair leaped into her heart, for she felt no pulse.

The knife must have killed him instantly.

The man on the ground had pleaded with her to help him. She had peered into the darkness where Pierre DuSault had disappeared and knew that the best thing was to flee.

She could remember so vividly how she had inched away from the groaning man and watched him begin to crawl along the ground toward her. In the moonlight she had seen the trail of blood that he left behind.

A part of her had pitied the man, yet that part of her that hated him for having a role in Black Bear's death, had made her turn her back on him and his injuries.

She had gazed at Black Bear one last time. She had planned to send someone for him as soon as she returned home. Even now, she still blamed herself for his death. Had she not brought him with her. . . .

Worrying about Pierre, and what his next move might be, Summer Hope had clutched her pistol to her side as she ran into the darkness of the forest, opposite from the direction she had seen Pierre going.

It had not taken her long to realize that she was lost. Even before she had been ambushed, she had known that she and Black Bear would not be able to find their way back home until daylight.

Alone, it became even worse for her, for every direction she turned, everything looked the same. All she could see were shadows and blackness with only a rare stream of moonlight shining down through the autumn leaves of the trees.

She had traveled one way, then turned another, until she was too exhausted to go any further. She had all but collapsed beneath a tree and then fallen into an exhausted, restless sleep.

But now, as she heard horses approaching, she realized that she had allowed herself the luxury of sleeping for far too long. The sunlight was bright and Summer Hope could see a path through a break in the trees. She had only lived in the area for a short time, but she recognized the path as one having been made long ago by voyagers.

And since she now knew where she was, she knew that she was not all that far from her village.

The horses were so close now. She inched her way beneath a thick covering of forsythia bushes and waited until she finally could see who was approaching.

Tears of relief flooded her eyes when she found friends, not enemies, only a few feet away. She knew they were friends, for the five white men were dressed in black robes, which meant they were holy men. The Ojibwa called them "Black Robes."

She grabbed her small firearm and slid it into her pocket, then rushed to her feet and stood in the path, waiting for the men to reach her.

When they saw her, she could see surprise leap in their eyes.

But it was the ensuing friendly smiles that they gave her that made her breathe more easily. She knew they would be eager to escort her safely to her village.

When Father Herschel Davidson reached

Summer Hope, he drew a tight rein, then slid out of his saddle.

His gaze skimmed over Summer Hope and took in the dirt and grass stains on the skirt of her buckskin dress, and the blood.

He looked into her eyes and reached his arms out for her. "Come to me, my child," he said softly. "Let me help you in your time of trouble."

Summer Hope had learned to trust Black Robes long ago. Sobbing, feeling nothing like a chief at this moment, she found comfort and safety within the man's long, thin arms.

"Tell me what happened," Father Davidson murmured, gently stroking her long, waist-length hair. "I see blood on your clothes, but I see no injury on your person. Would you like to tell me about it?"

Wiping tears from her eyes, Summer Hope backed away from Father Davidson. "My dear friend Black Bear was murdered last night when we were ambushed," she said. Saying the words made it all the more heartwrenchingly real to her. "I . . . I had to leave him. I—I—had to flee those men."

Father Davidson eased a comforting arm around her waist and gently led her beneath a tree, where he sat down next to her.

The other four Black Robes had dismounted and stood with their horses, their eyes filled with sympathy as they listened to Summer

Hope. She opened up to Father Davidson and told him everything.

"I am to blame for my warrior's death," she said, tears again rushing from her eyes. "I should have never asked him to go with me to follow Sun Hawk."

"Who is Sun Hawk?" Father Davidson asked, raising an eyebrow.

"Like myself, he is an Ojibwa chief," Summer Hope said, seeing the surprise enter the man's eyes at her confession of being a chief. "We just recently became acquainted. But I have not yet been to his village. I wanted to see where it was located. I asked Black Bear to join me on the excursion."

"Could you not have just asked Sun Hawk to take you there himself?" Father Davidson asked, searching her eyes.

Summer Hope didn't respond, for she felt that she had already said too much to this white man who, in truth, was no more than a stranger to her.

She most certainly did not want him to know that one Ojibwa chief did not trust another enough to show her his village.

If she didn't understand Sun Hawk, how could she expect a white man to see the reasoning behind his secrecy?

"Why are you in the area?" she asked, her gaze moving over him. He was a tall, thin, frail man, whose gray-bearded face was grooved with age and whose gentle gray eyes revealed a kind, generous nature. His hair was snow-white and hung down around his shoulders.

And he had a voice that could soothe anyone's heartache away.

"Why am I here?" Father Davidson said, slowly nodding, seemingly lost in thought.

He looked into Summer Hope's eyes. "I am a minister of the Lord who has come a long distance looking for a place where my services might be needed," he said.

He glanced around him with much interest, noticing the loveliness of the trees and land. But it was the path that he had been traveling on that truly interested him. He knew that this was a voyagers' path, made purposely for convenient land travel when a certain place could not be reached by water.

He knew that he had finally found a spot where a house of the Lord was needed, for voyagers traveling here were a long way from their homes. They could use a place of solace and prayer while journeying through land that was mainly occupied by the red man.

"There will be plenty of time for me to tell you more about me and why I am here," Father Davidson said, moving to his feet. "If you would allow it, my companions and I would like to see to your safe return home."

"It is not far, but, *ay-uh,* yes, I would appreciate you accompanying me there," Summer Hope said, her voice breaking. "One man is still at large. I am afraid that he will not rest until I am dead, for he must know that I aim to see him punished for all the wrong he has done me."

"The blood on your dress," Father Davidson said, eyeing it. "Is it his?"

"*Gah-ween,* no," she said, lowering her eyes. "It is the blood of his companion. After Pierre DuSault knifed my warrior, this other man forced me to the ground. I knew that their intentions for me were not good. I . . . I had to defend myself, or die. I shot the man."

Father Davidson's eyes widened. He stroked his beard. "Did you kill him?" he asked softly.

"He is probably dead by now," Summer Hope admitted, her eyes searching his for understanding.

"Do not carry guilt inside your heart for something you were forced into," Father Davidson said, reaching a hand out for Summer Hope. "Come. Let us get you home. Your people are surely sick with worry."

"They might not even know yet that I am not there," Summer Hope said as she moved to her feet. "When Black Bear and I left, we told no one. And it is still early morning. Those at my village are only now stirring and preparing themselves for the long day ahead."

She sighed and went to Father Davidson's horse with him. She stroked the steed's brown mane. "Can I ride with you?" she asked. "I am so weary, I am not sure how far I can walk."

She realized that she was not behaving as she normally did. Very rarely had she allowed anyone to see her cry. Since she was a chief, she knew the importance of appearing strong, especially in the eyes of strangers.

But she trusted Black Robes and had learned they did not look for ways to trick red skins.

"Most certainly," Father Davidson replied. He helped her onto the horse, then mounted behind her as the others slid into their saddles.

She pointed the way to her village and said nothing more as they rode toward it.

But inside her heart she felt so many things, mainly a deep remorse over the death of her longtime friend. She and Black Bear were the same age and had grown up together as friends and allies in everything.

When she had been appointed chief, he was the first to hug her and congratulate her.

From then on he had been her right-hand man, someone she could always depend on.

At one time she had toyed with the idea of them marrying, but after much thought decided that it would not work. There was too much friendship between them to ever become romantically involved.

And now that friendship had been robbed from her.

She must see that her warriors retrieved Black Bear's body. He must be buried with all the rites of their people.

Oh, how she would miss him!

As they entered the village, Summer Hope saw that mourning had already begun for their fallen warrior. She was stunned to see his body being taken into his lodge. It was apparent that she had been missed and a search party had found Black Bear.

Everyone swarmed around her. Summer Hope slid from the saddle and allowed herself to be hugged and fussed over.

When her people finally stepped away from her, she asked Father Davidson and the others to join her in her lodge. The Black Robes dismounted their horses while her people stood silently watching.

"If you don't mind, we'd rather sit by the outdoor fire," Father Davidson said softly. He glanced at her dress before looking into her eyes. "Please go on to your lodge. We will wait for you by the fire."

Summer Hope nodded, then addressed her people. "These holy men are our friends," she said. "Bring them food and drink."

She went on into her lodge, but she didn't immediately change her clothes. She sat down beside the slowly burning fire, and hung her head and cried.

More and more she doubted that it was wise for a woman to be chief. Surely a man would not be as easily overwhelmed. Every time she found herself in jeopardy, she realized that her people's welfare was also placed in jeopardy. With Pierre still out there, her people were in danger. Because of her.

Although she hated to even consider it, perhaps it was time for her to step down.

Although she was courageous and brave, sometimes that was not enough, not when a man's muscles could better protect his people.

She hated the fact that she had been forced to use a firearm to protect herself. The thought of having killed a man made her heart feel cold and strange.

"Black Bear would have made such a wonderful chief," she whispered to herself, wiping tears from her eyes as she thought of her fallen warrior.

She would always feel responsible for his death. This guilt weighed heavily on her heart, making her doubt whether or not she should still reign as chief.

"I must get hold of myself," she whispered, rushing to her feet.

She removed the small firearm from her pocket and gazed at it as it lay almost obscenely in the palm of her hand. She shuddered as she placed it in a small buckskin pouch and tucked it away beneath her bed.

Summer Hope hurried out of her dress, went to a basin of water, and gave herself a quick sponge bath.

With a clean dress on, her hair brushed and hanging long down her back, she slid her feet into new moccasins. A voice outside her entrance flap caught her attention.

For a moment she forgot last night's ambush

and thought the voice belonged to Black Bear, for it was always he who came to her with messages while she was alone in her lodge.

She swallowed hard when she realized that Black Bear would never come to her lodge again, nor would she ever again hear his voice. It was agony to think about.

Shaken, she went to the entrance flap and pushed it aside.

Another favored warrior, Eagle Wing, stood there looking down at her from his tall height.

"Chief Summer Hope, you should know that we are holding a prisoner for Black Bear's death," he said, his eyes flashing. "I will take you to him."

She was taken aback by what Eagle Wing had said, thinking that they had found Pierre DuSault and had brought him to their village.

"How did you find him?" she asked, stepping outside and walking with Eagle Wing toward the prisoner's wigwam. "Where did you find him?"

"We found him standing not that far from Black Bear's body," Eagle Wing replied. "Of course, he denied killing him. But we knew better. We brought him back and his fate will be decided in council."

"But I thought Pierre DuSault would have more sense than to be anywhere near the death scene," Summer Hope said, glancing up at Eagle Wing.

"Pierre DuSault?" He stopped and stared

down at her. "I did not say that Pierre DuSault
is the prisoner. It is Chief Sun Hawk. He is the
one we found near Black Bear's body."

The color drained from Summer Hope's face.
Her footsteps faltered, then she broke away
from Eagle Wing and ran the rest of the way to
the wigwam. She sucked in a deep, quavering
breath, then placed her hand on the latch and
slid it quickly aside.

Sunlight flooded the interior of the wigwam
and it revealed Sun Hawk standing there, his
fists on his hips, his legs slightly parted. Summer Hope smiled weakly up at him.

Although overjoyed to see her, he could not
forget his anger so easily.

"Again I am your people's prisoner?" Sun
Hawk challenged, his eyes narrowed.

"Again you have been wrongly imprisoned,"
she soothed. "I know that it was not you who
killed Black Bear." She stepped aside and gestured with her hand toward the door. "You are
free to go. I apologize for those who have
wronged you."

Their eyes met and held.

"If you know who killed Black Bear, that must
mean that you were there," Sun Hawk said,
lowering his hands to his sides.

"*Ay-uh,* I was there," she said. "But something tells me that you already knew that."

"*Ay-uh,* I did. And I also know that you were
trailing me last night to find my village."

"You are right," Summer Hope said, her voice breaking.

"For now I will say no more about that," Sun Hawk promised, stepping closer to her. "You have enough on your mind without me badgering you about your actions."

She stepped aside to allow him to leave the wigwam.

Outside, he saw the black-robed men sitting among the Ojibwa people.

Seeing the preachers caused Sun Hawk to be thrown back in time.

He saw his father at the pulpit in his black robe. He saw his mother standing beside his father as she led the congregation in singing hymns. He saw himself as a little boy being held in his father's loving arms.

His heart ached as he pictured them lying dead on the ground, their hands almost touching, the bell that his father was so proud of only inches away.

Sun Hawk's eyes went to the face of the gray-bearded Black Robe who seemed to be speaking for the group. He was too far away to get a good look at him, and most of his face was obscured by whiskers and wrinkles.

Sun Hawk stiffened when the man looked over and caught him staring.

He thought he could see a look of wonder in the black-robed man's eyes. Perhaps he saw that Sun Hawk's tanned skin was not the true color of an Indian.

Perhaps he wondered why Sun Hawk was there among Indians, dressed as one of them, as one with them?

Unnerved by the holy man's sudden attention, and by remembrances of so long ago, Sun Hawk turned away. He gazed a moment at Summer Hope, then hurried into the shadows of the forest.

Summer Hope noticed Sun Hawk's reaction to the holy man and wondered about it. The Black Robe seemed to spark something inside Sun Hawk's mind. But what? She watched Sun Hawk until he disappeared among the dense forest trees.

The Black Robe's eyes had also followed Sun Hawk into the forest.

She went and sat down on a blanket close to Father Davidson. She was not at all surprised when his first question was about Sun Hawk.

"Who was that man?" he asked, his eyes again searching the forest for Sun Hawk. "He is a man who is white, yet he dresses like a red man. Why is that?"

"He is white by birth, but now lives among the Ojibwa," she explained. "I mentioned him to you before. He is Chief Sun Hawk of the Enchanted Lake band."

"He is white, yet he is chief?" Father Davidson asked, his intrigue of the man peaking. "How can that be?"

"As a young boy, he was taken in by a band of Ojibwa. His adoptive father was chief. Sun

Hawk was grown and revered by everyone by the time his chieftain father died. It was easy for his people to name him as their next chief."

"Interesting . . . interesting," Father Davidson said softly, stroking his beard. "I wonder where he came from. And why he was so alone that he was taken in by Indians?"

Summer Hope gave Father Davidson a questioning glance. She wasn't sure if she had the right to disclose so much about Sun Hawk to a stranger, even if this was a holy man who could be trusted. Sun Hawk's business was his own, and she already had been guilty of prying into it.

But she had a good reason to. Her people and his could come together as friends once trust was earned among them.

As for the white man? He, also, had to earn Sun Hawk's trust enough for Sun Hawk to divulge his past to him.

It became obvious that Summer Hope was not going to willingly share anything else about Sun Hawk. But even without more information, Father Davidson had thought of a possibility that made his heart race. His son had been small when he had been abducted by renegades. Could his son have traveled this far before being taken in and given safe refuge by a friendly Ojibwa tribe?

He scoffed at the very idea of this white Indian being his Jeffrey. He knew the odds were against him finding his son after searching for so many years, ever since the day he fully recovered from the blow to his head.

No. Surely not. Besides, his son would have never turned from his faith and joined those who did not worship God.

"His name," he blurted out anyway. "Do you by chance know what he was called before his name was changed to Sun Hawk?"

"*Gah-ween*," Summer Hope answered.

"Was that his name?" Father Davidson asked eagerly.

"In my language I spoke the word 'no' to you," Summer Hope said. "I said no to your question about knowing Sun Hawk's white name."

She felt empathy for him when she saw him bend forward in utter disappointment. But she decided not to interfere. She wouldn't even mention this man's interest to Sun Hawk. If the Black Robe wanted answers, he would have to be the one to question the only man who could give them to him!

11

The lords of life, the lords of life—
I saw them pass
In their own guise.
   —RALPH WALDO EMERSON

Limping, Pierre stumbled toward the British fort. He had twisted his ankle while fleeing the wrath of the Indian woman. He sighed with relief when two soldiers came out and helped him inside.

He gladly accepted a chair when it was offered to him in Colonel John Green's rugged office. He sat stiffly as the colonel raked his eyes slowly over him.

"Pierre, I see you've made a new enemy," Colonel Green said, smiling as he laced his fingers together. "Who is it this time?"

"A woman, a squaw," Pierre said bitterly. He reached a hand to the slight crease on his left arm where Summer Hope's bullet had grazed his flesh. "I need help finding her. She's trouble, John. Trouble."

"I imagine you gave her cause, now, didn't you?" John said, frowning. "Did you rape her, Pierre?"

"Naw, nothing like that," he answered. "But I did enough to rile her into wanting to see me dead."

"And is she the one who grazed your arm with a bullet?" John said, leaning over his desk, looking more closely at the wound.

"Yeah," Pierre grumbled. "And not only that. She shot my companion." He gestured with his hand toward the window. "He's out there somewhere. I imagine he's dead by now. And the other bush ranger who was in on this with us? I won't even waste time lookin' for him. I'm sure he's taken off for parts unknown with his and his friend's pelts."

"The Indian squaw. She's a feisty one, huh?" John said, a look of quiet amusement in his cool blue eyes.

"Too feisty for her own good," Pierre said angrily. "Can I get cooperation from you? Will you help me find her?"

"I doubt that I can help you," John said, gazing down at a journal, idly flipping its pages. "I'm here to keep peace with Injuns, not turn them into enemies."

"Well then, can I seek refuge here for a spell?" Pierre pleaded. "I'd as soon not show my face in these parts for a while. That squaw had a warrior with her last night. I killed him. She's out for my blood now. I don't aim to let her spill any more."

"Stay as long as you like." John shrugged.

"Just as long as you don't do anything foolish that might bring the wrath of the Injuns here."

"I'll keep my nose clean," Pierre said, standing. "I'm mighty tired and hungry, John. Can you oblige?"

"Certainly." He pushed himself up from his chair. "While I take you to your room, tell me more about this spirited lady."

"There ain't much to tell," Pierre said. "But I'm sure that you'll become acquainted with her, yourself, sometime soon. She'll probably even come to you and ask your help in findin' me."

"Don't worry, I'd never turn you over to the Injuns," John said, opening the door to a room and motioning for Pierre to go on inside. "That is, unless you give me cause to want them to scalp you for me."

Pierre's blood rushed from his face as he stopped and stared incredulously at the colonel.

"Just joshin' you," John said, laughing heartily. "Now go on inside and make yourself comfortable. I'll send food and fresh water."

"*Merci beaucoup.*" Pierre looked questionably at John, suspicious of his kindness. He had to wonder why the colonel was so eager to please someone he had never shown a fondness for.

He wondered if he had made the right choice in coming to the British for help after all.

Only time would give him that answer.

At least for now he was safe from the savages!

12

Too coldly, or the stars, howe'er it was,
That dream was on that night wind—let it pass.
—EDGAR ALLAN POE

Now that Sun Hawk was gone from the village, Summer Hope went into a serious council with Father Davidson. They sat beside the roaring outdoor fire after the sun had slid behind thick, white clouds.

It was hard for Summer Hope to think about anything but Black Bear's death, and how she already missed his companionship. When councils were held, he would always be at her right side, giving her strength whenever she felt hers waning.

So many decisions sat like a heavy weight on Summer Hope's shoulders. If she backed away from her role as chief and let a powerful warrior take over the duties, Black Bear would have been her first choice.

Now that he was gone, and without his trusted advice, she was not sure what she should do.

As the white men dressed in black sat with

her in council, she pushed everything but them, and their kindness toward her, from her mind.

Even Sun Hawk.

Spreading the skirt of her dress around her as she crossed her legs beneath her on the soft blanket, Summer Hope forced herself to be attentive and to smile at Father Davidson.

"Again I thank you for escorting me safely to my village," Summer Hope said, nodding a thank-you to a young brave as he handed her a wooden cup of hot sassafras tea. She waited to say anything else until the white men had their own cups of tea in their hands.

She took a slow sip, then set her cup aside.

"We are glad to have been of service to you," Father Davidson said. "I must tell you, though, we had seen your village through a break in the trees yesterday as we rode past it. We were going to return and make your acquaintance, for after surveying the land in this area, we have finally found the perfect place to build our church. If you would not mind, we would like to build our church on Lake Superior—close to your village, yet not too close. We know you value your privacy. We would want to do nothing to interfere with it."

Summer Hope's insides tightened, for although she found this man and his friends to be gentle, she wasn't sure if she wanted to be this friendly with them. The more association she had with whites, the more she found that she could not trust them.

She needed to associate herself with the British at Fort William. Trading could be good between her people and the Englishmen. But the men who sat in council with her now offered no such worth for her people.

Yet they were holy men, and they already had proven to be trustworthy. How could she possibly see any harm in them establishing their church of God?

"I see that you hesitate, and I understand," Father Davidson said, resting his hands on his knees as he crossed his legs beneath his robe. "I feel that you must know that my companions and I were here even earlier than yesterday. Weeks ago, before you came and established your village, we wanted to make our residence in this area. The only reason we did not stop then was because we wanted to be sure. We went farther south and then we were on our way back to the chosen land when we came across you in the forest."

"Our village has been here for only a short time, that is true," Summer Hope said. "We had planned to move further south, ourselves, but when we saw Fort William just inside the Canadian border, we could not pass up the convenience of having a fort so close by."

"We did not go that far north, for we did not wish to establish a church in Canada," Father Davidson said softly. "We are loyal Americans, through and through. When we have the need to replenish our supplies, we will travel south to find a trading post."

"My people, too, will seek out those trading posts, but for the most part, we will be dealing with the British at Fort William," Summer Hope explained. "I plan to meet in council with them soon."

She leaned closer to the Black Robe. "Please tell me more about yourself," she said, finding this small talk a way to forget momentarily what pained her heart. She looked over her shoulder and gazed at Black Bear's lodge. As she sat in council with the white men, her friend's body was being prepared for burial.

"There is not much to tell," Father Davidson said, drawing Summer Hope's eyes and attention back to him. "I have been a traveling minister for many years, since the death of my wife and the abduction of my son."

He did not tell Summer Hope about the massacre that he had somehow survived long ago. He had regained consciousness and had crawled down the road to a neighbor's house.

He had blacked out again before he was able to tell them what had happened to his son, and when he had regained consciousness several days later, it was too late. His son was gone.

He had always hoped that in his travels, God, in His mercy, might lead him to his son.

"And your friends?" Summer Hope asked, smiling at the other men. "They have been with you from the beginning of your journey?"

"Yes, they were young deacons in my church who did not yet have wives," Father Davidson said. "They dedicated their lives to the service of the Lord and offered to travel with me on my journey north."

He cleared his throat nervously and raked his long, lean fingers through his white hair. "I am too old to travel any longer," he said. "I want to build my church on the shores of Lake Superior, close to where voyagers portage across land to and from Canada. These men are far from their houses of God. I will offer them temporary refuge and prayer."

"You are a kind man with a big heart," Summer Hope said. "But you must know that my people have their own God. Because you helped me, and I see you as a man of utter goodness, I will not frown upon your desire to build your house of worship in this area."

She straightened her back and sighed heavily. "But you must promise not to try and convert my people to your faith."

"I would never interfere in your people's religion," Father Davidson said. "But know that, as they were in the past, the doors of my church will always be open to whoever wishes to enter, no matter the color of their skin."

"Please allow my warriors to help you with the building. It will be my way of thanking you for helping me in my time of trouble."

He was thankful that this woman who was a chief of a proud tribe of Indians had become his friend. It easily could have been otherwise, for so many red skins resented men of the cloth.

Father Davidson smiled. "I think we have a bargain," he said, his eyes dancing. "When my church was built in Kentucky, everyone in the area pitched in. It was built in no time. So, yes, I welcome as many hands as you can lend me."

"Kentucky?" Summer Hope said, raising an eyebrow. She had heard the name mentioned recently, but couldn't remember when, or by whom. "Where is this place called Kentucky?"

Proudly, Father Davidson began describing a land that he would always yearn for, where his wife's body was resting in peace. "It is a land of plush, waving bluegrass," he said, but even as he spoke, his mind was wandering to the young man that he had seen in the village that day.

Oh, surely not! he argued to himself. He couldn't be Jeffrey. He must put his search for his son from his mind and be content to have finally found a place to plant his roots again.

13

If I worship one thing more than another,
It shall be the spread of my own body
Or any part of it,
Translucent mold of me it shall be you!
　　　　　　　　　—WALT WHITMAN

One of Sun Hawk's warriors found a dead man floating in a stream and discovered that he had been shot before he had drowned. Concerned that another man had been killed in an area that usually was peaceful and serene, Sun Hawk had decided to go to Summer Hope to tell her the news.

But he had waited several days in order to give her time to bury her fallen warrior and mourn before having to learn about another death.

Today, though, he felt that he had waited long enough. He was on his way to meet in council with Summer Hope.

He hoped to have some questions answered about how Black Bear had died. Because the timing wasn't right, he had never asked her how she had been able to survive the ambush, and Black Bear had not.

Sun Hawk was certainly relieved to know that

she was all right. Had she died, he knew that a part of him would have died also.

Having kissed her and held her was all that it had taken for him to lose his heart forever.

And today he hoped to find a way to create a gentle peace between them so that he could take her to his village soon. He knew that until he proved he trusted her, he could not expect much more from her than quiet hostility and resentment.

Also, he needed to talk to her about the Englishmen at the fort. He hoped to be able to convince Summer Hope into shunning them, especially since the British were planning to abandon their fort soon.

Should her people show too much interest in them, and supply them with too many pelts, then they might decide to remain in the area after all.

Even the thought of that happening made Sun Hawk feel bitter. If the British were to leave the area, his people would be free of them and the greed they brought into Indian territory.

Just because the fort had been established in Canada, that did not prevent the British from crossing over into America to trade illegally.

But there was one concern that he could not shake. Should the British move from the fort, would Summer Hope and her people follow them and establish a new camp near wherever they planted their new fort?

If so, Sun Hawk might never see her again!

It was imperative, then, to persuade her against allying with the British.

He firmed his jaw and chided himself that perhaps he was putting too much thought on Summer Hope and what she would, or wouldn't do. He had lived without her up until now.

So shall he when she was gone again.

He must remember that his people came before any woman, especially a woman who might alter his destiny, which in turn might alter that of his people.

Until this point, no woman had been that important to him.

There was danger in allowing one to be now!

Yet he knew that no matter how hard he tried, he could never put her from his mind and heart.

He would have to find a way to work out everything with her so that they came together as allies in every way.

If he could make his midnight dreams come true, she would even be his wife. Yet too many things pointed to the impossibility of that ever happening.

She was a chief with duties to her people.

He was a chief who had vowed loyalty to his own.

Ay-uh, yes, today he was going to seek private council with Summer Hope. It was necessary that it was private, for he planned to speak very candidly with her about many things, and he could not do so in front of her warriors.

Alone they could speak man to woman, as well as chief to chief.

A sound came to him through the forest and stilled his thoughts. He stopped abruptly, stiffened, and listened. What he heard sounded like hammering, which meant that someone was building something up ahead. The Ojibwa did not use hammers and nails to build their lodges.

Then who . . . ?

He thought of the British, that they might be repairing or expanding their fort, that they might have decided to linger in the area now that a new band of Indians was near to trade with.

But, *gah-ween*, that could not be. As the sound of the hammering echoed through the forest, he realized that it was coming from a direction much farther south than the fort.

He was relieved. But whenever nails and hammers were being used, that could only mean one thing. White men were planting their roots on land that, by treaty, solely belonged to the red man.

When one white family came and established their residence, would that not lure many?

That meant the Ojibwa would have to share their forest and its animals with the interlopers.

Sun Hawk knew what had happened in other parts of the country. When white people came and interfered, they took over and the red man was pushed into finding a new home elsewhere.

He had even heard the ugly term "reservation" used when referring to Indians, a place where they would be herded like animals and treated even worse.

"I must see who has pushed their way into my people's lives!" he said to himself. "I must find a way to encourage them to leave."

He ran stealthily onward, his moccasined feet making no more sound than a panther's, until he saw the shine of Lake Superior through a break in the trees beyond him. There he also saw the gray-bearded, black-robed man and his white associates busy erecting a log cabin.

Stunned at such a sight, he crept closer until he got a full view of everyone and what they were doing.

The gray-bearded man was nailing together a steeple for the roof of the new cabin, which meant that it would not be a typical place for someone to live.

These men were building a church on the shores of Lake Superior!

And not only that.

He could not believe what else he saw. Several red men were among the whites, helping them.

When he recognized a few of the red men, his insides went cold.

These were men from Summer Hope's village.

They were actually helping the white men establish their house of worship, and no doubt they also would be helping build them a place of residence.

That meant that Summer Hope was allying herself with more whites, first with the British and now with American holy men who were bringing their religion to the area.

The Black Robes must have come in hopes of converting the red man to his religion!

A sudden flashback jarred Sun Hawk to the very core of his being. He recalled the day of his baptism in Kentucky just prior to his abduction at the age of five.

Holding hands with his mother, he had gone with his parents and the full congregation of his father's church to a beautiful pond that sat not that far away.

When they had reached the pond, birds were singing their melodies in the trees overhead and colorful lilies were smiling up at him from the clear, blue water. He could so vividly remember how his mother had swept him into her arms and kissed him, and how his father had taken his hand and had led him into the water until he stood in it waist-high in a white robe his mother had sewn for him.

Tears came to his eyes as he thought of how his father had placed his arm gently around Sun Hawk's waist.

He would never forget how he had gazed up at his father just moments before the baptism and how heavenly the man had appeared in his own white robe. Or how his father had smiled at him when their eyes met, and how he had steadied Sun Hawk against his arm as he began lowering him into the water.

The last thing Sun Hawk remembered having seen before going beneath the surface was his father praying as he gazed heavenward.

Sun Hawk could feel it now, the wondrous peace that had come over him as he had been immersed, and how the sun's rays filtered down through the water, touching him as if God's hands were blessing him.

He had come from the water baptized and filled with a rapturous glory!

Sun Hawk swallowed hard, unnerved by the memory that had brought so much to the surface that had lain dormant for so long. He ducked his head and ran.

He knew that he should never resent a house of worship being built anywhere, for his father's faith also had been his own.

But that had been long ago, he thought sadly to himself. Everything had changed when the renegades had swept him from the only life that he had known.

Since then he had learned another way of worshiping and had felt blessed by the Great Spirit, even though he felt that *Gitchie Manido* was one and the same as the white man's God.

After Sun Hawk prayed, he felt whole and clean again.

And he knew that it was wrong to want to deny anyone that chance. How could he, a preacher's son by birth, ever tell a man of God that he was not welcome?

Would it not be as if he were denying his own father? Yet a house of worship would bring too many people to this area. He had to find a way to stop it now, before it was too late.

Finally seeing the outskirts of her village, Sun Hawk could not help but feel some resentment over how he had been treated by Summer Hope's warriors, not only once, but twice.

That, too, had to be put from his mind.

He was there today in hopes for the future, not to cast blame for the past.

Sun Hawk's heart skipped a beat when he saw Summer Hope only a few feet away, a short distance from her village. She was kneeling beside the lake, plucking shells from the rocky shore.

Never had he seen anything as beautiful.

Her long, waist-length hair was fluttering softly in the breeze.

Her curvaceous figure was even more pronounced, as kneeling molded her dress tightly against her body.

The way the fringed hem of the dress was hiked up past her knees gave him a full view of her shapely legs.

And as she reached down for another shell from the beach, he admired her long, lean fingers.

The heat in his loins proved just how much he desired her.

If he could, he would go to her and grab her into his arms and give her a hot, passionate kiss, and forget how they had not come to terms yet on so many things.

To him, at this moment, she was only a woman. Not a powerful chief!

That she could stir such feelings within him made Sun Hawk reconsider the council he had wanted with her today.

He wasn't sure if he could ever go to her again and speak with a steady voice, when in truth her mere presence scrambled his thoughts.

Just watching her, memorizing everything about her, made him know that he was lost, heart and soul, to this woman.

How could he be able to sit with her and debate with her as chief to chief?

Deciding not to test that today after all, too puzzled by how a woman had the power to do this to him, he started to turn and retreat to the safe haven of his village.

But he had waited too long.

Summer Hope had apparently sensed his presence, for her eyes were suddenly on him and she caught him standing there.

As their eyes met and held, Sun Hawk was mesmerized into silence.

14

I felt her presence,
By its spell of might,
Stoop o'er me from above.
—HENRY WADSWORTH LONGFELLOW

Summer Hope could not believe that after thinking so much about Sun Hawk this morning that he would actually be there. It was as though she had willed him to her and he had responded.

Her knees had grown instantly weak at the first sight of him, and now her heart was thumping so hard inside her chest, she felt lightheaded.

But she was plagued with knowing that too many things could keep them apart. They were chiefs, and both had duties to their own people, unless she asked her people to appoint a new chief so that she could be free to love, and be loved!

Sun Hawk's gaze swept over Summer Hope, again seeing how feminine and alluring she looked in the lovely beaded dress that clung to her curves.

Through the copper coloring of her face he could see a slight flush and knew it was caused by his presence.

He felt tongue-tied and could not even say hello to her—a first for him. In truth, he was known to be open, talkative, and articulate.

"I have found many beautiful shells today," was all that Summer Hope could say. She was still so in awe of his presence.

She actually dreaded for him to speak, for she knew that he had not come today for small talk. She had been expecting him to come and sit in council with her and her warriors. She had no idea how he would act, especially since he had been wrongly imprisoned twice by her men.

"I know a place where there are many shells and other unusual things like gulls' eggs," Sun Hawk said at last, having almost forgotten his reason for having come today. For a while he just wanted to be a man impressing a woman. "There you will also find families of turtles. Would you like to see them? We could go there now, unless your duties beckon you back to your village."

"*Gah-ween*, no, I am not duty-bound to my people today. I am doing things that please me, for I need time to put these last few days behind me, where I have given my all to mourning Black Bear," Summer Hope replied, intrigued. She found herself caught up in unfamiliar feelings, since she had always put her loyalties to her people before her loyalties to herself.

She felt a total trust in Sun Hawk today and could not deny how badly she wished to be alone with him.

"Then you wish to go with me to this island?" Sun Hawk asked, his pulse racing at the prospect of finally being alone with her and knowing that she wanted to be alone with him.

"Island?" Summer Hope said, raising an eyebrow. "Where is this island?"

"It is not far." Sun Hawk glanced over his shoulder in the direction of Turtle Island and smiled. "By canoe we will reach it in a very short time."

"Mine is beached over there," Summer Hope said, nodding toward the canoe that rested on the rocky shore.

She bent and let the shells roll from her hands. "*Mah-bee-szhon*," come. I am anxious to see this island." She laughed softly. "It sounds almost as mysterious as the name of your band of Ojibwa."

When she saw the guarded expression that entered his eyes, and knew she had just reminded him of the one true tension between them, she wished that she hadn't mentioned it.

"Let us go to my canoe," she murmured. "I am so anxious to see the shells and the turtles. But eggs?" she asked. "Are you certain there will be eggs in nests this time of year?"

"Gulls nest in spring after returning from the south, and in autumn, before their long journey," Sun Hawk said. "We shall see how our luck holds today at finding eggs. If not? We shall come in early spring and gather them."

She lifted her hand, offering it to him in a

gesture of peace. Sun Hawk's lips formed a slow smile.

He tried to keep his hand from trembling as he reached out for hers, but the thought of touching her made him feel strangely warm and weak inside. The instant their flesh touched, there was no denying how his hand trembled as she twined her fingers through his. She looked quickly up at him, her eyes searching his.

If her village wasn't so close, and there wasn't a possibility her people could see them, he would pull her against him and kiss her.

Even the steady drone of hammering in the distance didn't break the sensual spell between them.

And if he didn't get her in the canoe soon, so that he could busy himself rowing to the island, he knew that nothing could stop him from embracing her.

"I am so anxious to see the island," Summer Hope said, her pulse racing as she gazed into his eyes dark with passion. "Do you not think we should go now, or else . . ."

"Or else what?" he asked huskily.

"I am . . . not certain," she said, hating it when she stammered and blushed.

"Come," Sun Hawk said, walking with her, hand in hand, until they reached her canoe.

He wanted to lift her into his arms and place her in the canoe, but seeming to know what he was thinking, she shook her head slightly and climbed in on her own and smiled.

And when he got inside and didn't row immediately away from land, but instead took the time to address the Great Spirit, she felt a tingling up and down her spine. It showed her that he was more Indian, than white, even though he had been born white.

She listened with affection to him performing the same ritual she had so often performed, loving the tone of his voice. The duty and conviction in it proved he saw himself not only as a red man, but also as a powerful Ojibwa chief.

"*Gitchie Manido,* Great Spirit, hear me as I speak to you today," Sun Hawk said as he looked heavenward. "You have made this water and you have made us, your children."

He looked down at a small buckskin pouch at his waist and removed it. He opened it and held it over the water and shook tobacco into the lake. "Spirits of the water," he said softly. "Here is our offering to you today so that the water shall remain smooth enough for us to pass over it in safety."

Touched by the sincerity of his prayer and the strength of his faith, Summer Hope felt herself being drawn more and more toward this man.

She stiffened when she heard the hammering in the distance grow louder and knew that Sun Hawk had to have heard it also. He had not questioned her about it, but she realized he must have seen the house of worship being built with her warriors' help. She had to wonder whether his silence meant that he accepted it, or whether he was waiting for the right time to question her about it.

She also wondered what his faith had been as a child, while he was still living in the white community.

Could he look past his dread of whites moving to this area and allow a white man of God to live there?

If so, would it be because that part of him that would always be white might crave something of his original people, for him to be a part of?

She watched him drawing the paddle through the water as he took the canoe farther away from shore. Wishing to take full advantage of the moment, she pushed everything from her mind except the two of them.

Wearing only a breechclout and moccasins, much of his beautiful, muscled body was exposed. Each time he pulled the paddle through the water, his shoulder, back, and arm muscles flexed, giving Summer Hope a full view of just how strong he was.

Although she knew that his skin was white, it was bronzed so dark. And his long hair! It was sleek and black, like her own warriors' hair. The breeze was fluttering it along his back so beautifully.

She wished to reach out and run her fingers through his hair, then move her hands to trace his noble, perfect facial features.

He had kissed her only once, but that was enough to make her hunger for more.

And her breasts grew hot at the thought of him touching them.

Her face warmed with a blush when she realized where her thoughts had taken her. Yet she could not feel ashamed of how brazen she became in the presence of this wonderful man. It was heaven to have been awakened sensually, feeling things she had never felt before.

Her shoulders swayed as she closed her eyes and envisioned lying in a bed of blankets with him. Although she was not all that familiar with a man's anatomy, since she had never seen a man undressed before, what she had seen defined beneath the tightness of a man's breeches gave her an idea of what to expect when a man finally took her to his bed.

To think that she might be with this man in this way anytime soon made a strange yet wonderful feeling stir between her thighs.

It had happened only once before.

When he had been kissing her!

"We are almost there," Sun Hawk said over his shoulder, drawing Summer Hope from her deep, wondrous thoughts. "Look. You can see Turtle Island as we approach it."

She looked past him and her eyes widened when she saw what might be a paradise spread out in the water a short distance away. Eagles were soaring over the thick, tall trees. The leaves on the trees were of various bright colors, like one large patchwork quilt spread out beneath the blue heavens.

"It is breathtaking," she said, moving to the edge of her seat. "I am so glad you are taking me there."

"I will take you there as often as you wish," Sun Hawk said. "It is a place where one can forget troubles and stress. It is like a piece of heaven amidst this large body of water."

"One needs a place like that when times grow hard," she said, thinking of how she had lost Black Bear forever.

"*Ay-uh*, and that is why I am introducing it to you, so that whenever you need to be alone with your thoughts, the island will be yours," Sun Hawk said, his loins stirring when their eyes locked in silent understanding.

He knew that he would not leave that island without having kissed and held her. He could see in her eyes that she, too, was envisioning it, and wanting it.

"I will remember, always, this moment," Summer Hope blurted, stunned by her boldness, and by allowing him to know just how deeply she felt about being with him like this. Only yesterday—even today, before they entered the canoe—there were tensions between them.

"As will I," Sun Hawk said, touched deeply by how she allowed herself to be so open with her feelings.

For a while they could both pretend there

were no problems on this earth, or reasons to resent one another.

For a while they would be lovers, feeding each other's sensual hungers.

Blushing anew, Summer Hope looked away from Sun Hawk and focused on other things. If she didn't watch herself, she might not need blankets on which to lie with this man.

Anywhere would do. She just wanted him, no matter where, or how. She knew that she would not deny this man anything today!

Her heart hammering inside her chest, she tried to think of something else, to brush aside, at least for the moment, the way she felt about this man.

Her canoe. *Ay-uh*, she would concentrate on her canoe.

The canoe in which they were traveling was her own private vessel, very light, made by her own hands out of white birchbark.

With a fair wind, it could skip on the water. Going very fast, it could withstand even heavy waves.

She carried a kind of mat inside the canoe to spread on the ground, on which one could lie or sit. Her mats, woven for her by the women of her village, were beautifully made out of different colors and closely woven of well-prepared bulrushes.

She had watched how they were made. To prepare the bulrushes, they had been cut when they were green and steamed after being bleached by the sun. They were colored before they were woven.

"We are there," Sun Hawk said, bringing Summer Hope back to him. He began steering the canoe closer and closer toward land, where the waves lapped slow and clear onto the white, sandy shore.

Sun Hawk leapt from the canoe into waist-high water, grabbed the vessel by the side, and dragged it onto the sand.

Then he turned and gazed into Summer Hope's eyes.

As she reached her arms out, giving him silent permission to lift her from the canoe, his heart skipped a beat. He knew that once he had her in his arms, he might never be able to let her go.

All that he wanted was to make love with her and to know that she wanted it as badly.

At this moment, it seemed to him that they were the only couple on the earth.

His pulse racing, Sun Hawk went to Summer Hope and slid his arms beneath her and lifted her from the canoe. When she twined an arm around his neck, Sun Hawk could not help but lower his mouth to her lips.

As they kissed, their tongues meeting in a sensual dance, Sun Hawk felt splashes of heat rising in his loins.

He heard Summer Hope's quick intake of breath when he cupped a breast, gently kneading it through the buckskin fabric of her dress.

He pulled his lips only partially away from

hers. "I cannot help but love you," he whispered huskily, looking into her eyes.

"As I cannot help but love you," Summer Hope said, choking back a sob of joy on hearing him say how much he cared for her.

As he carried her to dry land, he kissed her again and again, then laid her down on the thick, green, swaying grass, beneath towering oak trees.

"I want you," Summer Hope whispered. "Please, Sun Hawk, make love to me. I . . . so . . . badly want you."

Forgetting everything keeping them apart, Sun Hawk knelt down beside Summer Hope.

His heart pounding, with gentleness and adoration he slowly began sliding her dress up her legs. . . .

15

Do! I tell you, I rather guess,
She was a wonder, and nothing less!
—OLIVER WENDELL HOLMES

Having never been naked in front of a man, Summer Hope felt herself tightening when Sun Hawk stopped raising her dress.

But then she closed her eyes as pleasure spread through her body. She gave herself up to the rapture when Sun Hawk began gently stroking her womanhood with slow caresses of his fingers.

She found herself quickly lost to him, for never in her life had such feelings been awakened inside her.

She felt as though she might melt on the spot as the warmth spread, leaving no place on her body untouched with the deliciousness of it.

She even began to feel disappointed when he stopped the caresses and continued slowly inching her dress upward until he pulled it over her head.

Sun Hawk removed her moccasins and set them aside.

He twined his fingers through hers and lifted her hands above her head and gently held them there. His loins were on fire as he slowly raked his eyes over her.

Never had he seen anything as awesome as Summer Hope's body. Her breasts were large, round, and firm. Her belly was flat, and her waistline was tiny. Her legs were tapered perfectly down to her ankles.

"Do you know how beautiful you are?" Sun Hawk asked as he bent low, only a breath away from her lips. "You are like a delicate flower."

"One that needs plucking?" Summer Hope asked, blushing when she realized exactly what she had said, and the implication of it.

"Very much," Sun Hawk replied huskily, lowering his hands to cup her breasts. He slowly ran his thumbs over her nipples, causing her to suck in a breath of rapture and close her eyes.

Then he crushed her lips with his and kissed her heatedly, one hand sliding down to where he found her wet, throbbing, and ready for him.

When he began caressing her again, this time she slowly parted her legs so that he could have easier access to her.

Sun Hawk could feel Summer Hope's building excitement in how her heart raced and her breathing quickened.

She slid a hand down his back, slowly, caressingly, until she reached the waist of his breechclout. He held his breath, waiting to see what she would do next.

But believing that she was not so practiced with men, he reached for her hand and led it around to that part of him that was achingly hot with need.

Summer Hope's breath caught in her throat and her fingers trembled when Sun Hawk encouraged her to touch the bulge in his breechclout. She was stunned now that she had, realizing just how large and thick his manhood was.

A part of her was eager to feel him inside her, yet another part of her was afraid. If she was so tiny, would she be too small for him? This was her first time with a man in such a way. She did not want anything to take away the pleasure, or cause her to fear her next encounter.

Realizing her hesitance, and understanding it, Sun Hawk lifted her hand away from his hardness. He saw the wonder in her eyes as he removed the sheathed knife at his waist and slid his breechclout down his muscled legs.

He pulled it away from him and laid it aside, and quickly removed his moccasins.

His heart thudding wildly inside his chest, he was dizzy from wanting her. Yet he knew he must take it slow and easy, since it was clearly the first time that she had been with a man in this way, so he reached out, drew her up against him, and gently hugged her.

"I will go slow," he whispered into her ear as his hand moved in slow caresses on her back. "It *will* hurt, but only for a moment."

When he felt her stiffen, he leaned away and gazed into her eyes. "Should we wait until later?" he asked, unable to hide the huskiness in his voice. "Are you certain you even want me in this way?"

He scarcely breathed as he awaited her response. He thought he would die if she actually said that she did want to wait, or that she wasn't certain she wanted him at all.

His eyes searched hers, the whispering of the breeze and the distant warbling of songbirds the only sounds around them.

"Do I want you?" Summer Hope murmured, placing a gentle hand on his cheek. "Never have I wanted anything as badly. Do I want to wait? *Gah-ween,* no. If I had to, I would not be able to stand it."

He placed his hands on her cheeks and drew her lips to his. "My love," he whispered against them, then kissed her again, this time long and deep. He carefully positioned her on the grass, moving over her until his body blanketed hers.

He continued kissing her as he reached for his manhood and circled his fingers around it, slowly placing it at her woman's center.

His heart pounded so hard inside his chest from the building rapture, he found it hard to breathe.

But still he did not rush into taking her. He wanted to be gentle and caring, to get her past the initial pain that gripped a woman her first time, so that she would feel the joy of their coming together.

He entered her slowly, understanding when her body tightened that she was waiting breathlessly to become a true woman.

He still found it hard to believe that he was actually there with her, making love, with no thoughts of what had drawn them apart earlier.

All that he wanted now was not to please himself, but to make certain that she felt the ultimate of pleasure.

But it was not an unselfish wish because he knew that if she reached the highest peak of pleasure today, she would always hunger to be with him again, and again, as he would always hunger to be with her.

"I love you," he whispered against her lips as he wrapped his arms around her and gently anchored her against his body.

He groaned in ecstasy as he slid himself further inside her, her tightness gripping his manhood, arousing him even more.

When he broke through her virginal wall, causing a sharp pain, she cried out, then melted into his arms again when he smothered her cry with another deep, passionately hot kiss.

And then, as he began his slow, deep, rhythmic thrusts inside her, she discovered the rapture a man and woman felt when they made love.

As though practiced in ways of making the pleasure more intense, Summer Hope instinctively wrapped her legs around him and rode with him, thrust by thrust.

She gasped when he slid a hand down to her breast and cupped it, his thumb slowly caressing her nipple.

But she discovered an even greater passion when he covered her nipple with his mouth and flicked his tongue around it.

She twined her fingers through his hair and drew his mouth even closer.

With a moan of ecstasy she closed her eyes and allowed herself to feel everything to its fullest. She was truly alive now, for the first time in her life.

Her skin quivered from the building rapture as his strong arms surrounded her. Their bodies moved in unison, as though they were one.

Suddenly she felt a frantic passion overwhelm her. She had never felt anything as beautifully delicious as this new sensation sweeping through her.

And then she felt an explosion inside her that made her dizzy with euphoria. She knew that Sun Hawk was experiencing the same as his body jerked and spasmed into her, his lips on hers now fierce and demanding.

After she and Sun Hawk had matched passion with passion, and she felt as though she had returned to earth again, Summer Hope gazed into his eyes.

She was stunned to know that being with a man could be this beautiful.

She reached up and ran a finger across his lips, which seemed somewhat swollen from having kissed her so long and hard.

He, in turn, ran a hand over her body, his fingers trembling as he felt her swollen womanhood.

He smiled at her as he gently stroked her, a haziness in her eyes proving that she was not through yet with her sensual awakenings.

Nor was he.

He rolled away from her to reach down into the lake and bring a handful of water up to her body where the evidence of their lovemaking remained.

He drizzled the water onto her, laughing huskily when the shock of the water on her tender place made her suck in a quavering breath.

After washing her off, he knelt between her legs. As she watched with a guarded yet hungry look, he spread her with his fingers, then leaned low and swept his tongue over her.

When he heard her sigh, he knew that she was receiving pleasure in this new way from the man who adored her.

His tongue flicked.

His teeth nipped.

He blew his hot breath onto her, then sucked and licked until her body shook with sexual release again.

Summer Hope opened her eyes and gazed with question at Sun Hawk. "What you just did . . ." she said, somewhat embarrassed over having enjoyed so much what seemed a forbidden way of making love.

"What I did pleasured you?" he asked, slowly stroking her with his hands. Not to arouse her, but only to ease the soreness that he knew she now must be feeling.

"So very much," she replied, appreciating how he knew to be so gentle with her.

"This is only the beginning," Sun Hawk said. "That is, if you wish to be with me like this again."

"I could not live without you." Summer Hope reached her hands out for him. "*Mah-bee-szhon,* come. Lay with me. Let us just enjoy a few more moments like this before we have to enter that other world where we often are at odds with one another."

"It does not have to be that way," Sun Hawk said, drawing her against his body and hugging her to him.

"We must take it slowly," she said. She ran her hand down his back in caressing strokes. "There *is* so much that we do not agree on."

"Let us not spoil this moment by talking about those issues now," Sun Hawk said, gasping in pleasure when she reached down and twined her fingers around his manhood, making it grow again against her flesh.

"It is strange how that part of you can change so quickly," Summer Hope said. She moved away from him so that she could look at him.

Her fingers continued to stroke him until he was at his peak of fullness again.

"It only grows when a man is aroused," Sun Hawk said huskily, closing his eyes. He was afraid that she would not finish what she had started because she might not know that it would make him ache unmercifully if she didn't.

"I have aroused you?" Summer Hope asked, still watching him as she held him in her hand, truly in awe of that part of him that had awakened her to such heights of pleasure.

He chuckled. "*Ay-uh*, you have aroused me," he said, his heart pounding.

Summer Hope looked at Sun Hawk innocently. "Now what do I do?" she murmured, afraid that she might be too sore to have a sexual encounter with him again.

"There is something that you can do," Sun Hawk said, looking into her eyes.

"Please tell me." Summer Hope so badly wanted to please him since he had awakened her to a side of life that was so sensually wonderful.

"I will show you," Sun Hawk said. He reached his hands to her hair and twined his fingers through the long, black tresses.

"You will show me?" Summer Hope asked, her eyes wide as he slowly lowered her mouth toward him.

"If you do not wish to do this, I understand."

"You wish for me to do what you did to me?"

Summer Hope asked, scarcely breathing. She gazed at his manhood, which was only a breath away from her tongue and lips.

"Well, not exactly, but something similar," Sun Hawk said, his voice so deep from sexual need, he hardly recognized it.

"Show me," Summer Hope said, not hesitating to do what she could to give him the ultimate of pleasure.

He guided her mouth down over him, then closed his eyes and groaned when her tongue flicked on him. His euphoria was already so great, he felt as if he were floating.

He had never experienced such pleasure as he had today with the woman he would love forever and ever. . . .

16

On this green bank, by this soft stream,
We sat today a votive stone;
That memory may their deed redeem.
                    —RALPH WALDO EMERSON

Dressed, Sun Hawk and Summer Hope laughed and ran around gathering gulls' eggs like two children.

The scant few they found, they placed in a makeshift bag that Summer Hope had made by tying together the ends of a blanket that she had taken from her canoe.

Always carrying a spear in her canoe for protection, she had given it to Sun Hawk.

The many fat sturgeon he had speared lay in the bottom of the canoe alongside the many shells they had gathered from the rocky shore.

Summer Hope had asked Sun Hawk to go with her to her lodge after they returned from the island. She knew nothing of cooking, but she did want to attempt to cook the sturgeon for Sun Hawk, hoping to prove that she could.

Suddenly it seemed important to her to know the things that were required of a wife. She wished to make a life with Sun Hawk and be with him *ah-pah-nay,* forever, praying they could work out their differences.

As the sun dipped lower and lower in the sky, and the breeze picked up and caused goose bumps to rise on Summer Hope's flesh, she gazed at Sun Hawk. She knew they should leave now and get to the other side of the lake before night began to fall.

Yet she found the words so hard to say. She didn't want to disturb these moments of paradise yet. Deep down inside something told her that they might never be together like this again, no matter how much she or he desired it. When they came down from the clouds long enough to talk as chiefs, she could not see that things would change only because they had made love.

Nothing would take away the fact that they did have differences, and that they each had their own people.

As long as she was chief, she must always put her people's best interests before anything she might want out of life.

When she had agreed to be their chief, she had agreed to . . .

Her thoughts were stilled when she noticed Sun Hawk take his knife from its leather sheath at the left side of his breechclout's waistband.

He turned to her and beckoned with his free hand, his smile resembling that of a child who was ready to do something mischievous. She felt as though she were a child herself, and went to him, giggling.

"What are you going to do?" she asked as he took her by a hand and led her into the dense forest, away from the water. "Where are you taking me?"

She looked guardedly around her at the deepening shadows as the sun crept lower behind the far horizon. "It is scary in here," she said, her voice drawn. "The shadows too often look like men crouched and ready to pounce out on us."

"No one is here but you and I and the birds and animals," Sun Hawk encouraged, again giving her a devilish smile. "Come on with me. I must find that perfect tree."

"You are searching for a tree?" she asked, raising an eyebrow. She glanced down at his knife, then looked up at him again. "You have your knife drawn and you are looking for a tree. Why is that? You cannot fell a tree with a tiny knife, and why would you even want to?"

He chuckled and his eyes danced as he gave her another quick smile. "My knife is drawn for a reason other than felling a tree," he said. "I wish to carve something into the bark of the tree. I recall my mother showing me a carving on a tree in the woods not far from the home my father built close to his church in Kentucky. I wish to carve something similar."

The mention of a church and the name Kentucky made Summer Hope's heart skip a beat.

Her smile waned as she gazed questioningly at Sun Hawk.

When the Black Robe had mentioned that he was from Kentucky, Summer Hope had known that she had heard the name of the place before. At the time, she couldn't remember when.

Now she did!

It was Sun Hawk. He had mentioned it when he had spoken of being abducted from his home there.

And it was there that his parents had died.

Then, no. There could be no connection between the Black Robe and Sun Hawk. The fact that Kentucky had been a part of both their pasts had to be a coincidence. His father had died that day. That made it impossible for this holy man to be anything to Sun Hawk. Mentioning the connection could only bring back bad memories for Sun Hawk.

Her thoughts were interrupted when he stepped up to a huge hard maple tree, its autumn leaves appearing even a more brilliant crimson as the sun slanted its last evening rays onto them.

"This is the sort of tree my mother pointed out to me that day," Sun Hawk said.

In his mind's eye he recalled that very moment she had placed her tiny hand on the carved initials in the tree, her fingers like a caress as she ran them over the heart shape that his father had carved into the trunk.

"A hard maple," Summer Hope said, nodding. "What are you going to do, now that you have found the tree you were searching for?"

"Watch me," Sun Hawk said, his eyes twinkling. He placed the sharp tip of his knife to the tree's mottled trunk.

Then he pulled it away and slightly frowned as he gazed down at Summer Hope. "Have you learned the alphabet?" he asked. "Do you know one letter from the other?"

"Do not be insulting," Summer Hope said, squaring her shoulders. "Do I act as though I am an uneducated woman? Do I?"

"*Gah-ween*, no," Sun Hawk replied quickly, realizing his mistake in asking such a question of a woman who displayed her intelligence every time she opened her mouth to speak.

And she was a great leader.

Ay-uh, yes, she would know how to read and probably even how to work with numbers, to make sure no white man ever cheated her or her people.

"Then why would you ask me such a thing?" Summer Hope said. She relaxed her shoulders when she saw in her lover's eyes the hurt she had inflicted by her coldness.

"I was not sure if schooling was available while you lived in Canada," Sun Hawk was quick to explain.

"My people do not need a white man's school to learn what we must to survive among whites," Summer Hope said softly. "There was one man, when I was small, who came in his black robe and stayed among my people for some time. It was he who taught us what we needed to know to make certain that white man's treaties would not cheat us."

"A preacher came and lived among you?"

"A Jesuit priest. That was what he called himself. He traveled from place to place."

She glanced over her shoulder toward the shine of the lake before looking carefully into Sun Hawk's eyes. "Someone like that white priest who has come to our land with his entourage of holy men," she said. "He told me that he has been a traveling minister, going from place to place."

Not wanting to destroy these precious moments with her, Sun Hawk gently placed a hand over her lips. "Let us not talk about that now," he said. "We have some minutes left before we must head back to life and its demands. Let us not speak of the holy man who has come and caused even more tension between you and I."

She reached up and eased his hand away. "*Ay-uh*, you are right," she murmured. "Now is not the time to discuss such things. Please show me what you plan to do with the knife."

Sun Hawk once again placed the sharp tip of the knife against the tree. "Watch as I immortalize our love for one another," he said. "First I will place your initials into the tree, and then mine." She gazed in awe as he carved their initials.

"I never thought about it before, but notice how our initials are the same," she said, reach-

ing a hand and running it over them. "It is like
we are one and the same."

He placed a hand to her cheek and turned her
eyes to meet his. "We are, you know," he said,
brushing a soft kiss across her lips. "I am you.
You are me. We are of one heartbeat. One
desire."

She twined her arms around his neck. "I shall
cherish this moment *ah-pah-nay*, forever," she
whispered, lost in bliss when he kissed her, long
and deep.

When he drew away from her and again
placed the knife against the tree, just slightly
above the carvings, Summer Hope questioned
him with her eyes.

"Now what are you carving?" she asked.

Her eyes widened when she saw the shape of
a heart take form in the tree's trunk. It surrounded their initials, and in between them Sun
Hawk was carving the word "loves."

When he was through, and they had stepped
back to admire his handiwork, she saw how
beautiful it looked. The most wonderful of all
was the word "loves" that joined their initials.

"S.H. loves S.H.," she said, sighing. She
turned and gazed at him with adoration. "And
I do. Oh, so much."

"As I do you, *ah-pah-nay*, forever and ever,"
he said, drawing her against him, his heart
pounding as again he kissed her.

When the breeze grew stronger and colder,
and Sun Hawk felt Summer Hope shiver, he

thrust his knife into its sheath, swept her up from the ground, and held her against him.

"I shall always look back to today as if it were the first day of my life," he said, his voice breaking. "I will wish I were still here the moment I leave."

Summer Hope snuggled against him, lifting her head to gaze at their initials in the tree before he started carrying her away from it.

Overwhelmed by their feelings for one another, neither of them said anything else until the gulls' eggs were securely in the canoe. Summer Hope sat on the seat behind Sun Hawk as he gave an offering of tobacco to the water before heading back across it.

"You will come to my home and eat fried sturgeon and boiled gulls' eggs with me?" Summer Hope asked eagerly. Sun Hawk turned and nodded.

"I will prove that I can cook," she said, her words bringing a twinkle to Sun Hawk's dark eyes.

"I *can*," Summer Hope said, giggling, for she knew that her chances were not good. The fish probably would fall apart the moment she placed them in a skillet, and she probably would break all of the eggs before she even got them into boiling water.

She again vowed to learn how to cook, for she so wanted to impress Sun Hawk in every respect.

The enchantment of the island today had

woven itself inside her heart and she knew that it would be with her until the day she took her last breath of life.

Sun Hawk also was reliving everything they had shared today. He loved Summer Hope with an intensity he had never known, and promised that nothing would ever cause it to waver. Whatever came between them he would fight to get past with all of his might.

For her, he must learn how to accept things he might not want to.

He wanted to please, not antagonize her.

But halfway across Lake Superior, Sun Hawk saw something against the backdrop of the evening sky.

His heart stopped for a moment as he stared at the tall steeple that was now in place on the roof of the church, pointing heavenward.

Sun Hawk could not help but become angry all over again when he recalled how Summer Hope's warriors actually helped build the white man's house of worship.

He fought it inside his heart, the bitterness he felt over Summer Hope's eagerness to please the white man. If one settled there, more would follow. Soon it would be the white man's land, not the Ojibwa's!

Blinded by his anger, his feelings of only moments ago were forgotten. He turned and glared at Summer Hope.

Even after he saw her reaction, that the color had drained from her face, he still could not

push his anger aside. That quickly, he had forgotten how their names were carved for eternity
in the tall maple tree.

Now he was a chief worrying about his people, not the man who had vowed to do anything
to make things work out between himself and
the woman he loved.

"Why do you look at me like that?" Summer
Hope asked, cold with dread.

"You need ask?" Sun Hawk growled. She
looked past him, and he could tell that she, too,
saw the steeple.

When she turned her eyes back to him, and
in them he saw a stubborn defiance, he knew
that again they were two opposing chiefs. In a
sense, they were enemies!

17

When you have done, pray tell me,
That I my thoughts may dim;
Haste! lest while you're lagging,
I may remember him!
—EMILY DICKINSON

The world was a cloud of color, the sun a large disk of orange as it clung to the horizon like an upturned saucer. Sun Hawk could not help but continue to stare at the church steeple as he rowed slowly away from the island.

He stiffened when the sound of hammering reached him over the calm water, indicating that the church was not yet completed.

But the steeple was enough to make Sun Hawk feel torn with emotion.

As so many times before, he was taken back in time. Long ago, his father had proudly stood between him and his mother, the three of them holding hands and gazing up at the steeple on the roof of his father's brand-new church, only a few miles from the city of Paducah, Kentucky.

To him, the looming steeple had seemed like the connection between his preacher father and the Lord. When his father would preach and pray before his small congregation on Sunday mornings, it was as though that steeple would send forth his father's words to the Lord, and receive the Lord's blessings in turn.

Sun Hawk thought of the church bell. As though he were there now, standing with his parents, he could see the bell where it lay on its side on the ground, soon to be lifted to its new resting place in the belfry of his father's church.

His father had had his family's names engraved in the inside wall of the bell, to be there for eternity.

Eugenia, Herschel, and Jeffrey, Sun Hawk thought to himself, recalling how he had run his fingers over those words that day.

Although he had only been a small child of five then, he would never forget the tears of pride and joy in his mother's beautiful brown eyes, nor how she and his father had hugged for so long a time.

Not to leave Jeffrey out, his father had soon swept him up into his arms and gave him a fierce hug. . . .

Now at the age of twenty-eight, he was still torn over how to feel about the Black Robes' presence. Sun Hawk had only lived with white people as a child, when he knew nothing of how other people worshiped. He had been raised by a preacher father. His mother had taught Sunday school.

Deep inside, he could still remember the feelings of that young boy who loved hearing about Jesus. But as an adult, he carried within his heart resentment toward the white community over how they treated all people whose skin was red.

"Sun Hawk, you have stopped rowing," Summer Hope said, bringing him quickly back to the present. "Why?" He could not answer.

Just because a holy man reminded him of things past that made his heart ache, how could he change his feelings toward whites and their church?

And how could he not help but feel angry that Summer Hope had sided with the holy man?

Was her hunger for white man's trinkets so deeply imbedded that she would allow more and more whites to come to this land so that she could trade with them?

"Sun Hawk, please say something," Summer Hope said, reaching a hand to his shoulder, gently touching him. When she felt him flinch, she withdrew her hand as though he had shot her. And when he turned and gave her a scowling look, she recoiled and shuddered involuntarily.

"Why are you behaving in such a way?" she asked guardedly.

"I am trying to see inside your heart and truly know you," Sun Hawk answered, his voice cold. "Moments ago we shared something beautiful, which I thought was enduring, yet now I am not sure how to feel about anything."

"What has changed?"

"It is not that so much has changed, it is that for a while I just forgot."

"Forgot what?" she asked, her voice breaking, her heart thudding. She felt as though everything she had shared with Sun Hawk was a lie. If not, he would not be treating her as though he loathed her . . . as though she were a stranger.

And still she did not understand why.

Her eyes returned to the church steeple outlined against the beautiful evening sky. She had no doubt that Sun Hawk had also seen it, as well as heard the hammering. Had he seen her warriors helping . . . ?

"You are wrong to encourage the Black Robes to stay in the area," Sun Hawk said finally. He turned his back to Summer Hope and continued to talk in a scolding fashion over his shoulder as he rowed quickly toward the shore. "I saw your warriors helping the Black Robes. You are inviting other whites to the area, for a church is also a place of refuge for travelers. Do you not see that just one night in this area will be long enough for whites to see the wonders of this land? They will never want to leave it."

"But—"

"You are wrong to have come to this area to align yourself with the British at Fort William," he interrupted, his voice tight.

He began to tell her that the British were planning to abandon the fort in the near future, but he was too close to shore to continue the discussion. He dropped his paddle to the bottom of the canoe, leaped out, and yanked the boat onto the rocky shore.

Summer Hope climbed from the canoe. Furious at Sun Hawk's tone and his refusal to give her a chance to speak, she reached into the canoe and grabbed her makeshift bag in which were the gulls' eggs. She left the shells and sturgeon in the birchbark vessel, then stamped angrily over to Sun Hawk.

Before he had a chance to apologize and let her know he wanted to discuss their differences in a more civilized fashion, Summer Hope was there, fire in her eyes.

What she did next surprised him so much that he was rendered speechless. One by one she took the gulls' eggs from the bag and threw them at him.

"You can have the eggs!" she screamed. "Now go! *Mah-szhon*, leave! Take your lectures with you. You have proven to be someone I do not want to be around. Ever! Do you hear me? I want no part of your life!"

Stunned that Summer Hope would be this angry over his words, he only now realized just how harsh and authoritative he must have sounded to her, another chief. He was shocked that she would actually throw the eggs at him, breaking them all, and he could not think of what to say to stop her as she haughtily turned and left.

He should have been more guarded in how he reacted to the Black Robes' arrival, to not allow this matter to stand in the way of their new-found happiness.

When they should be celebrating their love for one another, he had made her angry instead.

His gaze moved slowly over himself. He cringed as he tried to smooth the runny mess from his bare chest with his fingers, flicking it from them. It dripped in sticky streams from his fingertips to the grass.

Suddenly a low rumble of laughter came from deep within him, which turned into a loud guffaw. He could see the humor in what she had done.

By now, she must be past her anger enough to think back at the astonished look that he must have had on his face while she threw one egg after another at him. Surely she was laughing, as well, which he hoped would help lift the anger from inside her heart.

Still smiling, he waded into the water, and when it was deep enough, he dove in headfirst and swam hard until his body was clean.

When he turned back to shore, he found several Ojibwa children from Summer Hope's village standing around her canoe, gazing down at the catch of sturgeon inside it.

As he came dripping from the lake, their eyes moved to him.

He smiled and reached down and picked up the fish that he had secured on a buckskin thong. "Do me a favor?" he said, holding the sturgeon toward the brave who seemed the oldest of the group, perhaps ten winters of age. "Will you take the sturgeon to your chief?"

Twin Arrows nodded eagerly and took the fish. "I will do that for you," he said.

"Thank you, young brave," Sun Hawk said, placing a hand on the young man's shoulder. "What is your name?"

"Twin Arrows," the boy replied, his dark eyes wide. "And you are Sun Hawk, chief of the Enchanted Lake band of Ojibwa."

"*Ay-uh*, I am Chief Sun Hawk," he said, not having to ask how the child knew who he was. Sun Hawk had been in the child's village enough times that surely everyone knew him.

"I am glad you are no longer a prisoner," Twin Arrows blurted, then turned and ran with the other children toward their village.

"So am I," Sun Hawk whispered, sighing.

Yet, in a sense, he thought to himself, he was still a prisoner . . . a prisoner of love. He knew that he must do everything to make things right between him and Summer Hope. Never to hold her again, or feel her lips on his, would be to die!

The hammering, which had stopped for a while, resumed, reminding Sun Hawk of the source of tension between him and the woman he loved. He longed for a quiet, wondrous peace, where they could sit together and prepare the fish, as planned.

If she accepted the fish from Twin Arrows,

knowing where they must have come from, he would be surprised.

For even though she loved Sun Hawk as much as he loved her, he suspected that she would be stubborn in her love.

He hated to think of how long it might be before she agreed to talk to him again.

He hated to think about how long it might be before he had the chance to make love with her again.

Sighing, absolutely certain that it was not the right time to try to make amends with Summer Hope, he followed the sound of the hammering. He never wanted to be put in the position of looking like he was begging for her attention.

When he got close enough to see the church through a break in the trees a short distance away, he crept through the forest, making sure that no one saw him spying on the activities.

He hunkered behind a thick stand of bushes and grimaced when he discovered that the warriors and white men were just now putting the finishing touches on the church.

He froze when he saw a bell being lifted from a wagon.

In flashes, like bursts of sunlight, he could not help but again remember another bell . . . another time . . . and the last time that he had seen it.

He closed his eyes and tried hard not to picture his parents' bodies, so still on the ground,

the bell not that far from where they had taken
their last breaths of life.

After Sun Hawk had been pulled onto a horse
by a renegade, the bell was the last thing that
he had seen before he had been carried away.

Three men now set down the bell close to
where Sun Hawk knelt, momentarily leaving it
resting upright on the ground. The warriors and
white men went to the embankment of the lake
and sat down. He scarcely breathed as he studied the bell.

Although he was quite small that day of the
massacre, he remembered the bell well enough
to know that this one was exactly in its image.

He glanced at the men who still sat talking,
the sunset no more than an orange glimmer behind them, then stared at the bell again.

He had to take a closer look.

Breathing hard, feeling strangely weak in the
knees, Sun Hawk crept from the protective
cover of the bushes toward the bell, his eyes
never leaving it.

His hand trembled as he reached out to touch
it. As his hand lay flat on the outside surface,
he swallowed back a lump in his throat. His
memory of that day was engraved in his heart
for eternity. He recalled how his father had
placed one hand next to his, and as they had
knelt there, touching the bell, his father had explained its importance. Every Sunday its peals
would beckon the community to the Lord's
house.

Tears filled his eyes. He could hear his father's voice as though it were only yesterday when he had last spoken to him.

Something urged him to turn the bell on its side.

As he did so, he almost fainted. The remaining light from the sunset splashed onto the engraved names.

"Eugenia, Herschel, Jeffrey," he whispered, totally stunned by the discovery.

Wondering how this could be, he stared and stared at the names. *Ay-uh,* yes, it had to be his father's bell. It must have been found that day by someone, and sold . . . or taken . . . ?

He was so engrossed, he did not hear footsteps approaching, and then stopping. Sun Hawk realized that he was no longer alone. He looked up into the weather-lined face of a black-robed man, and was mesmerized by the man's blue eyes. His father's eyes were just as blue . . . !

How often had he sat on his father's lap and gazed into his blue eyes as he had told him stories of Jesus?

Sun Hawk suddenly became that boy Jeffrey grown up into a man. Something grabbed at his heart and made him realize the truth—that his father had somehow lived through the massacre after all, that although it had looked like he was dead as he lay beside his wife on the ground, he must have still been alive!

"Father . . . ? It is I, Jeffrey," Sun Hawk managed to say, his heart racing.

He saw the Black Robe's eyes widen in disbelief. Sun Hawk gasped when the man's shoulders began to sway. He leapt to his feet just in time to catch the thin, frail man as he fainted dead away.

18

Ask me no more; the moon may draw the sea;
The cloud may stoop from heaven and take the shape,
With fold to fold, of mountain or of cape;
But, O too fond, when I have answer'd thee?
Ask me no more.
                                    —ALFRED, LORD TENNYSON

Summer Hope stood at the entranceway of her wigwam, her eyes wavering when she saw why the children had called her from her lodge.

She gazed down at the string of sturgeon, and in flashes remembered having watched Sun Hawk spear each one of them.

They had made plans to eat them in her lodge. She was even going to try cooking them. But that had been before he had insulted her.

She started to wave the children away, then dropped her hand.

How could she ever forget Sun Hawk's deep affection toward her while they were alone on the island? How could she ever forget his kisses and gentle embraces? How could she ever forget how he had awakened her body, when it was so vivid in her mind now that she could feel the ecstasy all over again?

She tried to fight these feelings. She was full of love for a man she knew she should deny herself.

They not only differed in opinions about so many things, they were of two bands of Ojibwa, two worlds.

Yet her heart could not let go of the ecstasy she had discovered today while with Sun Hawk. She knew that she could not live without it, or him, ever.

Sighing heavily, she took the fish.

She went inside and guessed how to clean and cook the catch, but felt forlorn and alone as she sat beside her lodge fire. She felt ashamed for having become so angry with Sun Hawk, and for having showered him with eggs.

She couldn't help but giggle as she recalled Sun Hawk's mortified expression. The eggs had broken and, as though they were melting, ran down his bare, muscled body.

Yes, oh, yes, she loved him. No matter what, she knew that she could not live without him! Whatever it took, she would find a way to be with him!

19

This world is not conclusion;
A sequel stands beyond,
Invisible as music,
But positive, as sound.
                —EMILY DICKINSON

Colonel John Green stood at his office window, staring out at the serenity of the sunset. It had been a beautiful day at the fort, with only a slight breeze ruffling the autumn leaves.

But with that breeze had come the sound of hammering. He had sent men out to see what was being built, and where. When they had come back and reported that a church was being erected near the voyagers' path, he had felt some hope for his future at the fort. He had been considering leaving, but a church in the area might create much interest, bringing more people and a better opportunity for trade. He had to think hard about whether to stay or move onward.

He turned and looked at Pierre, who stood at another window. "I'm going to be meeting with the Northern Lights band of Ojibwa soon," he said, sitting down behind his desk. "And I might go and have a talk with the preacher who's building a church in the area. It's too bad you're hiding out, or you could come and help translate. You've been in the area long enough to know most of the varied languages."

"Yeah, I've got to stay hidden for a while longer," Pierre grumbled. "Then I'm gonna find that squaw. She's still a threat to me. If she points me out to the warriors of her village, I'm a dead man."

"She might be from the Northern Lights band," Colonel Green said, nodding. "Describe her. I'll see if I can spot her at the village while I'm there."

"Aw, there's no way for me to describe her," Pierre said. "One Injun squaw looks no different from another. But I must say, this one was awful pretty and petite." He shrugged. "No, only I can point her out. And I will, when I feel safe enough to go lookin'."

"You think she'll forget about you?" Colonel Green asked, laughing sarcastically.

"No, as I won't forget her," Pierre said tightly. "But I won't give her the chance to find me first. I'll be the one doin' the huntin'."

"Just remember not to bring your trouble back to my fort," John said as he began entering figures in a ledger. "There's only me and my five soldiers. The red skins outnumber us too much to rile them over anything."

"Why are there so few soldiers here at this fort?" Pierre asked sullenly.

"There used to be more," the colonel said,

pausing to look at Pierre. "When I received word from my superior to send most of the men back to England, I had no choice but to comply."

"Your commander told you to plan on returning to England soon?" Pierre asked, reaching for a book on the colonel's desk and thumbing through it.

"If I could begin trade with the Ojibwa, and with the whites who might come to settle around the new church, it wouldn't be necessary for me to abandon this fort," Colonel Green said, returning to his ledger. "I'm sure men would be sent back to this fort, then, perhaps even their wives. I know that I miss mine."

"A woman is nice to have around," Pierre said, so low, the colonel didn't hear him.

Pierre's eyes narrowed as he watched the sun lowering in the sky. Soon he would go looking for that squaw, but not because he wanted her as a companion for his bed.

He wanted her dead.

And he hoped that he was the one who got the opportunity to sink a knife into her heart!

20

Whene'er the fate of those I hold most dear
Tells to my fearful breast a tale of sorrow,
O bright-eyed Hope, my morbid fancy cheer;
Let me awhile thy sweetest comforts borrow.
—JOHN KEATS

As Sun Hawk stared down at his father, he found himself surrounded by Summer Hope's warriors.

Two of the warriors grabbed him from behind and wrestled him to the ground.

Eagle Wing stood over him, glaring, his arms folded across his bare chest.

Sun Hawk could tell from their behavior that they must not have paid any attention to the Black Robe when he had left, only noticing him when he had fainted. They would assume that Sun Hawk was responsible.

"What did you do to harm the Black Robe?" Eagle Wing asked, his voice full of mistrust.

Sun Hawk barely heard Eagle Wing questioning him nor seemed to be aware that the other warriors were still holding him on the ground.

His main focus was on his father, who lay too quietly on the ground. One of the Black Robes had come and was leaning beside him, checking his pulse.

Sun Hawk watched as another Black Robe placed a damp cloth on his father's brow.

"Sun Hawk, you continue to prove yourself untrustworthy," Eagle Wing growled. He nodded at his men. "Take him. Lock him away! When he decides to answer questions, only then will he see sunlight again!"

Sun Hawk frowned at the two men who yanked him up from the ground, each of them tightly gripping an arm. They started walking him away.

Sun Hawk knew that if he shouted to them that this man was his father and he would never do anything to harm him, they wouldn't believe him.

His own people probably wouldn't believe him if he confessed such a truth to them. When they looked at him they saw a man who had no white blood left in him. And he thought he had put that part of his life behind him.

Something told him to stay quiet about these truths. Could being reminded . . . would being seen as this white man's son weaken Sun Hawk in the eyes of all red skins? Worse yet, would it make him look less of a man in Summer Hope's eyes? Or would he seem weak if he did not admit the truth?

He wasn't sure how he should feel. For so long he had lived the life of an Indian. Because whites had been so heartless to the red man, it was hard for Sun Hawk to admit that his true heritage *was* white. So much about his past had lain dormant inside his heart for so long.

Yet there was his father. He loved him no less now than he had as a little boy idolizing the man who stood for everything good on this earth, the man who had been everything to everyone—a preacher, husband, and father.

His heart skipped a beat when the warriors stopped at the sound of a voice behind them speaking Sun Hawk's name.

It was his father's voice. He had awakened and had seen Sun Hawk being taken away.

Only Sun Hawk's father could prove that he had not been hurt by Sun Hawk. But Sun Hawk knew that his father could also reveal too much.

His father had called Sun Hawk by his Indian name. He waited breathlessly to see if he would address him by the name he had been given at birth.

With a pounding heart, he listened for Father Herschel Davidson to announce to the world that he was Sun Hawk's white father.

Instead, his father seemed to understand the need to be silent about such things. He came to him and gazed at him, smiled, and then eased the warriors' hands from his arms.

"He is not at fault for my being unconscious," Father Davidson said. It was as though he was looking clean into his soul and could see that child of long ago who was now a grown man, a powerful leader.

"No, this man is not at fault," he repeated. "My heart gives me trouble from time to time. It caused me to faint."

Hearing that his father had heart problems sent a shock through Sun Hawk. Surely fate would not reunite them after all of these years only to have his father die soon from a heart attack.

He wanted to move into his father's arms and embrace him and be a child again, but he kept his distance. When they were alone, they would share the embraces that they had been denied because of the wrongful acts of renegades those many years ago.

Somehow they would make up for those lost years.

It made Sun Hawk's heart swell with gladness to know that they had the chance, that his father had survived and that God had somehow led him there.

"I would like to talk with Sun Hawk in private," Father Davidson said as he looked slowly around him, first at the warriors, and then at his friends. He was bursting to tell his friends that this was his son, the son he had told them so much about. Of course, when he had spoken of his son, he had not known that his Jeffrey was called by an Indian name, or that his behavior was now more Indian than white.

To Father Davidson, that was not important. That God had reunited them was.

Sun Hawk looked guardedly at Eagle Wing

and his warriors, whose eyes revealed mistrust, even resentment. Perhaps they thought that because the Black Robe had singled out Sun Hawk for private council, he might favor Sun Hawk and his people over Summer Hope's.

What should that even matter? Sun Hawk argued to himself. These warriors should not care one way or another about this black-robed man's choices. They should not have allied themselves with him.

But now that Sun Hawk knew that this man was his father, and that he had a weak heart, he was glad that the warriors had given him a lending hand to build his church.

Sun Hawk would see to it that his own warriors came tomorrow and helped build his father a home in which to live.

He could no longer resent a church being built in this area, for it was his father's.

He glanced over at the bell. He had to fight back tears that threatened to spill from his eyes. He would be proud to help install that bell in its rightful resting place. He would be proud to hear its peals echoing through the forest, for it was his father's bell.

"Come with me?" Father Davidson asked, reaching a hand out and placing it gently on Sun Hawk's bare arm. "Will you come with me and talk?"

Sun Hawk looked quickly at his father. "*Ay-uh*, yes, I want to talk," he said, his voice breaking.

Forgetting everyone else, Sun Hawk walked with his father to the embankment and sat down beside the lake. As the sun sank behind the horizon and the sky quickly darkened, father and son became reacquainted.

His father explained how it was that he had not died that day, but had, instead, been knocked unconscious.

Sun Hawk swallowed hard as his father parted his snow-white hair and revealed a nasty scar on his skull. He could not believe that his father could have survived such a terrible hatchet blow, but he was so glad that God had made it so.

Father Davidson continued, relating how, as soon as he was well enough, he had searched for Jeffrey. As he traveled the country, he had spread the word of God.

Sun Hawk's eyes filled with tears when his father told him where his mother was buried. He said that if he had not found Sun Hawk now, he would have never found him, for his heart was too weak to travel any further.

The more his father talked, the more Sun Hawk felt guilty for strongly having opposed the Black Robes bringing their religion to this land, where the only religion was that practiced by the red man.

Yet Sun Hawk knew that no matter how hard he fought to accept his father and his religion in this area, it was not what was best for the people who were so dear to him . . . the Ojibwa!

He wasn't sure how to tell his father his true feelings when he suddenly understood so little about himself.

Sun Hawk explained to his father how he had been taken by renegades on that terrible day of heartbreak so long ago, how the red skins had all gotten sick, and how he had escaped them and been taken in by a band of Ojibwa.

He proudly thrust out his chest when he related how he had been named chief after his adoptive chieftain father had passed on to the other side.

"Son, I am so very proud of you," Father Davidson said, reaching over and taking one of Sun Hawk's hands. "To see you so well and strong, and to know that you were singled out to be a great leader of a great people, makes my heart soar. But, son, what are we going to do? Do you want to disclose the truth of our relationship to everyone?"

Sun Hawk was afraid that the warriors might see his father holding his hand. Even though he was so happy to see his father that he wanted to shout it to the tree tops, he knew that it was best to wait, especially now that he had a special woman in his life. If she saw his father in the flesh, it might make it too real inside her heart that the man she loved was white, and she might back away from him.

Sun Hawk knew that her outburst of anger when she threw the eggs at him was only temporary. Her having gotten that angry proved her deep feelings for him.

"*Gee-bah-bah*, I feel that we should wait until later to tell the truth," Sun Hawk said, his voice drawn. "I will know when the time is right for such truths. Do you mind that we wait?"

"I want to do what is best for you," Father Davidson said, then he looked questioningly into Sun Hawk's eyes. "You addressed me in Ojibwa. Sun Hawk, what was the word you used?"

Sun Hawk smiled. "In my people's language I called you 'father,' " he said softly. "For now I cannot address you as father in the presence of others. I only will do so when we are alone."

"Being called 'father' by you in any language makes me happy and proud," he said, restraining himself from hugging his son to make up for all of the lost years. "How do I say 'son' in Ojibwa?" Father Davidson asked.

"*Nin-gwis*," Sun Hawk replied, happy that his father truly understood things.

"*Nin-gwis*," Father Davidson repeated, stroking his beard. "Yes, and I would like to learn more of the Ojibwa tongue. Will you teach me?"

"I will teach you everything Ojibwa, if you wish to know it," Sun Hawk said, sighing contentedly.

"In time, my son," Father Davidson said. "In time."

"Father, I must warn you that life in this wilderness is both *nah-nee-zah-ni-zee*, dangerous, and *san-nah-gud,* hard," Sun Hawk said, quickly translating the Ojibwa words into English. He was just now realizing how real all of this was, how his father was where few white men ever traveled, much less lived.

White people were not permitted to build their homes on land that was protected by treaty for the red man. But Sun Hawk knew that if he did not complain about his father and his friends making residence there, the American government probably would not intervene and order them to leave.

"Son, do not fret over a father who has been a part of the wilderness for many years," Father Davidson said. "From the day I was strong enough to travel, I began my search for you. Since that time, I have never planted roots anywhere or made a permanent home. But my heart is no longer the heart of a young man. It will take only so much more before it stops and rests for eternity. It is by the hand of God that I am here with you now. He saw that I could go no farther in my search."

"Father, I wish that we could have been reunited sooner," Sun Hawk said. "But I am thankful that we will at least have this time together."

"When I saw you earlier, and asked Summer Hope about you, she said something about you living near an enchanted lake," Father Davidson said, squinting to see Sun Hawk as the sky darkened. Moonlight was beginning to flood the land with its silver light. "She said that you were of the Enchanted Lake band of Ojibwa. The name is intriguing. Where is your residence? I would like to see it, to see how you live. I would love to be introduced to your people."

Sun Hawk felt his insides tighten. He wanted to take his father to his home, but it would look suspicious to those who knew he never brought anyone there, and who knew he never associated with whites.

He would have to explain it to his father and hope that he understood, for he could not take his father to his village.

Not yet, anyway.

He would, but only when he felt that the time was right.

And only if he could do so without causing more tension between himself and Summer Hope.

"*Gee-bah-bah*, Father, the man who took me in and raised me as his son established his people's village in a special, hidden place," Sun Hawk softly explained. "He saw how whites were taking over other lands. He wanted no part of it. He wanted his people to live where they would not feel threatened, where they would not be awakened one day to the barrel of a white man's firearm. He wanted them to be a free, happy people for as long as possible. Establishing their homes on Enchanted Lake gave them wondrous peace in a place where they coexisted with birds and animals. It is a place that might be called a paradise."

Sun Hawk paused, then added, "Father, I hope you understand why I cannot take you to my village. Since no one but my people are ever permitted to go there, it would raise questions if I arrived with someone whom everyone considered a total stranger. Please give me time, Father, until it is right for you to come see my people's paradise on earth."

Father Davidson listened to his son, spellbound, hearing the love and devotion in Sun Hawk's voice as he described his people and their way of life. Father Davidson realized that everything had worked out for his son, even though the idea of Jeffrey living with Indians, and being their chief, was not something he ever would have imagined.

And he did understand his son's position. "Son, it is enough to know that you are alive, well, and happy," he said. "It is enough to know that we have been reunited. I will cherish our private moments together."

Sun Hawk looked over his shoulder at the church, the steeple defined in the moonlight. He was reminded of his earlier concerns about the church being built in the area.

"Father, I still cannot help but be concerned about your church and the possibility it will bring whites here to establish homes nearby."

"Son, as I have said before, I have not built my church here to bring settlers to your lovely land," his father said, his voice calm and filled with love. "It is only to help those who already do travel across this land. God is with me and my new church, as is God with you."

Sun Hawk's eyes wavered. "*Gee-bah-bah*, in my new life with the Ojibwa, I learned a different way of religion. Father, I now pray to the Great Spirit."

He could see the initial shock register in his father's eyes, followed by a gentle peace. His father smiled. "Son, whether you call the one above God, or the Great Spirit, He is one and the same," he said.

So glad that his father understood, Sun Hawk flung himself into his father's arms, for the moment forgetting everyone and everything but them. Once he was in his father's arms, he knew that he should not have waited or worried about who might see them.

It was everything to him, that loving embrace. He had been too long without it.

21

Love seeketh only Self to please,
To bind another to Its delight;
Joys in another's loss of ease,
And builds a Hell in Heaven's dispute.
—WILLIAM BLAKE

As Sun Hawk walked through the forest, filled with many emotions, he barely noticed the weather until a brisk breeze brushed against his bare chest and face. He hugged himself to ward off the autumn chill, realizing that it was time to exchange his breechclout for a full dress of buckskin.

The older he got, the more he became aware of how quickly time passed.

Even more so now, after seeing his father as an old man. The last time Sun Hawk had seen him, he had been youthful, his hair had been black instead of white, and there had been no trace of wrinkles on his narrow face.

"It is as though I blinked my eyes and those years passed by," he whispered. With his father complaining of an old, worn-out heart, it frightened Sun Hawk to realize that their time together might be short-lived.

He would make every moment with him count.

And, yes, he would soon take his father to his village and let his people know the man who had given him life. "Even Summer Hope will know one day soon that the man she has befriended is my father," Sun Hawk said to himself, smiling.

Being reunited with his father, knowing that he was alive, had filled Sun Hawk with such a peaceful joy. He had left his father to return home, only now realizing that he was headed toward Summer Hope's village instead of his own.

He wanted to make things right between them.

He wished to share the good news with her. And not later—now!

He could not forget how angry she had been when they were last together, but he smiled at the memory of her throwing the eggs at his chest. Even now, if he looked closely enough, he could see a faint stain on his breechclout.

"She does love me," he whispered, pride in his eyes. No matter what she said, or did, when she became angry at him over one thing or another, he always would know that behind that charade was a woman whose heart beat for him. She had returned Sun Hawk's love with such passion that it had to be real and enduring.

Wanting her so badly, hoping that they could get past their disagreement, Sun Hawk broke into a run. Through the trees, he saw the shine of her people's outdoor central fire.

He hoped his apology would do, for he wanted nothing more than to be with her at this moment. He was not going to share the news about his father with Summer Hope yet, but just being with her while he was so happy would be almost the same as being totally open with her.

Happiness was contagious.

Surely Summer Hope would feel his happiness and she would, in turn, be as happy.

His heart thudded inside his chest as he slowed his pace. He entered the outskirts of her village. Many women and children were sitting around the outdoor fire listening to a storyteller. Groups of men sat elsewhere, smoking their pipes, talking.

The entrance flaps of the lodges that sat closer to the outdoor fire had been drawn aside and tied, revealing women sitting inside, sewing.

Everyone grew quiet and turned to look at Sun Hawk as he stepped into the outdoor fire's glow.

He nodded a silent hello to the people, searching quickly to see if Summer Hope was among them.

When he did not see her, he ignored the stares and walked onward until he came to Summer Hope's wigwam.

Its entrance flap was drawn closed. The smell of something cooking wafted from beneath the flap. He raised his eyebrows in surprise, remembering that she had told him she knew nothing about cooking. Someone must be with her, cooking for her. But this seemed a strange time of evening to be preparing food.

And the more he smelled it, the more he recognized the smell of fried sturgeon!

He smiled broadly knowing that she had accepted the sturgeon. Not only had she accepted it, she was going to eat it.

"Summer Hope?" he said, only loud enough for her to hear him through the buckskin flap. "It is I, Sun Hawk. I have come for private council. Will you grant it?"

He waited anxiously, melting when she pushed the flap aside and gazed up at him without anger in her eyes.

A wondrous relief rushed through him.

"Why have you come?" Summer Hope asked, her voice soft, yet guarded. "Did not we part with much anger toward one another in our hearts?"

"You were *nish-ska-diz-ee*, angry, not I," Sun Hawk said.

"You were angry, and you said many angry, hurtful things to me," Summer Hope defended. "Or else I would have not gotten angry myself. The day had been too beautiful. I wanted to continue feeling the beauty of it up until I went to my bed tonight. But . . . but you changed that. Your words hurt me."

She took a step closer. "How can you hurt me so easily if you love me so much?" she said, her lips in a pout. She placed a palm on his chest and slowly ran her fingers down the front of him. Her lips quivered into a smile. "The eggs. Oh, how funny they looked as they ran down you."

Her hand moved lower, and he flinched when she touched a stain on his breechclout that was made by the eggs. "They even ran onto your breechclout," she murmured. "I am sorry about that. I should not have done it."

When she saw how his breath had quickened, and how his eyes had darkened with passion, she suddenly realized just where her hand was resting.

The presence of her hand had made that part of his anatomy become larger.

And now that she knew about a man and that part of him, she understood what was happening.

Standing beneath the moon and stars, innocently gazing up at him, her hand touching him, she sparked his desire.

In awe of his reaction to her, she jerked her hand to her side and blushed. She smiled awkwardly at him. "I did not mean to . . ." she began, but her words failed her, for passion had ignited her as well.

Her love for this man overwhelmed anything that she had ever felt before in her life. They must find a way to get past their differences. They could not love one another so much and ruin it with foolish pride!

"Come in," Summer Hope offered as she held the buckskin flap aside for him. "We do have to talk. I . . . I feel so many things. I cannot hold them inside me any longer."

Encouraged, Sun Hawk went into her lodge. It was clean and smelled of sage, flowers, and cooked fish.

She gestured toward a pallet of furs beside the fire pit in the center of the lodge, then blushed again when she caught him staring down at a pan sitting in the coals of the fire. The fish he had caught simmered in lard.

Sun Hawk sat down, looked up to smile at Summer Hope, then froze. In the brighter light of the fire he saw what preparing food had done to her. There were flour smudges on her face. There were grease spatters on her lovely buckskin dress. One of her fingers was red and slightly burned. And her hair was tied back from her face in a long pony tail.

"Yes, I look a mess," Summer Hope said, laughing softly as she wiped her hands on the sides of her dress. "And, yes, I accepted your gift of sturgeon and have tried to cook it."

She giggled as she sat down beside him and stared at the torn bits and pieces of the fish in the grease of the heavy, black pan. "I doubt that I will eat it, though," she said, giving him a quick glance. "I will not even offer you a bite. I would not want you to get ill from food cooked over my fire."

"You have slaved over the cook fire too long for no one to eat what you have made," Sun Hawk said, taking a wooden spoon and scooping up a small piece of fish from the pan. He blew on the fish until it was cool enough for him to eat, then sank his teeth into the small chunk. His eyes brightened and he quickly ate another bite.

When he finished chewing and swallowing, he turned to Summer Hope, who seemed to be waiting with bated breath for his verdict.

"Quite good," he said, smiling.

He snared another chunk of the fish with the spoon, then lifted it to her lips.

"Trust me, Summer Hope," he said. "It is *o-nee-shee-shin*, good."

Summer Hope hesitated, staring at the bite that awaited her, then closed her eyes and tasted it.

As she chewed, her own eyes opened and brightened, for she discovered that it actually was good.

In fact, it was delicious!

"Now no one can say that you are not a good cook," Sun Hawk said, eating more of the fish, enjoying their lighthearted moment together.

He hoped their disagreement was behind them and they would not get angry at one another so quickly again.

He sorely wanted to tell her about his father, and hated keeping another secret from her, yet he truly didn't feel the time was right for anyone to know the truth.

"Tell me about your family," he found himself asking, wanting to know everything about her even though he could not be as open with

her right then. In time, though, she would know
everything about him.

She leaned toward Sun Hawk. He reached an
arm around her waist and drew her against him.

His heart soared when she snuggled closer.
She stared into the fire and began talking about
her mother and father, who had died in a snowslide, and about how she had saved others,
prompting her people to name her chief.

As she was talking, his mind wandered to
something he had forgotten to tell her earlier in
the day.

The dead man that had been found in the
stream. Whoever killed him could be a threat to
her and her people! He waited for her to finish
what she was saying, then broke the news.

When Summer Hope heard about the man,
she hung her head. She had almost forgotten
about having shot both men, knowing that the
one would surely die. The other, Pierre DuSault,
barely had been wounded. She felt an emptiness
deep inside her soul now that she realized she
had actually killed the man. The body had to
be his.

"His wound was made by my pistol," she admitted, quickly looking up at Sun Hawk. "He
was the man who . . . grabbed me while Pierre
DuSault knifed my warrior. I sent my warriors
out to search for DuSault, but he has gone into
hiding. I even asked my warriors to find the
wounded man. They failed to."

Tears filled her eyes. "I had never killed a

man before," she said, rising and pacing. "That I have seems so unreal."

Seeing how distraught she was made Sun Hawk regret having told her. He hurried to his feet and placed his hands on her shoulders.

As she gazed up at him with tear-swollen eyes, he ran a hand across her cheek. "You only did so to protect yourself," he soothed. "And killing a man such as he is not something to be ashamed of. Be proud. You did the work a warrior brags about."

A voice outside the wigwam caused Sun Hawk and Summer Hope to step away from each other and stare at the flap.

"It is I, Eagle Wing, and I have come with news," the warrior said through the buckskin fabric.

"I must see what he wants," Summer Hope said, brushing tears from her eyes with the backs of her hands.

Sun Hawk's spine stiffened as she went past him and momentarily left the lodge.

Was Eagle Wing bringing rumors to his chief about Sun Hawk's meeting with his father?

If Eagle Wing told her about how attentive Sun Hawk was to the Black Robe, how he even showed some affection for him, would Summer Hope lose her trust for him all over again?

Were those sweet moments they had just shared to be this short-lived?

When she came back into the wigwam, her eyes wary as she stood before him, he knew

that what she had been told was not good. That
quickly things had changed again between
them.

"Are you a man who speaks with a forked
tongue?" Summer Hope asked, incensed over
what Eagle Wing had told her. He had seen Sun
Hawk act affectionately toward a white man, the
same man who earlier had been the sole cause
of Sun Hawk's anger toward her.

"Those who know me would say that I am a
man known for my honesty," Sun Hawk said
tightly. "Who has said otherwise?"

"Eagle Wing told me about the affection you
showed the Black Robe," Summer Hope said. "I
cannot understand a man who speaks ada-
mantly against a person in one breath, even
chances losing the love of his woman, then sits
and talks with him like he is a long-lost brother.
Explain, or leave and never set foot in my village again."

Torn, afraid that he would be damned no matter what he said, Sun Hawk gazed quietly at
her.

He chose to ignore her question, and the in-
sult of her asking him if he was a man who
spoke with a forked tongue.

If she truly loved him, she would learn to understand and accept everything about him.

But until he broke the news of his true father
to his people, he felt he could not tell Summer
Hope.

"You should trust me more than this," Sun

Hawk said, his voice tight. He turned and left her wigwam.

"*You* do not trust *me* at all!" Summer Hope shouted after him, her voice carrying to him on the wind.

Although it tore at the very core of his being to know that he had caused her such pain again, Sun Hawk could not return to her and make things right.

His people came first.

He must reveal the truth to them, and then, only then, to Summer Hope, the woman he chanced losing forever because of his silence!

22

Break this heavy chain,
That does freeze my bones around
Selfish! Vain!
Eternal bane!
That free Love with bondage bound.
—WILLIAM BLAKE

Anxious to be with his father again, and not caring who might see them together, Sun Hawk ran in a soft trot through the forest. Today he wore his full dress of buckskin.

Later he planned to bring many of his warriors to begin building his father and his friends a spacious, two-bedroom cabin. Sun Hawk would bring many pelts for their comfort, as well as much food prepared by the women of his village.

He wished that his father could live with him at his village, but because of his father's desire to open the doors of his church to wandering souls, Sun Hawk knew that it was impossible. Even though Sun Hawk understood his father's motives, he still found it hard to accept a church in close proximity to his hidden village.

But he would not fight it any longer inside his heart. He would not speak against it to Summer Hope again or question her decision. He knew that to fight it would be to fight the two most important people of his life. His father and the woman he desired with every beat of his heart.

He hoped to meet with Summer Hope sometime soon and begin the mending process all over again. Something had to be done about how quickly harsh words and mistrust flared up between them, threatening their love and their future together.

Yes, he must find a way, but he had never met such a woman as Summer Hope. She was both complicated and intelligent. And never had he seen such a fiery, beautiful woman. To look at her was to look at the loveliest rose in summer. And her skin was as soft as a rose's petals. . . .

Lost in his thoughts as he made his way to his father's new church, he was not aware of how close he was to Summer Hope's village.

A drone of voices carried to him through the thick brush and towering trees. He stopped and stiffened when he recognized whose voices.

British soldiers! They were at Summer Hope's village.

An instant rage filled Sun Hawk as he heard how congenial Summer Hope was being to the British. She was actually bargaining with them!

Sun Hawk could no longer just stand there and listen. He must make Summer Hope understand how wrong it was to ally herself with the British, not only because the British would take advantage of her people, but also because it would make her and Sun Hawk enemies.

He could not bring his people together with hers as friends if the British were a part of her people's lives.

That the British could cause such tension between him and the woman he loved made his eyes narrow with anger.

Doubling his hands into tight fists at his sides, Sun Hawk made a quick turn and stomped toward Summer Hope's village.

When he was close enough to see the soldiers, he could only stop and stare. Her people sat in a group facing the British opposite them, a roaring fire at their backs.

Between the British and the Ojibwa were beautiful glass beads of all shapes and colors, bolts of colorful cloth, fancy lace, iron kettles, and tools for butchering.

But worst of all, there was a stack of steel traps shining in the fire's glow.

Sun Hawk had done everything within his power to keep steel traps out of his beautiful forest. Illegal trappers and English soldiers placed them there.

Sun Hawk saw no choice but to intervene, even at the risk of arousing Summer Hope's anger. He rested his right hand on the sheathed knife at his waist, tightened his jaw, and stepped into the open so that everyone could see him.

As he moved closer, he saw that there were

six British soldiers, among them their colonel, the spokesperson in this area.

Summer Hope silently glared at him as he approached her. Sun Hawk could feel her anger as though she had slapped him in the face, and knew that the task before him was not going to be easy. It was not only a battle of wits, it was a battle of the heart.

He could tell by her expression that she saw him as an interloper in her life and in her people's.

But even that would not stop him.

He had a battle to win today, regardless of their personal, intimate feelings for one another.

What he must say was in the defense of her people and the Ojibwa as a whole.

It was time for him to put his selfish needs aside and be the chief of his people.

Finally standing amid the group of Ojibwa and the English soldiers, Sun Hawk was keenly aware of the strained silence all around him.

He could hear the popping and crackling of the fire, the distant bark of a dog, and the faint cry of a child from one of the wigwams.

"Sun Hawk, I have no time to have council with you this morning," Summer Hope said, her voice tight as she tried to find a way to make him leave without ordering him to.

He must have been walking past, perhaps on his way to the lake, and had heard the soldiers' voices.

So he had purposely come, uninvited, into her

village to interrupt—no, to stop, the trans-
actions.

Already angry with Sun Hawk after last night,
she could not see how anything between them
today could be civil.

Especially not if he had come to preach to her
about what she should or shouldn't do with the
British from Fort William.

No. She wanted no part of Sun Hawk today.
She needed more time to think.

For now, she wanted him gone. At least until
they could try to work things out between them
in private.

"I would like for you to let him stay," Colonel
Green said, rising, extending a hand of friendship toward Sun Hawk. "We have not had the
pleasure to meet. But I have heard of Chief
Sun Hawk."

Sun Hawk watched the Englishman's eyes
move slowly over him. The colonel would notice
how the color of Sun Hawk's skin differed from
the Ojibwa's, yet also how he wore his hair, long
and sleek down to his waist, and how he
dressed in a full outfit of buckskin, decorated
in beads representing the flowers and trees of
the forest.

Yes, Colonel Green would know that Sun
Hawk was white, but represented himself as
red. And he already knew, by how long Sun
Hawk had avoided meeting him, that Sun Hawk
had no interest in talking trade with him.

To show his disinterest, his loathing of the

English, Sun Hawk straightened his back, squared his shoulders, lifted his chin, and slapped his hands together behind him.

The Englishman awkwardly dropped his hand to his side, gave Summer Hope a quick glance, and took his place again on the blanket spread on the ground.

Sun Hawk turned to Summer Hope. "I see that the British have brought themselves to your village not only for talk, they have brought much to you for trade," he said tightly. "Summer Hope, do you approve? Did you invite them into council with you? Did you ask for these objects to be brought to you for trade?"

Suddenly Colonel Green was on his feet again. He gestured toward the things he had brought, which he thought would interest any red skin. "Although you did not respond to my offer of friendship, I would like to include you and your people in the trade today," he said. "My men and I have brought steel traps for hunting, and steel tools for butchering, and iron kettles that can be used at your maple sugar harvest."

Before Sun Hawk could say anything back to him, Colonel Green continued, "We have offered these gifts today to Chief Summer Hope's people to encourage the Ojibwa to hunt for us at Fort William. The rich pelts brought to us will be shipped and sold to the British people in England. If both bands of Ojibwa join the hunt, you could gather many pelts before winter closes in on us all. Two bands of Ojibwa can double the pelts for the British." He laughed awkwardly. "Although we are soldiers at Fort William, experienced with firearms, we lack the skills of the Ojibwa to hunt. At heart, we are soldiers, only soldiers."

Enraged by what the Englishman was proposing, insulted that the English thought they could dupe the Ojibwa into doing their dirty work for them, Sun Hawk doubled his hands into fists. He leaned his face closer to the colonel's and forcefully said, "*Gah-ween*, no!"

He grabbed a steel trap and hurled it into the air so far, it fell past Summer Hope's private dwelling.

"Traps are evil," he said to Colonel Green between clenched teeth. "You are evil. Never will my band of Ojibwa be drawn into such a deceitful bribe as you have offered today."

He turned on a heel and faced Summer Hope. He ignored the look of utter horror in her eyes, yet he made sure to speak more gently to her.

"You must listen to reason when I say to you once again why I have kept my people away from the British," he said. "I know how these men have tricked and cheated many tribes. I see the British soldiers as a lawless, unscrupulous group of men, whose acts would be denounced by their own government were England to know of them."

"Listen here," Colonel Green said hotly. "You had better watch what you say, or—"

"Summer Hope, you should never get caught

up in the deceptive ways of these men," Sun Hawk said, ignoring the colonel's angry outburst. "You will find your people hunting for trade rather than for your own use. Can you not see the wrong in that? The new hunting methods of the whites have diminished wildlife across our country. The beaver population is almost depleted. Fewer beaver means lower water levels—which means less wild rice, which, as you know, is a staple food of the Ojibwa."

Wanting to believe that Sun Hawk spoke out of love for her and her people, Summer Hope tried to reason with him. "Sun Hawk, even before my warriors have hunted for the British, these men brought us many things, things that were taken into our lodges already. They gave each household a colorful blanket, and each woman a glass-beaded necklace, vermilion, and fans made of feathers from birds I have never seen before."

Sun Hawk had not yet mentioned to Summer Hope that the British had been planning to move onward before she had arrived and planted roots close to their fort. Now, because she seemed intent on cooperating with them, Sun Hawk was truly afraid that the British would change their minds and never leave.

He wanted her to choose the right road on her own, to turn away from the foolish things the British could give her.

But the more she talked about all that the British had given her people and promised to give them in the future, the more Sun Hawk felt he had to speak against her.

It was the woman in her talking of such frivolous things as fans made of feathers, not that part of her that was a chief.

"Summer Hope, the British knew that you, a woman, would like such things, and used them to bribe you," Sun Hawk found himself saying. "Under these circumstances, you should think like a chief first, a woman second. You are putting trivial things above the interest of your people."

So incensed, so humiliated, by Sun Hawk's berating of her in front of the Englishmen and her people, Summer Hope's eyes flashed. "I will send out my warriors soon to begin a serious hunt for you," she said to the colonel, holding her chin defiantly high. She felt Sun Hawk's eyes on her and knew he would be stunned speechless over what she had decided to do even after learning how he felt about it.

Colonel Green chuckled. "Chief Summer Hope is the wisest of the two chiefs in this council today," he said, his eyes dancing. "Her people will receive many more rewards."

He turned to face Summer Hope. "The sooner your warriors hunt and bring pelts to the fort, the sooner those rewards will be handed out to your people," he said. With a glimmer in his eyes, he added, "And perhaps I can throw in a fancy medal or two for your trouble."

He turned to Sun Hawk and frowned. "Half-breed, your band of Ojibwa will suffer because of your ignorance," he warned.

Restraining himself, his anger so strong inside his heart, Sun Hawk returned the colonel's glare. "I am no half-breed," he hissed. "I . . . am . . . Ojibwa!"

Laughing, and without even saying farewell, the British left.

As Summer Hope's people watched, Sun Hawk grabbed one of Summer Hope's arms and pulled her quickly to the privacy of her lodge.

He turned her to face him and held her by the shoulders.

"Did you enjoy seeing me ridiculed by the British?" he asked, hurt shining in his eyes. "Do you not know that behind your back they ridicule you as well? All red skins in the eyes of the British are savages, no better than animals. Do you see yourself as a savage? Do you see me as an animal? Do you, Summer Hope? Do you?"

Sun Hawk couldn't believe it when Summer Hope suddenly broke down and cried. He eased his hands from her shoulders as she looked up at him through her tears.

His heart ached to know that he had caused those tears. Yet a part of him was glad to see them. They told him that she did still care about him and what he thought.

"*Ay-uh*, yes, I saw how the British humiliated you," she said softly. "I felt your humiliation deep inside my soul."

"I did not feel the humiliation that you

thought I did," Sun Hawk said. "My pride is not wounded that easily."

"Sun Hawk, everything about me has become very fragile since I met you." Summer Hope sobbed. "And, *ay-uh*, yes, sometimes I do feel more like a woman than a chief. I have desires of a woman that I have never had before. I think of nothing but you. Do you think of me often? Will you accept my apology for having allowed the British to believe you are my enemy?"

"My *ee-quay*, my woman, there are no words to express how much I love you and need you," Sun Hawk said, brushing tears from her face. "And as for the British . . . there is so much that you and I disagree on. I doubt that will change."

"It has already," Summer Hope said, searching his eyes. "I . . . I will never allow them in my village again. The way they insulted you before me and my people, enjoying it so much, you could see it in their eyes, told me that I could not tolerate being around them again."

"Not even for fancy fans made of beautiful *mee-gwuns*, feathers?" Sun Hawk asked, relieved when he saw her lips quiver into a soft smile.

"Not even for fancy fans or feathers," she said, giggling softly. "Not for anything, my love. They must go elsewhere for what they sought at my village. I will return their gifts and tell them we cannot hunt for them."

"They will not give up all that easily," Sun Hawk warned. "They saw your weaknesses. They will return and work on them."

"They may try, but they will soon learn that I am a stronger leader than I showed them today," Summer Hope said, proudly lifting her chin.

"I want you, Summer Hope," Sun Hawk said huskily.

Summer Hope was breathless as he swept her into his arms and gave her a long, passionate kiss, his hands on the hem of her dress, slowly raising it.

When she reached down to stroke his manhood through his clothes, Sun Hawk's heart leapt with bliss. All of their anger had melted away.

23

'Twere best at once to sink to peace,
Like birds the charming serpent draws,
To drop head foremost in the jaws
Of vacant darkness and to cease.
—ALFRED, LORD TENNYSON

A smug smile on his face, Colonel Green entered his office. As he yanked off his coat and hung it over the back of his chair, Pierre DuSault sauntered into the room.

"How'd the council go at the Indian village?" Pierre asked, settling down into a plush leather chair opposite the desk and propping up his booted feet.

"Like pure gold, that's how," Colonel Green said, chuckling. "That squaw chief fell hook, line, and sinker for everything I said. Little does she know that after I have a good supply of pelts piled high in my storage room, I plan to leave the fort. I have no intention of paying her what I promised."

"What's she look like?" Pierre asked, nodding a silent thank-you to the colonel as he handed him a cigar.

"Pretty as a picture," John said, chomping off the tip of his cigar and spitting it over his shoulder. "I've never seen such perfection, actually."

"Pretty, huh?" Pierre said. He leaned down close to the flames in the fireplace and lit his cigar, then sank back into the chair and puffed eagerly.

"Like I said, pretty as a picture," Colonel Green repeated, his cigar resting in the corner of his mouth. "Funny thing, though, how you could tell there was something between the white chief Sun Hawk and Chief Summer Hope. Yet they couldn't see eye to eye on anything."

"White chief?" Pierre asked, arching an eyebrow. "Ain't that a bit peculiar? A white man acting as chief?"

"I've heard of other white warriors." Colonel Green shrugged. "I imagine there's been plenty of mixed marriages between whites and red skins."

He smiled. "But you wouldn't take a squaw as a bride, would you?" he asked, chuckling. "You'd like to get your hands on that pretty squaw that you've talked about, wouldn't you, but not to bed her. Right?"

"I've good reason to want her dead," Pierre said, a plan already forming in his mind. If by chance this squaw chief could be the woman who got away, he would easily be able to track her down.

Tomorrow he would sneak up close to the village and observe. If she was there, beautiful as she was, she would stick out from all the others like a rose.

"I met briefly with the Baptist preacher

today," Colonel Green said, knocking ashes from his cigar into an ashtray. "I doubt that he'll be much good to us for long. He's got a sickly look about him. It's in the eyes."

"But there are others with him," Pierre said. "Can't you depend on them to bring settlers to the area?"

"Father Herschel Davidson, the preacher, seems to be the main reason they have planted their roots here," Colonel Green said, recalling how the others only sat and listened while the older man carried on the conversation. "When Father Davidson dies, the others probably will leave and find a better, more populated place for their church."

"So why did they choose this site for their church now?" Pierre asked. "I'm beginning to think there might be something in particular that drew them to this area."

"Only time will tell," Colonel Green said, shrugging.

Pierre was getting tired of waiting. Soon he would make his move, and when he did, he intended to leave more than one dead body behind.

24

O cunning love! with tears thou
keep'st me blind,
Lest eyes well-seeing thy foul
faults should find.
—WILLIAM SHAKESPEARE

Kissing Summer Hope with a fierce, possessive heat, holding her silkenly nude body against his own, it was easy for Sun Hawk to forget they had ever had differences between them. At this moment there was only the two of them, lovers. He moved rhythmically within her, causing her to moan in pleasure. He thrust more deeply into her, each stroke sending them closer to rapture.

A raging hunger pushing him, yet not wanting release just yet, Sun Hawk slowed his pace. He moved his mouth to the hollow of Summer Hope's throat and gently kissed her there.

Her heart was racing as Sun Hawk's body worked its magic on her. She arched in response as he filled her with his throbbing manhood.

She clung to his neck and swept her legs around his waist to bring his heat even closer to hers.

She was aware of the moans of the man she loved.

Her own senses were spinning.

When Sun Hawk stopped for a moment and leaned a fraction away from her to look down at her with his dark, stormy eyes, the heat of his gaze was scorching.

As though she were a fragile flower, he tenderly touched her face, then reached up and smoothed back fallen locks of her hair.

"I love you," he said, his voice low. "I will never be able to get enough of you."

"And I love you more than I ever thought possible," she murmured. "Were we given cause again to be angry—"

"*Shh,*" Sun Hawk whispered as he ever so lightly placed a hand over her mouth. "Let us just savor these precious moments of paradise, for soon I must return to my duties as chief, as must you."

"I am not certain—"

Again he stopped her from speaking her doubts, this time by brushing a soft kiss across her lips.

She trembled and drew in a ragged breath when he slid a hand over one of her breasts, his thumb teasingly circling her nipple.

She felt her temperature rise when he dipped his head and flicked his tongue where his thumb had been.

She closed her eyes and slowly tossed her head from side to side as he licked first one nipple, and then the other. When he thrust himself deeply inside her again and resumed his rhythmic strokes, his mouth on hers, Summer Hope was flooded with waves of bliss.

Overcome with feverish heat, she knew that the moment of sheer ecstasy was near. It was spreading like wildfire through her now.

She could hardly control her breathing.

Sun Hawk was almost beyond coherent thought, each thrust now sending hot, white flames through him.

He cradled her close and slid his mouth to her ear. "Feel how I want you?" he whispered urgently.

"*Ay-uh*, and I am yours, my love," she whispered back. Although her thoughts were clouded with passion, she knew that was how she truly felt. She was his, yet she could not forget that they both had duties to their people. Hers to her band. His to his.

Today, more than ever before, she had felt that someone else should be her people's chief. How could she forget her response to the British?

If she advised her people to choose someone else, wouldn't that free her to give herself totally to the passion that had been awakened inside her?

To marry Sun Hawk now seemed more important than life itself! She wanted him. She wanted what other women wanted.

A home, a child. . . .

These thoughts were swept away when, with

one final thrust, her mind splintered into many flashing colors.

She cried out her ecstasy and knew that Sun Hawk had also reached his. His body trembled as he spilled his seed into her womb.

Breathing heavily, yet still throbbing from the pleasure, Sun Hawk rolled away from Summer Hope and stretched out on his back beside the gentle flames of the lodge fire.

Not wanting to give him up so soon, Summer Hope snuggled close to him.

"I wish you did not have to leave," she said, "but I know that you must. As I must return to my duties that await me."

Not wanting to even think about such things, Sun Hawk remained quiet.

Especially since today he had planned to set aside his duties to his people long enough to go and meet with his father again. He would have been there by now had it not been for the British at Summer Hope's village.

For now it seemed like she had chosen his side, yet Sun Hawk expected the British to return and try to persuade Summer Hope to trade with them.

Forcing such thoughts from his mind, he gently stroked Summer Hope's back. "I love you, but I must leave now," he said. "I do not want to stay away from you for long. How can we arrange private meetings? I do not believe it is best for anyone to realize the strength of our love for one another just yet. We must enter into that gradually."

"But even when they do find out, what are we to do about loving one another so much?" Summer Hope asked sadly. "We are of two bands, two peoples. To become man and wife, one must . . ."

"*Ay-uh*, one must choose," Sun Hawk finished for her. "But this is not the time. We both must have time to think. What matters is our love for one another. The rest will work itself out in time."

"*Ay-uh*, yes, in time," Summer Hope said, sighing. She watched Sun Hawk rise and start dressing.

"I could never love anyone as much as I love you," she said, understanding that she probably would be the one to make the sacrifice to ensure their future.

And she would do it.

But when? How? She didn't want to lose the respect of her people by choosing a man over being chief. *Ay-uh*, she had a lot to sort out in her mind now that she knew what she must do.

She reached for a blanket, and as she rose to her feet, she draped it around her shoulders. "When you came into my village after having heard the soldiers' voices, where were you headed?" she asked.

She didn't like how her question made Sun Hawk's body tighten, or how his eyes slightly wavered as he gazed down at her from his tall height.

Could it be that so soon after their lovemaking and promises to one another he was keeping secrets that he did not want to share with her?

Not wanting him to feel as though he must tell her a half truth, she spoke again before he had responded.

"What you do is your business," she said. "I apologize for poking my nose into it so often."

Seeing how she was making such an effort to keep things good between them, Sun Hawk felt that he must do the same. Honesty was very important to him.

"Pretty one, I was going to have a private council with the Black Robes," he said, touching her cheek. "I am going to offer to send my warriors to help build their private living quarters. You were kind enough to offer your warriors. I wanted to do the same."

"If you listen closely, you can hear the sound of hammers at work," Summer Hope said, hating that she already had sent her warriors to help build the Black Robes' lodge. She was very surprised that Sun Hawk had wanted to lend his help, but had she known, she would not have interfered.

"Why is that?" Sun Hawk asked, raising an eyebrow as he recognized the steady rhythmic sound of hammers at work.

"My warriors are even now building the

lodge you intended to build," Summer Hope said, noticing that he flinched.

"Then I see that my good intentions came too late," Sun Hawk said, forcing a soft laugh. He could tell that Summer Hope had not wanted to cause tension between them again.

"I am sorry," Summer Hope said softly. "Had I known . . ."

"Since you sent your warriors to do this, it frees mine to hunt," Sun Hawk said, shrugging. He brushed a kiss across her brow. "I must go now. But we will be together soon. I could not stand it, otherwise."

The blanket fell away from Summer Hope as she flung herself into his arms, their lips meeting in a frenzy of hot kisses.

With a racing pulse, she stepped away from him. She smiled as he bent down to pick up the blanket and placed it around her shoulders again.

They exchanged another soft kiss, and then Sun Hawk left the wigwam.

Summer Hope held back the entrance flap far enough to see which direction Sun Hawk went. She was not at all surprised to see him walk toward the lake and the black-robed men.

She sensed that Sun Hawk had not told her the whole story about wanting to lend a helping hand to the holy men.

She hoped that one day he would open up and tell her what the connection was. She prayed that soon there would be no secrets between them, especially regarding the location of his village.

"I still need to know," she whispered to herself. "Perhaps he will just take me there one day."

Smiling, she turned away from the entrance flap. She sat down beside the fire and reached for a piece of cooked sturgeon.

She grimaced when she took a bite of the cold fish and wondered if Sun Hawk had only praised her cooking out of kindness, if she had allowed him to convince her that it had tasted good.

"I will give him cause to brag about my cooking and mean it," she said. When she was determined to do something, she always succeeded. Cooking was no more a challenge than all of the obstacles she had faced and conquered as chief!

25

Can I see a falling tear,
And not feel my sorrow's share,
Can a father see his child,
Weep, nor be with sorrow fill'd.
—WILLIAM BLAKE

When Sun Hawk stepped up to the church with its impressive steeple, he smiled at his father, picked up a hammer, and helped Summer Hope's warriors until the sun began to wane in the west.

Everyone stood back, proud, as they observed the near-finished cabin.

Its chimney of stone stood tall against the shadowing of stately evergreen trees.

"We have a real roof over our heads tonight," Father Davidson said. He smiled warmly as he went from warrior to warrior, giving each a hug of gratitude.

After they were gone, and the other Black Robes had stepped away, Sun Hawk gave his father a fierce hug.

"Did you see?" Father Davidson asked, gesturing toward the bell in the church's belfry.

"*Ay-uh*, the bell is ready to send its peals throughout the land." Sun Hawk gazed up at the bell that was a symbol of love once shared by his family. "It is *o-nee-shee-shin*, good, to see it there, Father."

He turned and placed a hand on his father's shoulder. "It is good to have you and your church here," he said. "I should have never resented it. But it was the fact that whites mean trouble to my people that made me show my resentment so openly to you."

"I understand," Father Davidson said, taking Sun Hawk's hand from his shoulder, holding it.

"*Gee-bah-bah*, Father, let me take you to *my* home," Sun Hawk said impulsively. He had not planned to take his father there just yet. He was afraid that it might renew problems between him and Summer Hope.

But now he decided that the next time he saw her, he would make her the same offer.

Although he would always fear bringing new people to his village, he knew that he had no other choice than to take Summer Hope there, or lose her love, forever.

"But you said earlier that—"

"Yes, I know," Sun Hawk said, interrupting him.

His father looked at his black-robed friends, who were picking up debris left from building the lodge, then turned to look at Sun Hawk. "My friends are included?" he asked.

"I hope you understand when I say that you are the only one of your group that I can take there," Sun Hawk answered.

"Yes, I do," his father said, patting Sun Hawk gently on the hand. "Let me go and explain things to my friends, and then I will be ready to go."

He cast his eyes heavenward. "Soon it will be dark," he said. "Should I tell my friends I will stay with you tonight so that we can avoid traveling in the darkness?"

"I would enjoy your company for a full night," Sun Hawk said. "As will my people. We can sit in our council house beside a fire and talk. They will learn about you, my father. They already have heard me talk about you, but it has been many moons. I believed it was best not to remind them of the white side of my character, so that they would see me only as Ojibwa."

"My son, that part of you that was borne of your mother and father's love will always be white," Father Davidson said softly.

"Yes, I know that, now that I am a part of your life again," Sun Hawk said. "And so shall my people know that, and, I hope, accept it."

He waited for his father to explain things to his friends, and then they set out walking through the darkening forest toward his home. He was not aware that someone was following them.

"Oh, and by the way," his father said. "A British soldier, a Colonel Green, came today and asked about things."

"Like what?"

"Like why we are here and how long we plan to stay."

"What was his reason for asking?"

His father went quiet, for he didn't want to tell his son that the British hoped he could lure many settlers to the area with his ministry. If so, the British would profit, and he knew that his son would not want this. Perhaps he should not have established his church in this area after all. He didn't want to cause any hardships for his son.

"Son, I've been thinking," he said. "It just might be time for me to retire."

"Retire?" Sun Hawk asked, his eyes widening. "What about your church? Your ministry?"

"Do you think you'd welcome an old man in your life?" Father Davidson asked softly. "I could move to your village, and urge the others to go elsewhere with their ministry."

Sun Hawk was stunned. "You must be certain about such a decision," he said carefully.

As they walked onward, Father Davidson studied Sun Hawk out of the corner of his eye. He wasn't sure how to take his son's response.

He tried not to take it as a rejection, knowing Sun Hawk needed time to work it out inside his heart. This could change many things for Sun Hawk and his people.

Father Davidson didn't want to interfere in his son's future. They had been separated for too many years, and he didn't want to do anything now that might destroy their new-found friendship.

Sun Hawk didn't know how to answer his father. He was afraid that he did not truly want to live with him at his village. He thought that his father was only offering to give up his ministry because he felt it was best for Sun Hawk.

He was torn, but soon he would have to give his father an answer. He only hoped it was the right one for them both!

26

O! he give, to us his joy,
That our grief he may destroy,
Till our grief is fled and gone.
—WILLIAM BLAKE

Twilight had turned to night. The moon was a perfect, bright circle of white against the dark sky.

In the distance a coyote yelped, followed by another and another.

A breeze stirred the autumn leaves above him as Sun Hawk continued to lead his father toward his village.

"I had given up on finding you," Father Davidson said. "I had lost hope long ago, yet I could not give up . . . until recently. My old body reminded me that I could go no further. When we arrived at this land, where everything is still untouched and beautiful, I knew that I had come home. I knew where I must plant my final roots."

"*Gee-bah-bah*, I knew so long ago that I had found my home away from home here," Sun Hawk said, maintaining a slow place so that he would not tire his father. He was trying to keep the concern out of his eyes every time he looked at his *gee-bah-bah*, but deep inside his heart he knew that his father was not well.

Again he thought about what Father Davidson had suggested, that he come live with Sun Hawk. Sun Hawk and his people had done quite well for themselves, living away from others and using their own resources to feed and clothe themselves.

But Sun Hawk knew that most things changed with time. After he introduced his father to his people and brought Summer Hope to meet them and discover the true paradise of Enchanted Lake, the location of his village would no longer be secret.

"Son, you have gone quiet again," Father Davidson said, reaching over to touch Sun Hawk gently on an arm. "Are you regretting taking me to your home? If so, it's not too late to turn back."

"No, I hold no regrets for what I am doing tonight," Sun Hawk said, giving his father an easy smile. "I am eager for you to see how I live, how my people prosper. You will then know why your son's eyes show such happiness, such contentment."

Sun Hawk's smile deepened. "But I must confess, Father, the joy you see in my eyes is caused also by something else," he said. Soon he would announce to the world that he loved Summer Hope.

The more he thought about it, and about the

inevitability of change, the more he felt they should not keep such a thing from their people.

Once the truth was out, then he and Summer Hope would arrange things so that they could get married.

"Son, you are again lost in thought," Father Davidson said, drawing Sun Hawk's attention back to him. "And you haven't said yet whether or not you'd welcome me as a part of your life. I'd like to spend my final years with you, Sun Hawk. If you and your people would accept this old, tired man at your village."

He smiled at Sun Hawk. "But first, son, tell me to whom your mind drifted moments ago? What lady takes you into dreamland as your eyes dance?"

"You can tell?" Sun Hawk asked, surprised. "You know that I am thinking of a woman?"

Father Davidson laughed. "It isn't very hard to figure out. I might be old, but I remember what it is like. I'm happy for you."

Sun Hawk grinned. "Thank you, Father."

When they came to a place where flat slate rocks were used as steps, Sun Hawk took his father by an elbow and assisted his every footstep.

"Soon we will be at my home," Sun Hawk said. "That lady, Father? The one who invades my every waking thought? She is Summer Hope. We have only recently met, but we knew immediately of our love for one another."

"Summer Hope?" Father Davidson said, raising an eyebrow. "But I have been told by her warriors that there is much tension between you two chiefs."

"We have put all of our differences behind us," Sun Hawk said.

"But you are chiefs to separate bands of Ojibwa," Father Davidson persisted. "How can you see a future together?"

"It will be worked out, somehow," Sun Hawk said, with determination. "Somehow, we *will* work it out."

He quickly changed the subject. "See the glow of the fire through the trees up ahead?" he asked. He was glad that they were almost at his village, for how could he answer his father's questions about Summer Hope when he did not know, himself, how they could ever be man and wife?

"Yes, I see the fire, and now I even see the shine of a lake," Father Davidson said, watching his footing as he continued to travel downward. Tall spruce trees towered above them on both sides.

"Soon you will also see our lodges, and then my people," Sun Hawk said, gripping his father's elbow more tightly as the slant of land steepened. "Careful now, Father. Do not let the skirt of your robe cause you to trip."

"Although you have explained how you came to be an Ojibwa chief, I still find it hard to grasp when you call them 'your people,' " Father Davidson said. "Your family, your mother and I, were your people."

"I have never forgotten that," Sun Hawk said, stopping to gaze directly into his father's eyes. "Through the years I kept both you and Mother alive inside my heart. How could I not? You were wonderful, caring parents. When I refer to 'my people' today, I speak of my Ojibwa family. They became my life after I was orphaned, or thought I was orphaned. They, too, are wonderful and caring. They took me in as one of their own and looked after me all these years. They are my people. But you are my true father."

He wrapped his arms around his father and hugged him. "*Gee-bah-bah,*" he said, his voice breaking. "The Great Spirit blessed me when he led me to the Ojibwa, as he blessed you and I when we found each other again. I will forever be grateful."

They embraced again, and just before Sun Hawk led his father into the village, he turned to him and smiled. "Father, it would make me even more grateful if you were to come and live with me," he said. "We have been apart for too long." He reached out to touch his father's arm. "But are you certain? Are you giving up the ministry for all of the right reasons?"

"It is time, my son, it is time," Father Davidson said, his voice tight. "Now tell me. Are you certain that you want this old father living with you?"

"Father, I have missed you," Sun Hawk said.

"Please stay if this is what you truly wish to do."

"Then I shall!" Father Davidson exclaimed, beaming.

Sun Hawk smiled back. "When, Father?" he asked, his voice full of emotion. "When?"

"After I arrange things with my associates," he said, easing away. "Soon, son. Very, very soon."

Still smiling, Sun Hawk led his father into his village.

When his people came from their lodges and saw the old man with him, he could see an instant shock register in their eyes. Never had any white man been allowed.

But trusting Sun Hawk's decisions, they soon relaxed and sat in council to hear Sun Hawk's explanation.

As he spoke, his father sat next to him on plush pelts inside the large council house. Sun Hawk carefully watched the expressions of his people. Although he knew that he should not have to hold back the truth, he could not help but see that his people were wary of it.

Sun Hawk felt a twinge of uncertainty about reminding them that he had been born into the white world. Seeing that his true father was still alive might make his people think twice about having chosen him as their chief.

If they believed that the white man's presence might make Sun Hawk waver in his duties as chief, they might go into a private council, and discuss replacing him.

The fact that he had taken it upon himself to bring a stranger, a white man, into their village might give them enough cause to want to oust him.

But how could he be denied his true father? Surely his people would respect his honesty in not keeping his father's identity a secret.

And then there was Summer Hope. Soon they also would know about her! Would it be too much at one time for them to accept?

His fears about having brought his father into his village were soon laid to rest. His heart sang with gratitude when one by one his people came to his father and welcomed him.

He could tell that they were touched deeply by their chief having been reunited with his father after so many long years.

Sighing, an inner peace making his eyes shine, Sun Hawk joined his people in song. The women came and went from the lodge, bringing food for a celebration.

And after the celebration was over and everyone was in their lodges, Sun Hawk and his father went and sat on a bluff that overlooked Enchanted Lake and the wonders surrounding it.

"You have seen tonight how special my people are, and why I am so content to be among them," Sun Hawk said, sliding a blanket around his father's frail shoulders. "Although I regret having been taken as a child from the security of my true family, I am so happy to have had the chance to know this life with the Ojibwa."

'After being with them I understand everything," Father Davidson said, lifting a corner of the blanket so that they could sit beneath it together.

"And I feel so blessed that they understood," Sun Hawk said.

He frowned slightly as he glanced over at his father. "But we must be careful, *gee-bah-bah*, that until you have moved your things to my village, no one follows us when we travel back and forth."

He squinted into the darkness, realizing that he had been so caught up in his conversation with his father as they had come through the forest that he might not have been as careful as he usually was.

So far, he had eluded everyone who desired to know the location of his village.

Surely tonight was no different.

"Since it is such a problem, there is no need for me to come to your village until I have found a way to give the news of my retirement to my associates. Until then, it is much simpler for you to come to my lodge for our time together," Father Davidson said, then laughed. "Besides, this old ticker of mine might not hold out very many times traveling over the rocks and hills that surround your village."

"Father, your heart?" Sun Hawk asked, his voice filled with concern. "Just how bad is it?"

"At times its beat is erratic," Father Davidson replied. "Other times I feel it skip, and wonder if it is going to beat again. Sometimes, like yesterday when I first saw you, I feel lightheaded and faint."

"Have you gone to a doctor?" Sun Hawk asked, wondering if he should suggest allowing his Shaman to check him over.

Quickly thinking better of it, he kept silent. He knew that it must be difficult for his father to accept some things about his life as an Indian. Especially that his son never entered a house of worship anymore, and that when he prayed, he addressed the Great Spirit instead of God.

Sun Hawk suspected that his father would think that he had not owned, or had even opened, a Bible since he was a little boy.

In that respect his father would be wrong, for Sun Hawk had traded for a Bible once, when he had been old enough to catch his own game and skin a pelt for trade.

Although his people avoided traders, Sun Hawk had entered a camp of whites when he had seen a mother reading the Bible to her children beside an outdoor fire.

He had surprised them. Dressed in only a breechclout and moccasins, his hair waist-length, he had appeared more Indian than white even then.

But they had been kind enough to accept his beautiful doeskin pelt for the Bible.

Many a night Sun Hawk had sat alone in his wigwam, reading and remembering—his mother, whose face was that of an angel, and his father, whose holiness showed in his beaming smile.

"On my journey north, yes, I have stopped from time to time to get a doctor's advice about my heart." Father Davidson nodded. "Every doctor said there was nothing they could do to help. When I was a young man, as I began my search for you, the trouble started, and through the years it has worsened. One day it will just stop. That will be a blessed time for me, when I will join God, your mother, and all those I love who have passed on before me to the glorious heaven."

"But, *gee-bah-bah*, you must not plan to leave me any time soon," Sun Hawk said, swallowing hard. "I have only been reunited with you."

"God will comfort you when I say my last good-byes," Father Davidson said, reaching over to pat Sun Hawk's hand.

He looked away from Sun Hawk when wolves suddenly howled somewhere in the distance. "There is so much about this land that I want to know," he said, quickly changing the subject. "Listen to the wolves. To some they might sound threatening. To me their song is like music."

'To me, also. All of the animals in our forests have a purpose," Sun Hawk said, relieved to have something else to talk about besides his father's health. "Moose are dependent upon wolves to control their numbers, and upon beaver to provide dams and aquatic vegetation for food. Beaver serve as a summer food for the wolf, and beaver ponds eventually become meadows that support a variety of smaller animals."

In awe, Father Davidson listened attentively. "I have never heard it told in such a way," he said softly.

Sun Hawk continued, "The red fox eats the hare, who, if left unchecked, would destroy the forest that supports the moose, that supports the wolf. In such a system of delicate balance, no one animal or life is more important than another."

Father Davidson nodded, then chose his words with care. "Speaking of a delicate balance," he said, "I would like to know something else. I am aware that the British established a fort just past the Canadian border line. I have heard from Summer Hope's warriors, as they were building my church, that you are against allying yourself with the British. Is that true?"

"Very true," Sun Hawk answered. "For more than one hundred fifty years the French, British, and Americans offered axes, blankets, knives, kettles, and beads, and many other things, to entice the red man to bring them expensive furs."

He paused. "Profits to the fur companies were

enormous," he said bitterly. "At times a canoe-load of trade goods worth two thousand dollars was given to the red man in exchange for furs valued at more than thirty thousand dollars. The whites grew richer as the red man grew poorer and too often depleted the land of the animals he needed for his own survival."

"But this never happened to your band of Ojibwa?" Father Davidson asked with concern.

"Never," Sun Hawk said, his jaw tight. "And never shall the British fool my people into trading with them."

He thought of Summer Hope and how the soldiers from Fort William had tried to play their game with her people. And also with his father.

He knew that his father had ignored them and would do nothing to ally himself with them.

He hoped that Summer Hope's change of heart would make the British see the futility of staying any longer in the area.

"And how do you feel about the voyagers?" Father Davidson asked.

"They have never been much of a concern to my people, not like the bush rangers who, from time to time, invade our land," Sun Hawk said, in his mind's eye seeing Summer Hope being held captive in the bush rangers' canoe.

"Bush rangers?" Father Davidson asked, arching an eyebrow. "Those men who abducted Summer Hope were bush rangers, weren't they?

I have never made an acquaintance with such a man."

"Consider yourself better off for it," Sun Hawk said, then explained in detail who the bush rangers and the voyagers were. "As you might know, Grand Portage, where the British established a fort a short distance from the voyagers' travel path, used to be the center of the world for the voyagers. Once a year, in July, the 'pork-eaters' and 'winterers,' the names they called their separate groups, came together there to trade and celebrate. In the 1780s, the post contained many buildings, a canoe works, and several hundred Indians who worked at cleaning and packing furs to be sent to Montreal."

"Indians worked side by side with the British?" Father Davidson asked, his eyes wide. "They actually worked together?"

"That was the time of the Sioux, when that tribe outnumbered the Ojibwa. The Ojibwa never allied themselves with the British in such a way," Sun Hawk answered.

"The Sioux as well as the Ojibwa live in these woods?" Father Davidson asked. He looked warily into the thick forest on all sides of them.

"The number of Sioux in the area are few," Sun Hawk said. "There were wars between the Sioux and Ojibwa over the Sioux alliance with the French and British. The Ojibwa won. The Sioux scattered to parts unknown. Perhaps you will find a family of Sioux here and there, but never a large population in any one place in the Minnesota Territory."

"And so your people stayed apart from everyone else and relied solely on your skills at hunting," Father Davidson said, gazing at Sun Hawk.

"Trapping is an instinct to the Indian," Sun Hawk said, nodding. "The red man knows the ways of the wild. He uses this instinct, or skill, in the spring and fall to obtain pelts of muskrat, fox, mink, raccoon, and rabbits. Pelts are used for food, clothing, and lodging."

He smiled. "My favorite food is *zush-ka-boo-bish*, muskrat soup," he said, laughing softly when he saw his father shudder.

"You do not agree that muskrat could make a tasty dish?" he tested.

"When you talk of muskrat, I see a rat in my mind's eye," Father Davidson said, then laughed along with Sun Hawk when he realized that his son had been joking.

"Are you ready to go to your bed of blankets?" Sun Hawk asked, smiling gently at his father.

"Tonight I am so content, I will rest like a baby," Father Davidson said.

They sat quietly for a moment longer, enjoying the time alone with the stars, moon, and night songs.

27

My mistress bent that brow of hers;
Those deep, dark eyes where pride demurs,
When pity would be softening through,
Fixed me a breathing-while or two.
—ROBERT BROWNING

After having taken his father safely to his new home, Sun Hawk could hardly wait to get to Summer Hope's lodge.

There was so much to tell her—so much to share with her!

First he would tell her the wonderful news about who Father Herschel Davidson truly was.

Then he would tell her all about his father, and how he had taken him to his village.

He smiled when he thought of how he was going to invite her to his village in the very next breath.

Yes, today he would make all wrongs right between them so that they could talk seriously about a future together. When a man and woman loved one another as much as Sun Hawk and Summer Hope loved each other, there must be a way to find peace.

As he entered her village, the sun was mid-point between morning and the noon hour. Everyone, even the children, was doing their daily chores. He was glad that only a few people seemed uncomfortable at him being there again.

He stepped up to the entrance flap of Summer Hope's wigwam but did not have to speak her name to bring her there. She apparently had heard his footsteps. When she pushed the entrance flap aside, she didn't show a quick joy at seeing him, and he was taken aback by her cold demeanor. She looked beautiful in a white doeskin dress that was heavily fringed and beaded, with her hair hanging in two thick braids down her back. Their last parting had been a sweet one, after finding intense bliss in one another's arms. As he had left her lodge, she had been wrapped only in a blanket, her body still warm from their lovemaking.

So why would she now treat him as though he were no more than a stranger? Sun Hawk wondered.

His eyes searched hers questioningly, yet he was unable to read her feelings.

"*Mah-bee-szhon*, come in," Summer Hope said, her voice cold as she held the flap aside for Sun Hawk.

He hesitated, then sighed heavily and walked past her.

She dropped the flap and turned to face him, watching as the glow from her lodge fire cast dancing shadows on Sun Hawk's face. Seeing him was like being stabbed in the heart. Only moments ago Eagle Wing had brought news that made her feel as though she and Sun Hawk had never come together as a man and woman in love. She could hardly find the words that she knew she must say.

More than likely, when they were through talking, they would have no more councils, or moments of blissful ecstasy together. Blind trust and understanding could go only so far, and she had reached her limits.

His devotion to her had been tested last night and he had shown that the love he had professed was all false. He had proven to be—as she had once accused him—a man who spoke with a forked tongue!

"I see you are troubled by something," Sun Hawk finally said when he could no longer stand the silence. "Speak it aloud to me so that I will know why you are treating me like a stranger."

"And you are not?" Summer Hope asked, hating it when her voice broke.

"What do you mean?" Sun Hawk said, raising an eyebrow. When he reached out for her, to wrap his arms around her, she stepped away and defensively hugged herself with her own arms.

"Tell me what is wrong," Sun Hawk said, dropping his hands to his sides. "If I have done something that has upset you this much, it is only fair that I know what it is."

"Fair?" Summer Hope said, a sob lodging in

her throat. "What do you know about what is fair and what is not?"

"You are talking in circles," he said.

Frustrated, he again reached a hand out toward her. He winced when she actually slapped it away.

Deciding to change tactics, she gave him a forced smile. She would speak in a sweeter tone in order to see if she could get honest answers out of him by using a woman's deception. It was something she actually abhorred. In truth, she was a straightforward woman who never talked around things.

And she felt that she deserved everyone to be as honest with her, especially the man who claimed to love her. But she already had cause to believe he was not as he had seemed. He was a man she perhaps did not even know. She felt foolish for having given herself to him, body and soul, when she should have been more cautious.

"Oh, Sun Hawk, I am so *gee-mah-szhon-dum*, sorry," Summer Hope said sweetly. "I did not mean to make you uncomfortable."

"I am not uncomfortable," Sun Hawk said. "I am just puzzled by your behavior."

"Like I said, I am sorry," Summer Hope purred.

She reached a hand to his face. It was hard for her to touch his cheek gently, when she so badly wanted to slap it.

"Sun Hawk, can we start all over and forget

how I was behaving?" she asked. "I just had something on my mind. I have managed to get past that now. Can you forgive me? Can you?"

She stiffened when he reached out for her and drew her into his arms. Then she could not help but soften inside. Being with him, loving him so much, it was hard to remember why she should be angry.

His breath warmed her cheek as he brushed a kiss across it, and she shivered with passion.

Feeling herself becoming lost to him, yet needing answers, she sighed and eased from his arms.

She bent to a knee beside her lodge fire and shoved a log into the slow-burning flames.

"It is much colder this morning," she said, stalling. "I will soon have to have my firewood pile replenished."

"I shall do that for you," Sun Hawk said, moving beside her. "And when it becomes the dead of winter, I hope that you and I will be warming each other in our shared blankets every night and not have much use for fire."

She looked quickly over at him. "Have you come today to take me to your village?" she asked bluntly, knowing that she must not let this small talk continue.

She had to get answers from him. *Now!*

The suddenness of her question and the look of anger in her eyes made Sun Hawk realize that something still was not right.

Although he had come here today to take her

to his village, he no longer felt as though he should. Her temperament, her stiffness when he had first drawn her into his arms, the fact that she had slapped his hand away when he had reached out to touch her, all told him that something had happened.

And until he knew what it was, he was not about to open his and his people's lives to her by taking her to his village. He felt that must wait until another time.

"In time I will take you there, but as I have said more than once to you, it is a hard thing to do . . . to expose my village to outsiders," he said. "I want my people, as a whole, to be comfortable with my decision to bring outsiders among them."

Her eyes glaring, her hands circled into tight fists at her sides, Summer Hope leapt quickly to her feet. "Outsiders? You refer to me as an outsider after all that we have shared?" she screamed. She pointed to the entranceway. "*Mah-zhon*, go!"

She swallowed hard, then said, "And take your heart with you, for I no longer want it!"

Stunned by her outburst, and by her continued erratic behavior, Sun Hawk just stood there staring at her, his eyes wide.

"How could you deny me what you gave the white holy man?" Summer Hope asked, fighting back the urge to cry. "You took Father Davidson to your village last night. He was until two sunrises ago a total stranger to you, and yet you will not take me, whom you have vowed more than once to love forever?"

She pointed to the entranceway more determinedly. "I said to leave!" she cried. "Never come to my village again. I will order my guards to keep you away if you try!"

Finally understanding what this had been about, he quickly became hot with anger at her tactics to get answers from him. He now wanted answers himself. Sun Hawk's eyes flamed as he grabbed Summer Hope's wrists.

"How do you know about the Black Robe being at my village?" he hissed, his teeth clenched.

"You were followed," Summer Hope answered, lifting her chin defiantly. "Eagle Wing, my warrior who followed you, came and reported to me what he saw."

"You had me followed?" Sun Hawk said, his eyes widening in disbelief. He dropped her hands as though she were poison. He was finding it hard to accept that she had gone behind his back.

Like bullets firing from a gun, his words came forcefully and heatedly. "You are a deceitful woman."

"I am deceitful?" she cried out. "You are the deceitful one. You refused me something you gave the white man. How could you? Do you make love to a woman even though you see her as . . . untrustworthy?"

"*Ee-quay*, woman, would you refuse your own

father entrance into your lodge were he still alive?" Sun Hawk said, his voice tight.

"You know that I would not," Summer Hope said, looking questioningly into his eyes. "When he was alive, my *gee-bah-bah*, father, was always welcomed. But . . . what does that have to do with this?"

Sun Hawk leaned closer to her face. "The man who I took to my village and into my lodge is my blood-kin *gee-bah-bah*," he said. "Father Herschel Davidson is my true father."

She gasped as she stared incredulously up at him.

He gazed at her for only a moment longer, then turned and left her lodge.

"His . . . *gee-bah-bah*?" she whispered, in awe of the discovery, and feeling quickly ashamed for how she had tricked him into revealing the truth.

"He will hate me forever," she sobbed. She gazed at the entrance flap that still swayed from his hasty exit. "And he left before I could tell him that I had not given the orders for him to be followed! Eagle Wing did it because he wanted to please me."

She hung her head and sobbed into her hands. She was torn over what to do next. Go to him and explain? Apologize? Or just let it go and accept that it was for the best. It did seem an impossible thing . . . their coming together without either one of them finding a way to destroy the trust and love of the other!

She gazed through the smoke hole above and looked into the blue heaven. "What should I do?" she asked, hoping that her mother or her father might find a way to send her a sign.

"I feel so *gee-nay-ta*, so alone," she whispered, a tear sliding down her cheek. "If I have lost him, oh, how could I stand it, especially knowing that it was my own foolishness that sent him away?"

28

Ever drifting, drifting, drifting,
On the shifting currents,
Of the restless heart.
—HENRY WADSWORTH LONGFELLOW

Colonel Green stood at the window of his office and peered into the thick vegetation of the forest. "Where can he be?" he asked, then turned on a heel and glowered at Lieutenant Oscar Trower. "Oscar, didn't anyone see Pierre leave? You know that he could ruin things with the Ojibwa for us. If he goes snooping near Chief Summer Hope's village and is caught, he could tell the savages we gave him refuge at our fort, while knowing that he was a hunted man. If so, the Ojibwa certainly would never have another council with us."

"It doesn't look as though they will, anyhow," Lieutenant Trower said, lighting a pipe as he sat down in a plush leather chair beside the desk. "Chief Sun Hawk made sure of that."

"Chief Sun Hawk my ass," Colonel Green said, easing down into his chair behind the desk. "That woman chief is a beautiful lady who appreciates beautiful things. After she has time to think about what she's missing by not trading with us, she'll come knocking on our door. I know she'll soon make a deal with us."

He turned and looked over his shoulder at the window, then frowned at Lieutenant Trower. "Send out some men to look for that damn bush ranger," he said. "When you find him, tell him that if he wants us to give him a place to stay until he decides to move on, he'd best get back here, pronto."

Lieutenant Trower nodded and knocked out the ashes from his pipe into the fireplace. Colonel Green rose from his chair and held out a hand for his pipe. "Make sure the Indians don't see you out there," he said. "We don't want to associate ourselves openly with the bush ranger, and if you are seen searching the premises, you won't have any choice but to tell the savages the truth, or make them suspicious."

"I think we'd be better off if we send the bush ranger packing," Lieutenant Trower said, sliding his heavy blue uniform jacket on, the gold buttons gleaming in the glow of a kerosene lamp.

"No, not yet, anyhow," Colonel Green said, running his fingers through his shoulder-length golden hair. "I have an idea he'll come in handy, one way or another. He's very knowledgeable of the area."

"Most bush rangers are." The lieutenant chuckled. "They've set enough traps and stolen enough pelts from the Indians."

"Those damn bush rangers are an untrustworthy lot," Colonel Green agreed as he sat down again. "That's why if we need a scapegoat later on, why not let it be Pierre? No one'll miss him if he comes to a bad end while doing dirty work for us British."

"I see your point," Lieutenant Trower said. He stood stiffly, saluted the colonel, and left the room.

"Yeah, a scapegoat," Colonel Green mused. "Mine."

29

Breast that presses against other breasts,
It shall be you!
My brain it shall be your
Occult convolutions.

—WALT WHITMAN

Feeling frantic over what had transpired, Summer Hope paced her lodge, her braids bouncing on her shoulders.

Hoping that Sun Hawk was as upset, she kept glancing at the entrance flap. If only he would be there suddenly, his arms outstretched for her, she despaired to herself.

She couldn't understand how things kept happening to tear them apart.

"We are so much alike, that is why," she whispered to herself.

Ay-uh, yes, that was the true answer to their constant conflicts. They were of the same stubborn nature.

She knew that most of that came from their upbringings. Both of their fathers had been chiefs. As she and Sun Hawk were chiefs. Both were used to leading, not being led.

And she knew that was reason enough to keep them from compromise. They might never be able to find a gentle peace in their romantic relationship.

"That cannot be so!" she cried, aching inside at the thought of having to give him up, to give up a life of wondrous embraces and kisses.

"And children born of our love," she said, a sob catching in her throat.

What in life was fair? she argued, the inside conflict even worse than the battle that had only moments ago taken place.

"I must go to him," she decided.

She started to run from her lodge to try to catch up with Sun Hawk, then stopped and hurried to the bag holding her small pistol. She must remember never to travel again in the forest, or anywhere for that matter, without the protection of her firearm.

Especially today, for she would not ask any of her warriors to go with her. Black Bear's death was still too fresh on her mind and in her heart. Had she not asked him to accompany her on her search for Sun Hawk's village, he would not have been a part of the ambush. He would be alive, even now, for her to confide in, for her to take comfort from.

No, never again would she place anyone else in harm's way while she was working on her personal life.

Were it for the sake of her village instead of her own selfish, womanly needs, then she would feel it was right to ask her warriors to travel with her.

But this was for her own self. She hoped that, in the end, whatever happened regarding Sun Hawk would not also put her people in a compromising position.

She had always placed them first; her personal life second.

Now, as her heart ached for the man she loved, she knew that was no longer possible. She wanted different things now than she had before having met Sun Hawk. She wanted him.

Worrying that too much time had elapsed already since Sun Hawk had left, and having only Eagle Wing's verbal directions to Sun Hawk's village, she had to hurry. She must catch up with Sun Hawk, or else chance getting lost again in the thick vegetation of the lush wilderness.

After sliding her pistol into the pocket of her doeskin dress, Summer Hope went to the entrance flap and slowly drew it aside.

She looked around her and saw that everyone was busy with their morning chores. No one would notice if she left her lodge, not if she rushed around to the back, then sought shelter in the forest.

She wanted no one to know that she was going after Sun Hawk.

There would be too many questions . . . questions she did not want to answer.

Then, if she couldn't work things out with Sun Hawk, she wouldn't look the fool in her people's eyes. It would be a thing that she would carry around inside her heart, a rejection that would stay with her until the day she died.

She knew that no other man could ever take Sun Hawk's place in her heart.

And not only because she loved him so much, but because should she lose him, she would never trust having feelings for a man again.

In the dark shadows of the forest, where streamers of sunlight came through the tree's autumn leaves like golden ribbons, Summer Hope ran breathlessly onward. She wanted to cry out Sun Hawk's name in hopes that he would hear her and stop.

But she wasn't that far, yet, from her village. Her voice would carry back to her people. They would know that she was going after Sun Hawk.

Trying to recall everything that Eagle Wing had said about the different land markings to use to find Sun Hawk's village, and now and then seeing a freshly crunched leaf on the ground which indicated that Sun Hawk had passed by, Summer Hope hurried beneath the oaks, elms, and maple trees, and fled on past towering spruces and pines.

At least she was glad for one thing. The daylight was with her for many more hours. Should she not be able to find Sun Hawk, or his village, she would have plenty of time to turn back and return to her village before the blackness of night fell down around her like a threatening shroud.

A noise made her stop suddenly.

She looked slowly around her, and then upward.

She breathed a heavy sigh of relief and smiled when she saw that it was only an eagle. It was perched on a high limb above her. Its eyes were on her as it restlessly shifted its weight from foot to foot.

Having always been in awe of the majestic birds, Summer Hope watched how its feathers ruffled and rose at odd angles in the light, gusty breeze.

She was reminded of how she had felt the first time she had crossed over the border of Canada into this land of enchantment, how overwhelmed she had been by the exceptional beauty of the virgin hardwoods and cedars and pines, the intense mystical element of the place.

That first time she had seen many eagles soaring overhead, sweeping across the sky as though one entity, and then floating away in the wind and disappearing into the treetops. That was not far from where she was walking now.

As she admired the lone eagle, she almost forgot why she was there. When it extended its wings fully, then flew away into the sky, she was brought back to the reality of where she was.

Sun Hawk.

She had to find Sun Hawk!

But her spirits fell when she realized that he

was probably home by now and she would not find his Enchanted Lake.

"This is useless," she whispered, her shoulders sagging in defeat.

She turned and began walking back in the direction of her own village. After a few minutes she realized that she had accidentally taken a different route, for nothing seemed familiar to her.

She couldn't believe it. Was she lost again?

Tightening her jaw, determined to find her way back without mishap, she walked onward with her chin held high.

And then, suddenly, when she took another step, she found no ground there for her foot.

She found herself toppling downward into a hole in the ground, the shock stealing her breath away and making it impossible for her to scream out in alarm.

She had not seen the hole because it cleverly had been covered with branches and leaves. She didn't have time to think about how it had gotten there, because the moment she hit the bottom her head struck against the hard ground.

She quickly slipped away into the dark void of unconsciousness.

30

Pierre DuSault couldn't believe his luck! Just as he had arrived on the outskirts of the Ojibwa village to watch for Summer Hope, he had seen her leave her village.

Feeling victory close at hand, Pierre began following her. He wanted to make sure she got far enough from her village before he grabbed her, to be certain her screams couldn't be carried to her people.

He had stayed far enough behind her so that she would not realize she was being followed.

Pierre stopped when she stopped, caught in the spell of the eagle as it had sat, undisturbed, on the limb above Summer Hope.

Of all the animals, including birds, that he had slain in his lifetime, he had never downed an eagle. He had much respect for the creature. To look at it was to look at the best of a species.

He knew that even the red skins worshiped

the eagles and did not kill them for the feathers they used in their rituals and celebrations.

Pierre had come upon several Ojibwa warriors one day and stayed hidden as he watched them prepare a hole in the ground. The men climbed inside, then covered it with a thin layer of buckskin with the animal's fur left on it. They had scattered pieces of corn along the ground close to the covered hole. He wasn't sure what the Ojibwa were trying to lure into their trap, but he stayed and watched.

He had been surprised to see that it was an eagle.

The red skins caught the birds only to take certain feathers from them and then let them fly into the sky again.

Pierre had seen other warriors harvesting eagle feathers since then, realizing that most Indians took the feathers that fell from the birds when they molted.

After the eagle had flown off today, and Pierre's attention had been drawn back to Summer Hope, he had waited for her to walk onward. He was puzzled by how she had turned and headed back in the direction of her village.

Panic had seized him. He knew that if she got close enough, he would not be able to grab her without her screams carrying in the wind.

He had hurried his pace and had actually stepped out into the open and had outstretched his arms to take her, when suddenly she disappeared into a hole in the ground.

As he had waited for her to scream, he had stiffened, ready to make a fast retreat into hiding.

But she had made no sound, and even now, as he stood only a few feet from where she had fallen, she remained silent. She must have been knocked unconscious in the fall.

He inched his way forward and stood over the hole. "A wolf trap," he whispered. "A deadfall wolf trap that someone has dug deep in the ground."

He looked from side to side, wondering who could have made it. He knew of no one hunting in the area at this time. And he doubted that the Indians would prepare such a trap for wolves, for he knew they revered that animal and would do nothing to harm it.

He knelt down on one knee and studied the leaves and limbs that had been used to cover the trap. They were autumn leaves, which meant that they had been placed there recently.

He looked over his shoulder and slowly scanned the forest for signs of trappers. They had to be in the area. This sort of trap was even used by bush rangers. Although he had seen no other signs of them, he suspected that bush rangers were near. They, too, had learned the art of survival in this wilderness and how to keep one step ahead of the red skins.

For a moment he was torn over what to do now that he knew true allies were in the area, for he doubted that he could count on the British soldiers. He had begun to think he'd be better off elsewhere and had even planned to move onward, but only after he had finished off Chief Summer Hope.

He leaned over to look down into the hole. The break in the leaves and limbs provided enough light for him to see Summer Hope lying there, unconscious.

He started to clear away the rest of the debris, but stopped when he heard footsteps approaching.

Not wanting to be held responsible for what had happened to Summer Hope, Pierre's heart raced as he scrambled to find shelter.

He jumped behind forsythia bushes and sighed with relief when he saw who was approaching. Friends, not foe, were coming toward him.

He had to wonder why the British soldiers were this far from their fort, but at least he was not threatened by their presence.

Had it been red skins, he knew they had the skills to sniff him out.

He glanced through the branches of the bushes and gazed with a frown at the pit. He was not sure what to do about Summer Hope. If he told the British, would they see her safely back to her village to gain the Indians' favor? Would not the red skins then be eager to please the British as a way to thank them for their kindness?

But if the British did rescue Summer Hope, Pierre would lose his chance.

No. He would say nothing to the British about her. He would sneak away from the fort tonight and return to do away with the lady chief. Once she was silenced, he would be free again to roam the forest without fearing an attack from red skins, for they would only know he was the one who abducted their chief if she had pointed him out to them.

Once she was dead, that would no longer be possible.

Not wanting the British soldiers to find the wolf trap, Pierre scurried from the bushes and met them head on.

"What brings you so far from the fort?" Pierre asked, hoping that his voice did not sound too anxious. It took all of his willpower not to look over his shoulder at the pit, in it his prize!

"What took *you* this far from the fort?" Lieutenant Trower asked, looking warily at Pierre.

"I was squaw hunting," Pierre said, chuckling.

"Well, your squaw hunting is over," Lieutenant Trower said, laying a hand heavily on Pierre's shoulder and giving him a shove in the direction of the fort. "Colonel Green thought you might be up to no good. That's why he sent me to look for you. You, alone, could create a war between us and the red skins."

"I'm only after one measly Injun," Pierre growled.

"But that one is the chief of her people," Lieutenant Trower said. "Now if you want refuge at our fort, you must do what you are told, or else."

"Or else?" Pierre asked, stopping to glare at the soldier.

"Or else we'll see personally that you are handed over to the Ojibwa," Lieutenant Trower answered, his eyes gleaming.

Realizing just how serious the man was, Pierre cowered and turned, and walked silently in the direction of the fort. He could not help but smile at knowing that he had the upper hand, for after the soldiers were asleep tonight, he would return to the pit and finally see that Summer Hope took her final breath of life.

He would then fill the pit with dirt and rocks. No one would ever find her body!

31

Out of your whole life give but a moment.
—ROBERT BROWNING

Eagle Wing had called Summer Hope's name
outside her lodge enough times to know that
she was not there.

He turned and gazed at his people, who were
going into their lodges for their evening meals.
More than one of them had voiced concern
about having not seen Summer Hope for some
time now.

A short council had just been held about her.
Some spoke about having seen Sun Hawk enter
her lodge. But no one had seen him leave. Nor
had they seen her exit her wigwam.

They had come to one conclusion: They had
left together. Sun Hawk had taken Summer
Hope to his village.

And after figuring out where she was, the
people had seemed satisfied and even pleased,
for they knew of Sun Hawk's reluctance to reveal the location of his village to anyone.

But Eagle Wing knew that Sun Hawk had

taken the Black Robe there. Eagle Wing had given this news to Summer Hope. When she had faced Sun Hawk with this truth, he must have agreed to take her there. After that, he would also welcome her people at Enchanted Lake.

His people, in council, had assumed that the reason their chief had not told anyone that she was going there was because that was a part of the bargain between the two chiefs. After she returned, she would tell them that both bands of Ojibwa would now come together as friends, and councils would be held in either village, whenever there was a need.

But Eagle Wing was not among those who took Summer Hope's disappearance so calmly. He had witnessed the sudden bitterness that could arise between his chief and Sun Hawk. He had doubted that they could ever come together as true allies.

Yet he had silently observed how she felt about Sun Hawk. Eagle Wing had seen a side of his chief that he regretted. He knew when a woman was infatuated with a man. And Eagle Wing had seen it while Summer Hope had been with Sun Hawk. Even when she was angry with him, a look of quiet adoration had been in her eyes as she had gazed at him.

Turning to look up at the darkening sky, Eagle Wing frowned. He was torn about what he should do. Go, alone, and search for her, to make sure she was with Sun Hawk, and safe?

Or, as was agreed on in council, trust his chief to do what she thought was best?

Pierre DuSault's name had surfaced during council, a warrior wondering if he could be in the area and possibly have abducted Summer Hope a second time. But that was quickly brushed aside. Certainly no one could have come into their village and taken her by force. That meant she had left on her own, and willingly.

He walked away from Summer Hope's lodge, yet he could not help but still feel uneasy, even dispirited.

He knew he would look foolish if he searched for her and found her safely with Sun Hawk. He would be interfering in her private life, something she did have, even though she was chief.

Up until now she had not separated herself from her duties as chief in any respect, especially to be with a man. And Sun Hawk was not just any man, but an Ojibwa chief, and a man with whom she had many differences.

"What if she does not return at all tonight?" Eagle Wing whispered to himself, looking heavenward, seeing the stars now glimmering overhead. "What then should I do?"

He sighed heavily. He knew that he should not do anything, for most likely his chief was where she wanted to be, and with whom.

If she chose to stay the night with Sun Hawk, so be it.

But if she did, Eagle Wing suspected that soon she would announce to her people that she no longer wanted to be their chief. As a woman, she would need more than that.

Eagle Wing doubled his hands into tight fists at his sides, for he had silently loved Summer Hope for as long as he could remember. That was why he had not selected a wife at his age of thirty winters.

When he went to bed at night, he saw Summer Hope in his mind's eye.

When he dreamed, she was there.

But when he awakened, he found that his blankets only held his warmth within them.

He had never thought that Summer Hope would look past her role as chief and find favor in a man. That was the sole reason Eagle Wing had not pursued her as a man pursues a woman.

Now he realized how wrong he had been to keep his desires to himself. If she could love Sun Hawk, could she not have loved Eagle Wing?

Having lost at love, he would turn his focus on another sort of hidden desire. He had seen the wonders of being chief, first in Summer Hope's father, and then in Summer Hope. From time to time, he had hungered for the title.

It was not so much the power that was alluring to Eagle Wing. It was how being chief touched so many people's lives. He loved his people. He would do anything for them. And should Summer Hope exchange her title of chief

for the title of wife, he hoped that she would
see in him a man who would be a caring, devoted leader.

"What am I doing?" Eagle Wing whispered,
stopping and shaking his head slowly back
and forth.

He could not believe that Summer Hope's
brief absence could cause him to think such
things. He had Summer Hope not only resigning
her post as chief, but also marrying Sun Hawk.
And he had himself appointed to succeed her.

Yet none of that was impossible, was it? he
thought, smiling as he went on inside his wigwam. A pot of soup hung over the fire in his
fire pit, and beside the fire, wrapped in a colorful blanket, sat his beloved mother.

He went to her and gave her a tender hug.

"Is she home yet?" Shy Blossom asked in her
raspy, old voice.

"Gah-ween, no, but everyone agreed in council
that she is all right and that she is where she
wishes to be," Eagle Wing said, settling down
on a pallet of furs beside his mother.

He gazed over at her, his heart going out to
her as he took in the wrinkles on her leathery
face and the thinning of her white hair.

She had not only married late in life, she had
had her only child even later.

At her age of fifty winters she had given birth
to her son. When the villagers saw that Eagle
Wing had all of his ten toes and ten fingers, he
was called a "miracle baby." They had thought

that he might be born with all sorts of disabilities. Worst of all, they had thought that his mother would never make it through such a birth at her age.

But they had both fooled everyone.

And only now at the age of eighty did she have failing health. Her hands trembled as did her voice when she spoke, and she could no longer stand without leaning heavily on a cane. Eagle Wing knew that her days on this earth were numbered, and he cherished every moment that he could spend with her.

His father, who had been ten winters younger than his wife, had passed on to the other side some moons ago. Since then, it had been only Eagle Wing and his mother. Devoted so keenly to her, he dreaded her dying. A part of him would also be gone.

That, too, was why he hoped for something special in his life to help ward off the pain he would carry with him when his mother was gone.

He had only begun to think of searching for a woman who could fill that void in his life.

But being chief, should Summer Hope give up the title, was what he truly wished for.

"Where could Summer Hope be?" Shy Blossom asked, reaching for a wooden bowl, and then the ladle that rested in the pot of soup.

Although Eagle Wing worried about his mother burning herself while preparing their meals, he knew that she fought for her independence, especially when it came to cooking. Everyone had always said that she was the best cook of the Northern Lights band.

Even now, as the aroma of the soup wafted toward him, he could hardly wait to taste it.

And he had to hold back from helping her when he saw the soup sloshing around in the bowl, threatening to splash from it, as she held it out for him.

"You asked about Summer Hope's whereabouts," he said, taking the bowl. He told her that he thought she was with a man, and not just any man . . . the chief of the Enchanted Lake Ojibwa.

"Would she be this foolish?" Shy Blossom said, staring disbelievingly at her son.

Eagle Wing had to smile at her comment, and how she was still so opinionated. She had received her name Shy Blossom when she had been a tiny girl who was afraid of everything and hid behind her mother's skirts because of her fear.

But as she grew into a lady, she had become anything but shy. Anyone who knew her knew that she would always give her opinion about anything, whether it was good or bad.

She had criticized Summer Hope's judgment of things more than once, but out of respect had only voiced such opinions in the privacy of her home, and then only to her son.

"Why do you say that, *gee-mah-mah*, Mother?"

"Because Chief Sun Hawk is a man, and if he

and Summer Hope choose to marry, it will be Summer Hope who will have to give up her title of chief."

Eagle Wing's heart skipped a beat. "Why do you say that, *gee-mah-mah*?" he asked again.

"Because no man will give up his role of chief, not even for a woman," Shy Blossom said, her pale eyes dancing. "Then, my son, who do you think will be chief of our people?"

Eagle Wing's heart skipped another beat. "Who, *gee-mah-mah*?" he asked guardedly.

"I have prepared our people well, in private council, as to who should be chief after Summer Hope," Shy Blossom said, her lips quivering into a smile. "My son, it is you who will soon be chief."

Hearing his mother voice aloud what he had only silently wished for filled Eagle Wing with wonder. She never ceased to amaze him, how she could read him as though he were a book with printed pages of words.

"Eat your soup, son, before it gets cold," Shy Blossom said, ladling soup into her own bowl.

Eagle Wing nodded, yet his eyes never left his mother, whose mind had not aged along with her body. Perhaps he was wrong to think that she was soon to die. She was so headstrong, she would not allow it.

More than likely, he would even die before her.

32

Ah, what shall I be at fifty?
Should Nature keep me alive?
—ALFRED, LORD TENNYSON

Moaning, Summer Hope awakened. She reached up and found why her head ached so badly. There was a small lump exactly where she had been injured before.

She stiffened and her eyes widened when she noticed the darkness all around her, and heard wolves howling from afar.

In brief flashes she recalled having lost her footing, then relived the instant it took for her body to hit the ground.

"What is this thing?" she whispered, running a hand along the sides of the pit. "Where am I?"

She recalled hearing about pits that bush rangers dug to catch wolves for their pelts. Surely she had fallen into one.

She was reminded of those bush rangers that had abducted her not so long ago. This might even be one of their deadfall traps. If so, and if Pierre DuSault was anywhere near, might he check the trap and find her?

"I have to get out of here," Summer Hope said, moving slowly to her feet, the head wound making her somewhat disoriented.

She steadied herself, then peered upward and saw the opening overhead that her body had made when she had fallen through the layer of twigs, limbs, and leaves.

Moonlight filtered downward onto her face and all around her, revealing just how deeply imprisoned she was. While standing she could not even reach halfway up the pit.

And jumping got her no closer.

Panic seized her when she heard the wolves again, seemingly closer. She knew that if they were traveling in this direction, one or more of the pack might fall into the pit with her.

"*Wee-do-kow!* Help!" she screamed, searching the sides of the pit for roots to climb, finding none.

"Oh, please, somebody, help me!" she screamed again, yet afraid of who might find her. Pierre would make sure she was never found again.

"Oh, please, please, let him be nowhere near here," she prayed, gazing up at the dark heavens above her.

After again desperately trying to find something to grab on to to help her climb free, and again finding nothing, Summer Hope sank back to the ground.

Cold and trembling, she drew her knees up to her chest and slowly rocked back and forth. She tried to think of things that were pleasant in order to take her momentarily away from the terrible predicament that she was in.

"Sun Hawk," she whispered, tears filling her eyes. "I wish I had not been so hateful to you. You would not have fled my lodge, angry, and I would not have been put in the position of going after you, which led me, instead, to this dreadful place."

She closed her eyes and envisioned him standing there, wonderfully handsome, his voice gentle and loving as he spoke her name, his arms so warm as he drew her into them.

She was brought back to reality and the danger she was in when she heard the wolves again, even closer.

She tried to block out their howls and focus on something else, or chance losing her sanity from being so afraid.

She tried not to feel the coldness of the night as she listened to the marsh animals singing their songs from somewhere close by.

Frogs.

Yes, frogs did for the night what birds did for the day. They gave it a voice, and their music was welcomed by Summer Hope tonight. As they continued their serenade, she smiled and recalled how her father had taught her about the tiny evening vocalists, an innocent beauty of the night.

Summer Hope had been with her father one evening when he had captured a frog solely to show her what one looked like, so that she could enjoy envisioning them thereafter.

She had been in awe of this particular frog's dazzling markings. Her father explained to her that they were smart creatures, evolving their own distinct calls for specific situations, such as expressing alarm or distress.

She had been captivated when her father pointed out the frog's vocal sac to her, and explained how it inflated like a balloon. Her father had told her that in most cases the males were responsible for the crooning, which could reach a stirring crescendo. When hundreds of them converged to attract mates, beginning every spring, it was often possible to hear the marsh music from half a mile away or more.

He had also told her that although frogs were best known for their magical metamorphoses from tadpoles, they performed many other fascinating biological feats. For example, their bulging eyeballs, mounted near the top of the head and on opposite sides, not only provided an exceptional field of vision, but also aided swallowing by lowering into the roof of the mouth to force food down the throat. And they were not trapped anywhere easily, for they could jump their way out of danger.

"I wish I were a frog now," Summer Hope sobbed. "I shall never be free of this horrid place. Never!"

Shivering, her head still unmercifully aching, she slowly closed her eyes and fell into a restless sleep.

33

Forgive what seemed my sin in me,
What seem'd my worth since I began.
—ALFRED, LORD TENNYSON

Troubled, and regretting his behavior the last time he was with Summer Hope, Sun Hawk fretfully paced his dwelling.

As the fire cast dancing shadows on the walls all around him, he was torn over what to do.

If he returned to Summer Hope's village, would he even be allowed to enter?

If she had ordered sentries posted around the village to stop him, his humiliation would be fierce. He would not be a prisoner again.

Yet, should he not chance being humiliated in order to attempt to make things right with her?

No matter what they had each said to hurt the other, and no matter how their responsibilities as chiefs of two separate bands of Ojibwa divided them, they should have never allowed such things to stand in the way of their love for one another.

He swept the entrance flap of his wigwam aside and stepped out beneath the soft moonlight to gaze up at the stars.

"Where is she now?" he whispered, absolutely certain that she must be as upset as he.

Could she even this very moment be gazing at the stars, thinking of him? Could she be filled with as much regret? Could she be pining to see him? Would she eagerly welcome his apology?

"That is what I must do," Sun Hawk quickly decided.

Yes, he must go to her. He must demand audience with her and be allowed to see her.

He would then soften the mood between them by apologizing. But would she accept, or again order him from her lodge? From her village? From her heart?

The only way to answer those questions was to go to her and find out. And this time he would not talk in circles about things. If she asked to see his village, he would quickly comply. And then he would tell her that he wanted her to be his wife. They could work things out—they must!

Yet was this the right time to go to her? As he gazed around him and heard no voices coming from the wigwams, he knew that, for the most part, his people were asleep. Would it not be the same at Summer Hope's village? Should he risk going this time of night, possibly being taken as an enemy in the dark?

He squared his jaw and nodded. Yes. It would not be right to allow Summer Hope to go an entire night thinking he cared so little for her. He did not want to leave her alone for so long with remembrances of their last, troubled moments together.

"*Ay-uh*, yes, I must go," he whispered. "Now!"

Without alerting anyone, with a knife sheathed at his waist, he left the village in a run.

As he climbed the rocky steps that would lead him away from Enchanted Lake, all that he could think about was how he would be received by the woman he loved.

He tried to think positively. In the distance he heard wolves howling, as well as frogs sending off their lovely chorus throughout the darkness of the forest.

He cast his eyes heavenward. "Let my woman accept my apology . . . as well as my offer of marriage," he whispered in prayer.

34

So, take and use thy work;
Amend what flaws may lurk.
—ROBERT BROWNING

Colonel Green had badgered Pierre about having left the fort to search for Summer Hope, and now that everyone there was asleep, Pierre was adamant about leaving again to find her.

He didn't like anyone to dictate to him. Not even those who were temporarily giving him lodging.

If push came to shove and the British were forced to choose between Pierre and the Indians, he knew for certain who would come out the loser.

Pierre.

So he had to make sure to erase any reason why the British would be made to choose. No one but Summer Hope could identify him. Once she was silenced, Pierre would be free to come and go as he pleased.

Anxious to get back to where Summer Hope was trapped, Pierre grabbed a sheathed knife from the fort's cache of weapons, moved it in place at his waist, then walked stealthily toward the door and opened it.

He cringed when the hinges creaked ominously. He stopped and turned to see if anyone might have heard.

Except for men snoring, everything was still quiet behind him.

Smiling crookedly, he went out onto the small porch, slowly closed the door behind him, then ran across the moonlit courtyard, panting when he finally reached the cover of the trees on the outskirts of the forest.

Taking time to catch his breath, he looked over his shoulder and gazed intently at each of the windows of the fort. There was no lamplight. That meant that everyone was still asleep.

To make sure that he got back to the fort and in his bed before morning, he knew that he had to move hastily.

He would awaken Summer Hope and trick her into believing that he would not harm her, that he was there to help her. He would agree to save her if she promised not to turn him in for abducting her.

Once he had her pulled free of the pit, he would not waste any more time in shoving the knife into her belly. He wanted to see the expression on her face as she bled.

He would laugh triumphantly as he pushed her back into the pit and began filling it with debris, until not even the forest animals who sniffed out prey would be able to tell where she was buried.

His heart thumping excitedly, he hurried onward. He had made sure to watch for the different bushes and trees that would lead him back to where Summer Hope lay waiting to be rescued.

It wouldn't be long now. Soon he would be safely and contentedly in his bunk, the British no wiser when he was awakened for morning breakfast.

He smiled as he tasted victory deep inside his soul!

35

Those pretty wrongs that liberty commits
When I am sometimes absent from thy heart,
Thy beauty and thy years full well befits,
For still temptation follows where thou art.
—WILLIAM SHAKESPEARE

Hurrying through the forest, estimating that he was now halfway between his and Summer Hope's village, Sun Hawk was confident in what he had decided. Even if everyone at Summer Hope's village was awakened by his arrival, he would not hesitate going to her lodge and saying her name through the entrance flap.

Even if her warriors came and grabbed him, suspecting him of having come for the wrong reasons, he would not give up on trying to get her to pay him heed.

This time he would not leave her village until everything was settled between them, and in the only way that would make them both happy.

"Once she knows that I will give up my title as chief to have her, she will have no choice but to believe me," he whispered to himself. "How more could I prove my sincere love for her than to give up that which has been my sole reason to live . . . until I met her."

Yes, things would come to a head tonight. And he knew that she would finally believe that he loved her with all of his heart and being.

He would not even allow himself to think about how his people would react to his decision.

Anyone who had loved as he loved Summer Hope would surely understand why he would sacrifice so much to have her!

He was so lost in thought, he didn't notice the uneven scattering of leaves and limbs a few feet ahead of him. But when he took a step and suddenly felt nothing beneath his foot, he steadied himself and took a quick step backward.

Breathing hard, he realized that he had almost fallen into a deadfall wolf trap—a trap where a wolf restlessly pranced back and forth even now, since it was obvious that something had fallen into it. Sun Hawk stared at the broken limbs and hanging, loose leaves that surrounded the hole in the ground.

When he heard what sounded like a groan coming from the pit, he jumped.

Scarcely breathing, he slowly advanced toward the hole.

When he heard the groan again, and could tell that it came from a person, not an animal, he fell quickly to his knees and gazed down into the shadowy pit.

He was taken aback, his throat going quickly dry, when the moon's glow revealed who was there.

"Summer Hope?" he gasped. At the sound of his voice, her eyes snapped open and stared up at him disbelievingly.

"Sun Hawk, you came . . ." she said, her eyes filling with tears. "I do not know how you knew, but . . . you came!"

"I was on my way to your village when I almost fell into the pit, myself," Sun Hawk said, still too stunned to move.

"Help me out," Summer Hope said, reaching her hands up to him. Slowly she moved to her feet, the throbbing of her head making her lightheaded again.

Seeing her tottering, as though she might faint, and realizing that she must have been injured by her fall into the pit, brought Sun Hawk to his senses.

He bent low and reached his hands down for her. When she twined her fingers through his, holding on to his hands for dear life, he slowly drew her up out of the pit. When she was finally free of the trap, and he had her in his arms and was carrying her away, she sobbed out his name.

"Sun Hawk, I was coming to you when . . . when . . . I fell in that horrible thing," Summer Hope cried. "I have never been so afraid. Thank you, oh, thank you for coming."

"You were coming to me?" Sun Hawk asked, stopping to gaze tenderly into her eyes.

"Yes, I wanted to tell you so many things,"

Summer Hope said softly. "I want to apologize for so many things. Do you forgive me?"

"Forgive you for what?" Sun Hawk asked, overjoyed that she was as eager to seek his forgiveness, as he was hers.

"So many, many things," Summer Hope said, laying her head on his chest. "But I am too weak . . . my head hurts too much . . . to talk about it now. Please take me home."

"No, I will not take you to your home," Sun Hawk said thickly. "I am taking you to mine."

Summer Hope gazed in wonder up at him. "Your home?" she asked, searching his eyes. "But I thought—"

"I will take you to my home and then I will send warriors to tell your people that you are all right," Sun Hawk said. "I will also offer council to them, a council that will be held at my village."

"But that would open the doors of your village to the world, for you know that when others see my people coming and going to your village, they will follow," Summer Hope said.

"Let them come," Sun Hawk said. "It is tiring to fight what my people and I knew would happen eventually. Times change. People change. Although my people would like to keep their lives uncomplicated, we have talked in council and agreed that it is now all but impossible to live separately from everyone else."

"Your father was the first, and now I am the second," Summer Hope said, smiling. "Yet I still wonder if it is wise to break a tradition that your people have protected for so long. I do not have to go to your village. Having you love me is enough. If you still feel strongly about keeping your home a secret, please take me to my own."

"I am taking you to mine," Sun Hawk insisted, proudly lifting his chin. "I should have not waited this long to have done it."

"I should not have badgered you into it," Summer Hope said sadly.

"I am not taking you there tonight because of any badgering," Sun Hawk said. "I am taking you there because I love you."

Feeling wonderfully at peace, Summer Hope laid her cheek against his chest again. "I love you so much," she said. "But, oh, how my head hurts."

"Talk no more," Sun Hawk said softly. "Rest your head, even sleep. We shall be at my home soon."

"Your home?" she murmured. "It would sound more wonderful were you to call it ours."

"I shall, soon," Sun Hawk said, bringing her eyes to his again.

"Do you mean . . . ?"

"Yes, we must marry, and soon. We have waited too long as it is."

"I have done much thinking about that, myself," Summer Hope said. She had wondered if she could actually get the words out once confronted with the right moment.

"And?" Sun Hawk asked, still carrying her beneath the shadowy trees.

"I have made a final decision. I wish not to be chief anymore," Summer Hope said, bringing Sun Hawk to a quick halt. "I wish to be your wife, instead."

Too stunned to respond, having decided to give up his own chieftainship to have her, Sun Hawk stared disbelievingly into her eyes. His heart soared with the joy of loving her and knowing that she loved him as much, so much that she would give up everything for him!

"My woman, I was coming to tell you that I will give up my role as chief if that assures me a life with you," Sun Hawk admitted.

In shock, it was Summer Hope's turn to stare.

36

Some too fragile—
—EMILY DICKINSON

Breathless from eagerness, Pierre hurried onward until he reached the pit. He took slow
steps toward the opening, expecting Summer
Hope to be sleeping.

"What a surprise that red-skinned mademoiselle is going to get," he whispered huskily to
himself, laughing. " '*Ma chérie*, it's only Pierre,'
I'll say. She'll probably wish a wolf had come
along and dragged her away."

He dropped to his knees and tore away the
leaves to give him a better look.

One glance downward made his heart lurch.

He groaned and then cursed when he saw
that the pit was empty.

"Now how could that have happened?" he
said, having only been jesting about wolves carrying her out of the pit. There was no way a
wolf could have dragged her out if it had
fallen in.

He stood and looked around at the broken

limbs and smashed leaves, and concluded that someone had happened along and saved her.

"But who?" he said in a disappointed whimper.

He shrugged. "Well, it's too late to worry about it," he said, kicking at the leaves with his boots. "Damn it all to hell. Why'd the British have to interrupt me when I almost had the squaw finished off?"

He knew not to try and track whoever had saved Summer Hope. If the trail led to her warriors, he'd not live to see another sunrise.

As it was, he had better concentrate on getting back to the fort so that no one there would know that he had left after having been ordered to stay on the premises.

The way it was now, he only had the British to depend on for his survival. Until he found a way to see to Summer Hope's demise, his own life was in the balance.

"Damn her," he whispered angrily. "Why'd I ever grab her that day? She's been nothin' but trouble! And I'm sick to death of trouble!"

He broke into a mad run and did not stop until he saw the fort. As quietly as possible he went inside the cabin. His heart sank when he found Colonel Green standing in the dark, the glow of his cigar proof enough that he was there.

"You don't obey orders very well, do you?" Colonel Green asked as he stepped out from the shadows.

Pierre heard the shuffle of feet and knew they weren't alone.

"Lieutenant, seize him," Colonel Green ordered as he glanced over at Lieutenant Trower. "Tie him up. We've a package to deliver to Summer Hope. Pierre."

"You are taking me to Summer Hope?" he gasped, paling. "You're handing me over as though I am nothing but a worthless dog?"

"You *are* worthless," Colonel Green said, shrugging. "You're certainly not worth anything to me here at the fort."

"But why?" Pierre whined. "Why would you do this?"

"To bring Summer Hope over to my side, as an ally who will trade out of gratitude."

"When she hears that you've been harboring me for all this time, she'll be your enemy as well," Pierre said, snickering.

"And all I'll have to say is that you are lying," the colonel said, dropping his cigar to the floor and grounding it out with the heel of his boot. "Now, who do you think she'll believe? A thieving bush ranger? Or a British officer who can give her so many beautiful things?"

Colonel Green motioned with a hand. "Take him away," he said. "Lock him up until daybreak. Then we'll finally be rid of the filth he brought to our fort."

"You'll be sorry!" Pierre screamed as he was dragged away by two soldiers. "You will pay dearly for this! Just you wait and see! You will rue the day you ever made my acquaintance."

"You are certainly right about that," Colonel Green said under his breath. He went into his private bedroom and undressed for bed.

"I hope I haven't made a mistake," he whispered, crawling into his bunk. Somehow he just couldn't close his eyes. Pierre's whiskered face kept haunting him. He hoped that after he was handed over to the Ojibwa, they would take care of him once and for all, or else . . . ?

37

Stop and consider!
Life is but a day,
A fragile dewdrop on its
Perilous way!
　　　　　—JOHN KEATS

As the early morning awakened with its soft light, Sun Hawk gazed at Summer Hope where she lay peacefully asleep on his bed of blankets. He had seen to her head wound when they had arrived at his village last night.

He had held her cradled on his lap until she had fallen asleep, then had carried her to his bed and had covered her with warm pelts.

Sun Hawk had not been able to sleep for long, for he knew the importance of sending a warrior to Summer Hope's village at the break of dawn to assure her people that she was all right and would be returning home soon.

He would leave it to her to explain to them how he had found her in a deadfall trap.

And why he had taken her to his lodge instead of hers.

Soon both bands of Ojibwa would come together as one heartbeat to fight the wrongs whites tried to force on them. As the country became crowded with whites, more would come to this area. That was a day that Sun Hawk dreaded with every fiber of his being. But with both bands of Ojibwa working together, perhaps they could keep some semblance of privacy from the outside world.

Especially now that his father had decided to retire. But if those who had come with him felt differently and kept the church active, whites would be lured to the land of lakes where they could live in what Sun Hawk called paradise.

"Sun Hawk?"

Summer Hope's voice brought Sun Hawk from his thoughts. When she leaned up on an elbow, her hair unbraided and spreading out around her, Sun Hawk saw her as no less than a vision of loveliness.

And she was his. They had made up their differences. They would be married soon, he hoped.

He reached for Summer Hope and drew her onto his lap, facing him. She wore a gown that he had brought to her from a woman who was Summer Hope's size. Her smile was so sweet, her eyes were so filled with a quiet peace, that his heart soared with joy.

"I sent a warrior to tell your people that you are safe, and that I will be bringing you home soon," Sun Hawk said, gently stroking his fingers through her long, thick tresses. "But first I would like to talk further of our future plans."

"*Ay-uh*, we do need to talk," she said, her smile waning.

Seeing her smile fade, and hearing a seriousness in her voice that was not there only moments before, shot a warning through Sun Hawk's heart. If she was having second thoughts about them getting married, he was not sure if he could stand it.

His pulse raced as he waited for her to explain.

"Last night, when you were filled with such gratitude over knowing that I was all right, you said things that perhaps you did not mean," Summer Hope said, her eyes searching his. "You said that you were willing to give up being chief. Surely you did not mean that."

"I never say what I do not mean," Sun Hawk said, his voice tight. "Nor do you."

"No," Summer Hope agreed, placing a hand gently on his cheek. "And I truly believe you should not give up being chief for me."

"But if we are to marry, one of us has to make a compromise," Sun Hawk said, afraid to hear what else she was going to say. "Even though you have offered, I have chosen to be the one to do that."

"That is not necessary," Summer Hope said, easing fully into his arms, relishing being there, protected and loved. "I shall be the one who gives up being chief. It is not a quick decision. I have been thinking about it for a while now."

Hearing her say it, again, that she would give

her all to him, made Sun Hawk's heart skip a beat. He placed his hands on her shoulders and eased her away from him only far enough so that he could look directly into her eyes.

"You will? You will truly do this for me?" he asked. It seemed too much to comprehend, since he knew how much she loved her people.

"Did you not know that I would die for you?" Summer Hope asked, brushing a soft kiss across his lips. "I knew it from the moment I saw you. The part of me that has known nothing but being a leader wanted to deny the part of me that knew that, at long last, I had found my soul mate."

"I just cannot ask you to do this for me," Sun Hawk said.

"I will not allow you to do it for me," Summer Hope said. "A man's leadership is perhaps more important to a people than a woman's." She moved from his lap and drew a blanket around her shoulders as she sat facing the lodge fire. "I have a very dependable warrior who will make a great chief. He was always second in my eyes next to Black Bear. But now that Black Bear is gone, Eagle Wing is my first choice."

"Will he be your people's?" Sun Hawk asked quietly.

She turned slowly to look at him. "What I decide will be my people's decision," she said, smiling. "As I am sure whomever you would choose to take your place, should you ever give up your title, would be the choice of your people."

"*Ay-uh*, I have such a warrior in mind," he said. "Gray Eagle. He is a trusted, valiant Ojibwa who would make a powerful, noble chief."

"But are you not glad that you do not have to assign the task to him?" Summer Hope asked, dropping the blanket away from her as she moved back into his lap and gave him a soft, quick kiss.

"I still would, if you wished to remain chief of your people," Sun Hawk said, framing her face between his hands, their eyes filled with each other.

"I want to be your wife, and then a mother," Summer Hope murmured. "Please believe me when I say that for some time now I have pondered this. I had begun to doubt my true ability as chief, especially when I became enamored with you. Feelings for you clouded my judgment of things. My heart was no longer set on being a leader, and I saw that my future as chief would be short-lived."

"I did not think you could ever put anything above your people," Sun Hawk said, brushing her hair back from her face. "I am glad that if you feel that you must, that I am the cause, for I want the opportunity to love you forever. I wish to have many children with you."

"How wonderful it will be," Summer Hope said, sighing. "To be a *gee-mah-mah*, mother. To be a *gee-wee-oo*, wife! I have watched the women of my village and how fulfilled such a life makes them. I now will experience the same fulfillment."

"I understand that this is not something you can rush into," Sun Hawk said hoarsely. "I will be patient. Then when you feel the time is right, my arms will be open for you. I will eagerly wrap them around you and take you home as my wife."

"I have something to tell you that I should have, but forgot to," Summer Hope said. "You accused me of spying by sending my warrior to see where you make your village. I am not guilty of doing that. Eagle Wing went on his own. He did it for me, but not because I told him to."

"That is good to know, and I apologize for not having given you a chance to tell me," Sun Hawk said. He heard voices outside the lodge and turned his eyes to the entrance flap.

When Sun Hawk's name was spoken, he gently eased Summer Hope from his lap, then rose and slid the flap partially aside.

"I have returned from my mission to Summer Hope's village," Gray Eagle said. "I told them that she was with you and that you would soon bring her home."

"Thank you, Gray Eagle," Sun Hawk said, then arched an eyebrow. "But it seems by how you are behaving, so uneasy, that you have something more to say?"

"*Ay-uh*, I do," Gray Eagle said. "When I arrived at her village, I saw a man imprisoned on a stake in the center of the village. I soon discovered that it was Pierre DuSault, the man who abducted your woman."

Hearing Pierre's name brought Summer Hope quickly to the entrance flap. She pushed it completely aside and stood beside Sun Hawk, her eyes questioning Gray Eagle.

"The British brought him to your village," Gray Eagle continued. "They said they found him stealing things at their fort. They forced him to tell them why he was in the area, alone, and so in need of supplies that he would steal. Pierre DuSault told them he was there to kill you, not knowing that the British were trying to ally themselves with the Ojibwa. Colonel Green and his men brought Pierre to your village as a peace offering. They hope that you will now agree to trade with them as a way to thank them."

"Something does not sound right," Summer Hope murmured. "But we shall worry about that later. At least that man is no longer a threat. He will finally get what he deserves."

Gray Eagle nodded and turned to leave. "Thank you, Gray Eagle, for all that you have done for me," Summer Hope said, touching his arm.

She and Sun Hawk went back inside and began dressing, but Summer Hope felt that something was not right about why the British had brought Pierre to her village. The story about Pierre stealing just did not fit, somehow. He was too careful, and the British would have helped him if he needed supplies.

She could imagine him going there, seeking refuge while he worked out a plan to harm her.

"That is it," she said suddenly. She turned quickly to Sun Hawk. "Pierre was not caught stealing. I believe he went to the British to hide at their fort, mainly because it was close to my village. They allowed it. Then something went wrong. He must have done something to rile them. And when he did, the British decided to hand him over to us. They took that opportunity to use him as a bargaining tool."

She smiled. "Or they might have planned to use him from the beginning. That colonel seems capable of anything, especially double-crossing," she said. "At least Pierre is no longer a threat to anyone," Summer Hope added, shrugging as she continued to dress.

Sun Hawk remained silent. He had other concerns besides Pierre. The deadfall wolf trap had not gotten there by itself. It was the work of bush rangers. That probably meant that others had infiltrated this paradise of a land.

He tried to pretend he felt as good about things as Summer Hope. They left his lodge and headed back toward her village. Until news about Pierre's captivity, everything seemed to have been falling into place, where he could actually envision a future that was bright with hope for him and his woman.

But there were still obstacles to overcome. They would take them, one by one. And there was much to be patient about, for Sun Hawk knew that no matter what Summer Hope said, she could not give up her title as chief all that easily, nor would her people allow it.

In the end, if he saw no other way, he would do what he must to have Summer Hope, even if it meant handing his own chieftainship to someone else. He hoped that was not necessary, for he was convinced that his people still needed him.

But for her—anything!

38

It burned me in the night,
It blistered in my dream;
It sickened fresh upon my sight,
With every morning's beam.
—EMILY DICKINSON

Pierre was the first thing Sun Hawk and Summer Hope saw when they entered her village. He wore only his breeches as he hung on a stake a short distance from the outdoor fire in the center of the village, his ankles and his wrists tied to the column of wood.

When he saw Summer Hope, she could see an immediate fear splash into his eyes. And she knew why. He was responsible for some of the worst moments of her life when he had taken her captive and forced her into his canoe. She would never forget how he and his friends had taunted her, especially by saying what they were going to do to her once they made camp for the night. They had gone over their plan in horrendous detail. She was to be raped, then killed.

Sun Hawk heard Summer Hope inhale sharply. When he saw her shoulders begin to sway, he was afraid that she was going to faint from the trauma of coming face to face again with her captor.

He started to reach out for her just as she stepped away from him, her chin held high.

He smiled at her courage and strength, for a brief moment having forgotten that she had both. Although she was a woman with the same fears and apprehensions as anyone, she was still a brave, proud chief.

Seeing her in this light, Sun Hawk thought back to what she had said . . . that she would give up her title of chief to be with him, to be his wife, to be the mother of his children. He doubted that she could do that.

Her whole village was there now, standing in a wide circle around the captive and their chief. Knowing that she needed a moment alone with Pierre, Sun Hawk stood back with the others and watched Summer Hope go and stand before him.

Out of the corner of his eye Sun Hawk saw Eagle Wing take a step toward Summer Hope, then draw back, seeming to have thought better of it. This was the man Summer Hope had said would make a fine chief to her people, and Sun Hawk gazed at length at him.

He frowned, already very familiar with this warrior. It was he who had pushed Sun Hawk around and forced him into captivity at this village.

Sun Hawk tried not to resent the manhandling, for Eagle Wing had acted out of duty to his chief and had believed Sun Hawk had intended to harm her.

He smiled as he thought of how interesting it would be to go into council with Eagle Wing if he was named chief.

He wondered if Eagle Wing would enter into their relationship with humility. Or with the dignity that would be expected of him.

Of course, with dignity, Sun Hawk concluded, for he trusted Summer Hope's judgment that this man was fit to be named chief.

Pierre's voice came to Sun Hawk in a low whine. His jaw tightened as he listened to what the villain had to say.

Pierre said that the British had turned him over to the Ojibwa for their own selfish purposes.

"They have sheltered me for several days now," Pierre said, his voice growing anxious and much louder. "I went to them. I asked for refuge. I told them why. I told them that I couldn't allow myself to be seen anywhere near your village. I told them that you were out to get me because I abducted you. Had I known you were a chief, I—"

"Do not lie to me," Summer Hope hissed, interrupting him. "The British said you were stealing from them."

Although she felt triumphant that she had figured out the truth before hearing it from Pierre, she had to pretend otherwise to be certain. "And as for me, you thought you could get away with rape and murder. You would have received more pleasure in having abducted me had you known that I was a chief."

"That isn't so," Pierre whined. "But does any of that really matter now? You weren't raped. You weren't murdered. Have mercy on my soul. Let me go!"

"Tell me more about the British and how long you were with them," Summer Hope said, smiling over at Sun Hawk as he moved up next to her.

"I've been there for a couple of days and would still be there had I not gone against their orders," Pierre said, frowning.

"What orders?" Sun Hawk asked, drawing Pierre's eyes to him. Sun Hawk could sense that he was afraid to answer that question. It probably would condemn him even more in Summer Hope's eyes.

"I was told not to leave the premises," Pierre answered warily. "That's all."

"And why would they care if you did?" Summer Hope asked. "Surely you were nothing but a bother to them."

"I've said all I'm going to say," Pierre said, looking sheepishly from Sun Hawk to Summer Hope.

"Because what you have not said will condemn you in the eyes of the Ojibwa?" Sun Hawk said, his eyes narrowing angrily. "Is that why you refuse to say anything else?"

The three of them turned to look at the man who quickly stepped up to join them.

"Word came to me that a white man was being held captive here on a stake," Father Davidson said, his voice tight. On recognizing Pierre he stiffened. He recalled the other time he had heard mention of this man. The day he had found Summer Hope wandering the woods, this man was among them.

He was the one who got away!

"You!" Pierre gasped. "I know you! You're the one who—"

"Father, you shouldn't be here," Sun Hawk said, quickly silencing Pierre, but not before learning that the bush ranger recognized his father.

Although Pierre was a captive, and could cause no one else any harm, it gave Sun Hawk a feeling of keen apprehension to see the way he looked at his father, the man who had rescued Summer Hope.

Had Pierre known his whereabouts, surely he would have killed his father and friends!

"I didn't know that you were here," Father Davidson said, ignoring his son's obvious fears, yet understanding them. He, too, realized that had Pierre known how close he and his friends were, they would have been slain.

"Father, I will tell you everything that has happened later," Sun Hawk said, placing a hand gently on his shoulder. "Please return to your home. Stay until I come and talk with you."

Father Davidson nodded. "Yes, to make things less complicated for you and Summer Hope, I will go," he said. "It is good to see this evil man will be stopped. Let God have mercy on his soul."

He knew there was no actual court of law in the Indian village, and would not even consider how captives were brought to justice. He smiled weakly at Summer Hope, placed a comforting hand on his son's arm, then turned and left.

Sun Hawk and Summer Hope looked at each other, obviously both regretting that the bush ranger had discovered Father Davidson's presence. Yet they had to believe there was no actual threat to him. Sun Hawk nodded silently to Summer Hope as if to tell her that things were all right where his father was concerned.

Then they both focused on Pierre again.

"So you say the British handed you over to me for a purpose?" Summer Hope asked, her eyes glaring at Pierre.

"To trick your people," Pierre replied. "They thought that if you were given your assailant, you would, in turn, be grateful enough to agree to hunt and hand over pelts to them, so they could supply their countrymen with the riches of this land."

He slid his gaze over to Sun Hawk. "And since no other band of Injuns would ally themselves with them, you were their last chance," he said. "Otherwise, the British saw no choice but to move back farther into Canada. They would abandon Fort William, just the same as they were forced to abandon Grand Portage."

He smiled smugly at Summer Hope. "Yup, *ma chérie*, you were their last hope, and now they have none," he said, chuckling.

"If confronted by what you have said, they will just call you a liar," Sun Hawk said. "And how do we know what is the truth? No one would ever believe that someone like you, who would abduct innocent women to rape and kill, would be capable of telling the truth."

"And why would they turn on you now?" Summer Hope asked, taking a step closer to Pierre. "What did you do besides not follow their orders?"

"Like I said, they knew about me and you," Pierre said, swallowing hard. "They didn't want me to screw things up for them where you were concerned. They didn't want you to find out that they were harboring a man who abducted you. When I sneaked out, they followed me. That's when they decided to betray me."

"Where had you gone?" Sun Hawk said, moving up to stand beside Summer Hope again. "What were you up to that gave them no choice but to hand you over to Summer Hope's people?"

Pierre ducked his head, then raised his eyes and looked sheepishly at them. "I guess there ain't no harm in tellin' you that I was following Summer Hope," he said. "When I saw her fall into that deadfall trap, I thought I finally had her. Then the British came and dragged me away."

"Did they know I was trapped in that pit?" Summer Hope asked, trying not to envision how different things would have been had Sun Hawk not found her.

"No, only I knew," Pierre answered. "I . . . I came later and found you gone."

"Did you prepare that trap for the purpose of—" Sun Hawk began, but Pierre hurriedly interrupted.

"I had nothing to do with digging that pit," he said. "That's someone else's business. Not mine."

Sun Hawk and Summer Hope gave each other quick, frowning looks. They turned away from each other when they heard a commotion behind them, just in time to see Colonel Green enter the village on foot with his five soldiers.

Summer Hope's people stepped aside to allow the British to join the chiefs.

"I see you are interrogating your captive," Colonel Green said, resting his hand on a saber at his right side, his eyes locked in a silent battle with Pierre.

"And what he said was quite interesting," Summer Hope said. Sun Hawk stayed quiet, because it was Summer Hope's village and her place to respond to those who had trespassed.

"Of course, he lied," Colonel Green said, smiling smugly over at Summer Hope. "I have come to have council with you, Chief Summer Hope."

He looked over at Sun Hawk questioningly. "Chief Sun Hawk, also, if he wishes."

"I wish no council with you, ever," Summer Hope said, then smiled cleverly over at Sun Hawk. "As for you? What is your response, Chief Sun Hawk, to what the British propose?"

"My response?" Sun Hawk asked, taking a step closer to Colonel Green. "My response is to tell this Englishman he might as well return to his fort and pack his bags, for no Ojibwa will bring him pelts to send to the rich people of England."

"How can you both be so ignorant?" Colonel Green asked, his face growing red with rage. "Don't you know the money you are turning your back on for your people? All you have to do is bring us pelts. We will not only pay you in coins." He paused and smiled slyly at Summer Hope. "Like I told you before, we also pay in beautiful lace from Brussels, fancy feathered fans and hats, and beads that sparkle so much, they make your eyes burn."

"I was wrong to even for a moment be lured into wanting such foolish things from you," Summer Hope said, holding her chin defiantly high. "Do not believe that I am turning my back on your offer only because of what this bush ranger told me. It is because of you, and what you represent, that I am asking you to leave my village, and the area."

"I should have known better," Colonel Green said heatedly, glaring from Summer Hope to

Sun Hawk. The look he gave Pierre was much harsher. It was obvious that the Englishman blamed Pierre for his failure to get cooperation from the Ojibwa today.

It was very plain that were Pierre not the Ojibwa's captive, more than likely Colonel Green would kill him himself.

Colonel Green again glared at Sun Hawk and Summer Hope. "Yes, I should've known better than to ever believe I could talk sense to you savages," he spat out.

Having taken all that he could from this insulting man, Sun Hawk leapt toward him and grabbed his wrist. He twisted it behind him, while Eagle Wing and the other warriors disabled the British soldiers.

"Since you will not leave on your own, we will escort you from the premises," Sun Hawk said, glancing over at Summer Hope, seeing the pride in her smiling eyes.

"I thought I'd never applaud red skins, but were my hands free, I'd applaud you all today!" Pierre shouted, laughing as he watched the British escorted from the village.

Summer Hope, Sun Hawk, and the other villagers watched the British walk away, humiliated.

"I believe that is the last we will see of them," Summer Hope said, taking Sun Hawk's hand. "There aren't enough of them to retaliate."

Sun Hawk only nodded. He wasn't thinking as much about the British soldiers as the possibility that other bush rangers were in the area. They were more of a threat than the British. Ruthless and underhanded, they never tried to reach conclusions by bargaining.

He gazed down at Summer Hope. No, he wouldn't tell her his concerns about the bush rangers. She had had enough for one day. "Although there are so few British, I still believe that it would be a good idea to place sentries in strategic places around the village," he said.

She nodded, gave Eagle Wing instructions, and then walked with Sun Hawk back to where Pierre waited silently on the stake.

"What will his fate be?" Sun Hawk asked, sliding a comforting arm around Summer Hope's waist.

"For now, I believe he has been on the stake long enough," she said. She nodded toward two of her warriors. "Take him down. Lock him away. Tomorrow I will call a council. Together we will decide how to deal with the prisoner once and for all."

"Thank you for taking me from this lousy thing," Pierre said, his voice anxious as the warriors cut away the thongs at his wrists and ankles. "I'll forever be grateful."

"Do not be too quick to thank me for anything," Summer Hope said, glaring at him. "Your final fate is still in question."

She saw how that statement made the color drain from his face.

"I think you should go to your lodge and

rest," Sun Hawk said, already guiding her toward it, his arm still nestled around her waist. "And how is your head?"

"Pounding," Summer Hope said softly, reaching a hand up to the lump, slowly rubbing it.

"I shall soothe it with a cool cloth," Sun Hawk said, eliciting a smile. "Then I shall hold you until you feel better."

"I love you so," she murmured. "Thank you for understanding so much about me."

"How could I not?" Sun Hawk said. "I love everything about you. You are everything to so many, especially me."

They went into her wigwam, where someone already had fed logs into her lodge fire.

"Please—stay the day?" Summer Hope asked. "Your people are safe from the British. The British have no idea where your village is."

"I will stay, but there is one person I am certainly concerned about," Sun Hawk said, pouring water from a pitcher into a wooden basin. "Although Pierre is no longer a threat to my father, I wonder if the British might harm him."

"I shall send sentries to his home," Summer Hope said, going back to the entrance flap. "Then everyone should be able to relax, at least until the council to decide Pierre's final fate."

"And that will be tomorrow?" Sun Hawk asked, raising an eyebrow.

"As soon as the sun rises on the new tomorrow, yes, the council will decide Pierre's future," she said, then hurried away from the wigwam.

Sun Hawk sat down onto a pallet of furs beside the lodge fire, then smiled when a lady's voice spoke outside the entrance flap. He knew why the woman was there. He could smell a delicious aroma coming from a pot of food she had brought for her chief and male companion.

He rose, pushed the flap aside to take the pot, and thanked the woman.

By the time Summer Hope had returned, he had a bowl filled with rabbit stew, awaiting her.

They ate and smiled and talked of things far removed from their recent troubles. Sun Hawk lovingly bathed her wound with cool water.

He made sure not to bring up his concern about the bush rangers. When he returned home, he would send many warriors out to search for the interlopers on Indian land.

But for now, his heart was beating only for Summer Hope.

"Are you certain you feel well enough to make love?" Sun Hawk asked huskily. He gasped in pleasure when her answer was to reach down inside his breeches and wrap her hand around his manhood, her fingers stroking.

39

Thou art all fair, my love;
there is no spot in thee.
—OLD TESTAMENT
SONG OF SOLOMON 4:7

Wanting to join the council with Summer Hope, Sun Hawk had risen while the moon was still high in the sky.

He had rounded up the best of his warriors, leaving enough to guard his village. He walked through the forest with them, aware that day was just breaking along the horizon.

It was good to know that his warriors would become acquainted with Summer Hope's. It was the true beginning of an alliance.

He was anxious to see how well his warriors would be received this morning, with only Summer Hope's invitation to join her people in council today.

But by now she would have prepared her people for the upcoming changes in their lives, how these two bands of Ojibwa would come together as one force to fight injustice.

Before he left her in the late afternoon of the previous day, after they had made tender love, she had told him that she would talk to her people about the council.

But she had also told him something else—that she needed more time to prepare them for the other change, that they would have a new leader.

She felt they needed to adjust to one thing at a time.

Although she loved Sun Hawk, it was obvious that her transition from being a chief to a wife would not be as easy as she might wish it to be.

He would be patient, though, as promised.

As he continued to walk through the shadowy forest, well-armed with his bow and arrow and his knife, he looked guardedly around him and his men. They, too, kept their eyes moving from place to place, wary of every movement, every sound.

He had cautioned his warriors to be careful of their steps, for beneath their feet could be not only more deadfall pits, but the angry jaws of steel traps.

After the council today, Sun Hawk was going to send his warriors out in all directions to search for the newest intruders in their lives. They had to be stopped. He knew how lucky he was that he had found Summer Hope before they had come to check on their trap. It would have been a nightmare if she had been taken captive by bush rangers again.

Seeing the light of the outdoor fire in Summer Hope's village through a break in the trees a short distance away, Sun Hawk increased his pace.

But his mind had wandered to someone else.

He had gone to warn his father about coming alone to Summer Hope's village. He had asked him to always walk with an Ojibwa warrior escort as he moved from place to place.

Soon, he hoped, that wouldn't be a problem. His father would be living safely with Sun Hawk and his people by Enchanted Lake, where he could live out his life in peace and harmony with nature.

As Sun Hawk and his warriors grew closer to Summer Hope's village, Sun Hawk was aware of not having seen any sentries. There should have been several keeping watch over Summer Hope's people as they slept.

Sun Hawk's spine stiffened when he became aware of something else. He heard excited voices coming from Summer Hope's village, as well as wailing.

A sense of dread grabbed at Sun Hawk's heart, for he knew that people only wailed when someone had died.

Sun Hawk exchanged troubled glances with his warriors, then broke into a run.

When he finally reached the village, he stopped and stared in horror at the bodies of four warriors lined up on the ground in the light of the outdoor fire.

Beside the bodies were women and children, crying out their sorrow.

Summer Hope saw Sun Hawk.

She ran to him and grabbed his hands. "Four of my sentries were slain in the night. The one who was guarding Pierre and three who were standing around the perimeter of the village," she sobbed, her eyes red and swollen from crying. "This massacre was discovered only moments ago. Pierre is gone. He has escaped!"

Stunned, Sun Hawk drew her into his arms and held her protectively. His eyes again took in the tragic scene, the unspeakable loss of lives.

Eagle Wing stepped up next to Summer Hope. He placed a hand on her shoulder as she still clung to Sun Hawk. "There were many footprints where Pierre was being held. Whoever came had one purpose. They killed our warriors to get to Pierre. They forced the lock on the door, then fled into the night with him."

"Bush rangers," Sun Hawk choked out. "Those responsible for the wolf trap in which Summer Hope fell are surely responsible for releasing Pierre," he said. "They must have seen Pierre taken captive and known who he was. The bush rangers stand up for one another."

He eased Summer Hope from his arms then doubled his hands into fists at his sides. "They must be found," he hissed. "They must be made to pay for their heinous crimes against the Ojibwa people."

Then his heart skipped a beat. He swallowed hard as he stepped away from Summer Hope, his eyes staring in the direction of his father's home. "My *gee-bah-bah*, father!" he said, the color draining from his face.

"I thought of him the moment I saw how my warriors were so heartlessly murdered," Summer Hope said, wiping tears from her eyes with the back of a hand. "There are enough warriors there now to make sure he will be safe."

"You sent them?"

"*Ay-uh*, yes, I could not take a chance of you losing your father after having just been reunited with him."

"It might not have been bush rangers who did this," Eagle Wing said. "It could have been the British. You know they must blame Pierre for their failure to get us to agree to supply pelts for them. Because Pierre told us everything, the British might have decided to steal him away and kill him."

"There are only a few of them," Sun Hawk said, looking in the direction of the fort. "I doubt they would dare enter an Ojibwa village only to get back at Pierre."

"I believe they would," Summer Hope said. "And they would not hesitate at killing my warriors. Surely they hate us all now with a passion."

"Let us go to the fort and confront them," Eagle Wing said, resting a hand on his sheathed knife.

"They will deny everything." Summer Hope sighed.

"I think Eagle Wing is right," Sun Hawk

agreed. "We must go there. We cannot leave one stone unturned. We must go and check out the British, and if we are convinced they are not guilty of this crime against our people, then we shall hunt like never before, until we find those who are."

The wind had shifted suddenly to the north. With it came an instant chill, as well as a few flakes of snow from the sky.

Summer Hope hugged herself as she snuggled a blanket around her shoulders.

She puzzled over how ill she felt. When she had first awakened today, she had vomited more than once.

Now she again felt queasy. She knew that she was not up to accompanying the warriors to the fort.

"I will stay behind and comfort those who are in mourning," she said, glad when Sun Hawk and then Eagle Wing hugged her. They agreed that it was best that she stayed behind.

"Go with care," she said, watching as their warriors came together, heavily armed. "Be careful."

She waited until they left, then ran behind her lodge and threw up again. She was grateful when her favorite maiden came and helped her back to her lodge.

Once inside, she lay back as White Fawn lovingly bathed her brow with a damp cloth.

"I have had such a symptom as this," White Fawn said, looking sheepishly at Summer Hope.

"When I was with child, both times, I could hardly hold any food in my belly."

"With . . . child?" Summer Hope asked, her eyes wide. She thought of how recently she had made love for the first time. Surely she wouldn't be pregnant this quickly, or feel the affects of it so soon.

"My sickness came early in my pregnancies," White Fawn said, smiling at Summer Hope. Thirty winters of age, and entrancingly pretty, she and her husband made love often. She was exceedingly happy to have discovered that she was now with child again.

"Each time I had only missed my monthly by a few days and I was ill," she continued. "Have you . . . missed your monthly?"

Summer Hope's heartbeat quickened as she placed a hand on her stomach, for she had just missed it for the first time ever.

She said nothing more about it to White Fawn. This was something she did not want to talk about, not until she was certain.

But if she was pregnant, she must hurry and transfer the duties of chief to Eagle Wing!

She smiled at the thought of a tiny baby growing in the safe cocoon of her womb, a child born of a love so precious.

"Do not say anything to anyone of my illness," Summer Hope pleaded as White Fawn continued to bathe her brow.

"My chief, my friend, I would never tell anything as private as that without your permission," White Fawn said, dropping the cloth into the wooden basin. She drew Summer Hope into her arms. "I am happy for you if what we both think is true. I have seen you with Sun Hawk. I know that your love for him, and his for you, is real."

"It is a love that will endure, forever and ever," Summer Hope said, returning the hug.

She decided to reveal another truth to White Fawn. "As soon as our people are past their mourning for those who were killed last night, I will tell them that it is time for me to step down as chief," she said softly. "If it is approved in council, Eagle Wing will then take my place."

She could see how this news came as a shock to White Fawn by the way she had gone so quiet and stared at her.

Summer Hope swallowed hard. She now had a reason to believe that telling everyone was not going to be an easy task.

She could not help but dread it!

40

Deceit to secrecy confin'd,
Lawful, cautious, and refin'd,
To everything but interest blind,
And forges fetters for the mind.
—WILLIAM BLAKE

Just as Sun Hawk and the warriors approached the fort, snow began falling in blinding white sheets from the low-hanging gray clouds overhead, partially impairing their vision.

Sun Hawk moved closer to Eagle Wing. "The snow will help keep the soldiers from seeing us as clearly," he said, thankful that he had put on his warm bearskin coat before leaving his home. Suddenly, winter was upon them in its full-blown fury.

"I do not believe the English soldiers will fire upon us, or even refuse our entrance into their fort," Eagle Wing said, watching the fort carefully.

The fort was not protected by a wall. Each of its buildings stretched out in a tight-knit circle from the larger, main log structure. The Englishmen never had been given cause to fear an attack from the Ojibwa, so they never left sentries posted.

The Ojibwa were close enough to see everything within the perimeters of the fort, but Eagle Wing saw no one, nor any movement.

"Eagle Wing, we cannot take anything for granted. Things are different now between us and the soldiers," Sun Hawk said, his eyes studying the various cabins at the fort. "They have to be angry over our refusal to cooperate with them, even if they did not take Pierre."

"I know it was my idea to come here, but do you believe they would be angry enough about that to murder our warriors?" Eagle Wing asked, glancing over at Sun Hawk.

Sun Hawk reached a hand out and grabbed him by an arm. "What caused you to stop?" Eagle Wing whispered. "What do you see that I have not yet seen?"

"There is no smoke rising from any of the chimneys at the fort," Sun Hawk said, lowering his hand away from Eagle Wing's arm. His insides tightened as he continued to study the inactivity at the fort. "It is not likely they would not have fires today, not with the icy winds and blowing snow."

"Perhaps they decided to move on," Eagle Wing said hopefully.

"Perhaps they fled after they massacred four Ojibwa warriors," Sun Hawk said, his teeth clenched.

"Do you think they took Pierre with them?" Eagle Wing asked. Their warriors moved up closer behind them.

"Would you?"

Eagle Wing started to answer but stopped when a gunshot rang out from the main building.

Sun Hawk's heart went stone cold as he watched Eagle Wing's body lurch with the impact of a bullet slamming into his chest.

Eyes wide, Eagle Wing clutched at his chest. He gave Sun Hawk a look of disbelief that turned to horror, then collapsed at Sun Hawk's feet, his life's blood spreading out away from him, turning the snow a vivid red.

Everyone stood for a moment, shocked, then Sun Hawk looked over his shoulder at the warriors. "Run for cover!" he shouted, dashing for the thick forest at his left side.

Panting hard, taking cover behind a tall oak tree, Sun Hawk gazed in utter disbelief at the fallen warrior. From Eagle Wing's empty stare, there was no doubt that he was dead.

In a flash, he remembered how Summer Hope had talked so favorably of this warrior and how she had chosen to advise her people to name him as their chief when she gave up the title. He swallowed hard as he recalled how her first choice had been Black Bear.

Now both of her favored warriors were dead. And why? Because of the madness of men who did not value life. Of late, there had been too many deaths. After a long period of peace and tranquility in this area, death had come like a menacing, heartless giant, stamping out one life, and then another. Where would it end? Who else would die before those with cold hearts were stopped?

"Look!" Gray Eagle said, his eyes locked on the main cabin at the fort. "Do you see? A man! A soldier! He fell from the door, a rifle in hand, his chest bloody. He has been shot!"

A voice carried to them through the snow and wind. "Help . . . me!" it said. "Oh, Lord, help me."

"Do you think whoever shot Eagle Wing also shot the soldier?" Gray Eagle asked, looking guardedly from cabin to cabin. "Do you think it was Pierre? Did he get the best of the soldiers after they abducted him?"

"You there!" Sun Hawk shouted, hoping the soldier was still conscious enough to hear him. "Who shot you? Who else is there? Is it Pierre DuSault? Is he at the fort?"

"I . . . am . . . the sole survivor!" the soldier managed to say between moans of pain. "Please come and help me. No one else will fire upon you. I shot . . . your brave. I . . . did it in error. I thought you were the bush rangers returning to finish me off. Through the snow, and blinded by such pain, I could not see that it was the Ojibwa instead!"

"He killed Eagle Wing," Sun Hawk growled, doubling one hand into a tight fist at his side.

"He said that it was a mistake," Gray Eagle pointed out.

"And when did you ever believe what an English soldier said?" Sun Hawk snapped. "There could be others. They could be using the fallen soldier to lure us into a trap."

"Did you come to Summer Hope's village and kill her warriors in order to get your hands on Pierre DuSault?" Sun Hawk shouted at the man.

"No!" the soldier gasped. "The bush rangers! There were several of them! They released Pierre! Then they came and massacred my friends. Colonel Green is dead. I . . . am the only one alive."

"Perhaps he speaks the truth," Sun Hawk said, then looked over his shoulder at the warriors. He named off those who would stay and keep watch and those who would accompany him to the fort.

Sun Hawk ran stealthily through the snow, his eyes constantly darting all around him to guard against being ambushed. He knew that if what the soldier said was true, the bush rangers could be anywhere ready to claim more lives.

His heart leaped with fear. Summer Hope! His father! Were they safe? They were guarded, but was it enough?

The bush rangers seemed clever in their plans against their enemies. They had proven that, if they indeed had been the ones to release Pierre DuSault.

Just as he reached the wounded soldier, the man gave Sun Hawk a wild, frightened look, then gasped.

Sun Hawk knelt down beside him and placed his fingers at the man's throat.

There was no pulse. He was dead.

As others quietly came up beside him, Sun Hawk rose to his feet and slowly, carefully opened the door and crept inside.

Bitter bile rushed up into his throat at the sight before him. Dead men lay sprawled across the floor.

The bush rangers had massacred all of the British soldiers.

The rooms had been ransacked. All valuables had been stolen, including weapons.

With the help of the other bush rangers, Pierre had achieved vengeance against those who had turned him over to the Ojibwa.

Now Sun Hawk would have to do something that he dreaded. There was another English fort named Fort Regina some distance north of Fort William. The decent thing to do would be to transport the bodies of the fallen soldiers to that fort.

But first, he would try and round up the guilty parties, so that they, also, could be taken to Fort Regina. There they could stand trial in a white man's court. Although Ojibwa warriors had been slain by the bush rangers, now that they had murdered white men, they should be tried by whites. If the Ojibwa tried them and sentenced them to death and the white authorities got word of it, the Ojibwa could be punished. Best to let whites handle their own and leave the red men out of it.

He explained everything to the warriors. They agreed heartily to the plan.

They took blankets from the soldiers' bunks and covered the bodies.

Even the one who had mistakenly murdered Eagle Wing was treated with respect. He was taken inside the lodge and covered by a blanket.

While others stood guard, Sun Hawk took another blanket and went outside and knelt down beside Eagle Wing.

Overwhelmed by sadness and regret, he wrapped the fallen warrior in the blanket, then lifted him into his arms and slowly began the trek back to Summer Hope's village.

When they finally arrived, the body of their beloved warrior was taken and laid with the other slain Ojibwa. Grieving filled the air, sending off a chill worse than that brought on by the sudden winter weather.

Summer Hope came to Sun Hawk. She flung herself into his arms. "Will it never stop?" she cried, clinging to him. "How can such a man as Pierre feel so little for mankind? Until he is dead, no one is safe! No one!"

She leaned away from him and gazed up at him through tear-drenched lashes. "Eagle Wing was . . . was to be named chief," she sobbed. "Now that he is dead . . ."

She slowly lowered her eyes. "Things change," she said, causing Sun Hawk's heart to sink, for he thought that she was referring to their marriage plans. Did she think it was impossible now to marry him because of what had happened?

He gently placed his hands on her shoulders. "Summer Hope, tell me what changes you are referring to," he said, his voice tight.

When she looked up at him and tears rushed from her eyes anew, he saw that she could not find the words to tell him. He felt that he had lost his woman to Pierre DuSault, for it must be that she could not find it in her heart to abandon her people after what they had lost already.

She could not tell them that they were also losing their chief, especially since the warrior who was to take her place was now dead.

41

How the world is made for each of us!
How all we perceive and know in it,
Tends to some moments' produce thus,
When a soul declares itself—to wit,
By its fruit, the thing it does!
—ROBERT BROWNING

"There is no need for you to say anymore," Sun
Hawk said, reaching for Summer Hope's hands
and gently holding them. "You are distressed
and it is true that your people need you now.
My warriors and I will leave you and your people to your grieving. I must go and see that my
father is all right."

"Life can be so *o-neesh-skin-ah-wan*, so cruel,
so heart-wrenching," Summer Hope said. She
wanted to hold on to these few moments with
Sun Hawk, for she wasn't sure when they could
be together again, or if they could even talk
about a joined future.

She wanted to ask him to stay, to help her in
her time of sorrow.

She wanted to tell him how badly she
needed him.

But she couldn't.

And perhaps what had happened today had

been for a purpose . . . to show her with whom her true loyalties and devotion must lie.

Her people!

How could she turn her back on them?

"I will stay away long enough for your people to get through their burials, but I cannot stay away the full length of time that it will take for them to mourn their fallen warriors, for you know they will never stop mourning them," Sun Hawk said, his voice breaking. "Life must go on. Ours, Summer Hope. Ours."

He gave her hands a final loving squeeze and bent low and brushed a kiss across her brow, which almost broke her heart with want of him. He turned and walked from the village with his warriors.

As Sun Hawk walked farther and farther away from the woman he would love forever, he feared that she had just closed the door on their relationship. His heart felt as though it was turned inside out, the pain of possibly having lost her was so intense.

And he could not get the sight of the slain, blanket-draped warriors off his mind.

But he knew that he must!

He tried to think of more innocent times when he was able to smile and look to a future that was sweet and filled with hope.

Tears filled his eyes as he thought of the joy on Summer Hope's face when he carved their initials on that tree.

He closed his eyes for a moment and could

actually feel her joy, her happiness, matching his.

He opened his eyes and continued to trudge through the ankle-deep snow.

The snow was no longer falling.

But it had spread a *mee-kah-wah-diz-ee*, beautiful, serene blanket of white over everything.

In the distance he saw the steeple of his father's church looming into the gray sky.

The bell.

He gazed at the bell that hung quietly in the belfry, recalling another time, a place, a woman.

His *gee-mah-mah*, mother.

She had been such a tiny, fragile woman with deep dimples on each cheek.

She had almost never looked at Sun Hawk without smiling.

In her arms he had found such love and peace.

"Oh, if you were only here now," he whispered, knowing that she had always been able to take away his hurt.

But he doubted that the hurt he was carrying inside his heart would ever heal, not unless Summer Hope changed her mind.

If not, he would have to learn all over again how to live without her.

Arriving at his father's cabin, he knocked on the door.

When his father opened it, the warmth from the fireplace that filled the interior splashed invitingly onto Sun Hawk's cold face. His father reached out and drew him into his arms and gave him a long hug. He was so relieved to know that his father's life had been spared the hate of the bush rangers.

At least for now, he thought.

He looked around and saw that his father had started packing his bags with his personal books and journals.

"You are readying yourself for your journey to my home?" he asked.

He looked at the other men in black who sat before the fireplace on blankets, reading books by the light of the fire. As he stood there, they gave him occasional glances, then returned to their reading.

"I have explained things to my friends," Father Davidson said, placing a hand on Sun Hawk's arm to lead him away from the others. "They understand."

He glanced down at his friends, then back up at Sun Hawk. "When spring arrives they will move onward," he said. "They are not as old as I. They have much life left in their hearts and legs, enough to spread the gospel from town to town instead of staying in one place waiting for people to come to them."

"I know that you would rather go with them, because I know that teaching the gospel has been your life," Sun Hawk said, looking over at his father's time-worn Bible that lay on a table.

Its cover and its pages were frayed.

He could see many ribbons sticking out from the pages of the Bible.

He knew his father had placed those ribbons at his favorite Bible verses over the years, the ribbons giving him quick access when he felt the need to quote to a person hungry for the Lord's word.

"There comes a time in life when one must step back and re-evaluate things," Father Davidson said. "Come in, my son." He looked past Sun Hawk and motioned with a silent nod toward Sun Hawk's warriors for them to also enter.

As they crowded into the room, the door closed behind them, Father Davidson smiled. "Please warm yourselves while I speak with my son," he said, then stood aside with Sun Hawk.

Sun Hawk didn't remove his coat, for he did not plan to stay long.

Picking up on what his father had said earlier, about stepping back to reevaluate things, Sun Hawk gazed remorsefully into the flames of the fire.

"*Ay-uh*, yes, I could never be more aware of how one must, time and again, reevaluate one's life," he said, his voice low and filled with emotion. "I could never be more aware of that than now."

He felt his father's eyes on him. "*Gee-bah-bah*, Father, a short while ago my warriors, as well as several of Summer Hope's, went with me to the British fort," he said, his voice breaking. "We discovered a slaughter there."

He saw an instant look of horror in his father's eyes.

He reached over and placed a hand on his father's arm. "It was not the British who came and released Pierre DuSault, killing four of Summer Hope's warriors to get to the Frenchman," he said. "We went to the fort. We found all but one of the soldiers dead. He lived long enough to shoot and kill Summer Hope's warrior named Eagle Wing, and to tell us who came and left death behind. It was bush rangers."

"There was a slaughter? And . . . Eagle Wing was shot? But why?" Father Davidson asked, filled with anguish over hearing about more needless deaths. "Why would the bush rangers kill the British? Why was Eagle Wing killed?"

"Eagle Wing was shot by a dying British soldier because he was mistaken for a bush ranger," Sun Hawk said. "The British soldiers were attacked apparently because bush rangers were in the area and saw Pierre being held captive by the Ojibwa. Bush rangers will do anything to protect one of their kind. They rescued Pierre. He must have talked them into retaliating against the British for betraying him," Sun Hawk explained.

"Did you know there were other bush rangers in the area?" Father Davidson asked, raising an eyebrow. "None have come to our church for prayer."

"The bush rangers who do such things as this would not even know the meaning of prayer," Sun Hawk said. "They are a group of men intent on only one thing. Illegally killing our forest animals for the money they can get from selling their pelts. It makes no difference whom they might have to kill to achieve their goal."

"But where do they come from?" Father Davidson asked. "How could they be in the area without anyone being aware of their presence?"

"By the white man's law, and by treaty between the Ojibwa and white government, it is illegal for any white man to hunt on this land," Sun Hawk said. "So those who do come, especially bush rangers, would make sure not to be seen. But when a trap is discovered, like the one I discovered only recently, everyone knows to be on the alert. It seems we were not alerted early enough this time to hunt the bush rangers down and make sure they left the area."

"And so the bush rangers knew about Pierre, and came and rescued him," Father Davidson said, slowly nodding.

"*Ay-uh*, yes, that has to be the answer," Sun Hawk said, also nodding.

He walked past his warriors and went to the door and slowly opened it. When he saw snow swirling from the sky, he closed the door and turned back to his father. "We must go now before the snow worsens again," he said, his voice solemn. "I have been gone from my people for too long already. I hold a deep fear in my heart that the bush rangers might discover our Enchanted Lake village. If they do, they would heartlessly kill my people and take everything for themselves.''

''Then go, my son, and when you return, I shall be ready to start my life anew with you and your people,'' Father Davidson said. ''Do not concern yourself about your father's welfare. God is with me.'' He patted Sun Hawk's cheek. ''As is He with you. Every step you take on your journey home will be guarded.''

''And you are being guarded, as well, not only by God's caring, but by several warriors who are standing outside your lodge. Some are mine. Others are Summer Hope's,'' Sun Hawk said. He drew his father's lean, frail body into his arms and hugged him fiercely. ''You will be safe, *gee-bah-bah*. No one will be able to get close to this cabin without being stopped.''

''Summer Hope?'' Father Davidson asked softly. ''How is she accepting the loss of life at her village?''

Sun Hawk swallowed hard. ''With a very heavy, even guilty, heart,'' he answered. ''What happened today might change my entire life.''

''Why do you say that?'' Father Davidson asked, searching his son's eyes.

''Summer Hope and I had made plans,'' Sun Hawk said, then turned and hurried to the door, because he did not want to talk about it anymore. Carrying it in his heart was hard enough without confiding in someone, even his father.

Matters of the heart were not easy things to talk about, especially when a man felt as though he might have lost at love, the only love he would ever allow himself to know.

Sun Hawk would never reach out to another woman if Summer Hope turned her back on him and their love.

"I must go now," he said, opening the door. He stood aside as his warriors went ahead of him into the gray, heartsick day. He gave his father a wistful stare. "Tomorrow? Be ready tomorrow? I will bring a dogsled for you."

"Yes, unless you feel as though you should spend that time hunting the bush rangers," Father Davidson said, going to the door, gripping it.

"I will see to bringing you safely to my home, and then I shall join my warriors on the search for the bush rangers," Sun Hawk said. "But knowing how they would be hunted down, they would be ignorant not to have fled."

"But if they have, will they not then spread more death and destruction across the land?" Father Davidson asked.

"*Ay-uh*, yes, so I hope they did not get far enough before the snowstorm arrived in its intensity. They will have searched for a safe, warm shelter. I am sure they are somewhere close. I can almost smell their stench in the wind."

As the snow began falling more rapidly, the flakes large and white, Sun Hawk frowned at the low-hanging gray clouds. "Any footprints will soon be covered by what is falling now," he said disappointedly.

He turned to his father, gave him one last hug, and hurried from the lodge.

His warriors moved in closer around him, some following behind, others flanking his sides. They ducked their heads into the blowing snow and rushed onward, ever alert for footprints.

42

Why should the private pleasure of someone
Become the public plague of many?
—WILLIAM SHAKESPEARE

Sun Hawk was relieved when the snow had
stopped again. He welcomed the shine of the
sun as it crept through the clouds that were
breaking up in the sky. Halfway between Summer Hope's village and his own, he ran at a
steady trot, his warriors keeping pace with him.

He stopped dead in his tracks when suddenly
he saw someone coming from a cave a short
distance away.

He nodded to his warriors and motioned for
them to take cover.

Just as they hid behind a thick stand of snow-
laden bushes, a familiar voice came to Sun
Hawk from the direction of the cave. He and
his men observed several bush rangers coming
from it, talking, laughing, and carrying large
packs of firearms across their shoulders.

Sun Hawk did not even need to hear the voice
to know who was with the burly men. Dragging
a supply of firearms thrust into a large buckskin

bag, no doubt stolen from the fort, was none other than Pierre DuSault.

The bush rangers apparently had taken cover in the cave during the earlier snow fall. They had probably taken the time to build a fire for warmth, and had perhaps eaten while talking over their latest victories against the English and Ojibwa.

Even now they laughed about having left everyone dead at the fort. Sun Hawk's teeth ground angrily together, his breathing sharp and fierce.

When one of the men patted Pierre on the back, bragging about how they had bested the Ojibwa by killing the sentries and releasing him from bondage, Sun Hawk could not stand to stay there any longer, listening.

He turned to his men. "They are bragging about ambushes and deaths?" he thundered. "Let us show them who laughs last! Set your firearms aside. Load your bowstrings with sharp-pointed arrows. Our silent weapons will not give the bush rangers the chance to escape before arrows riddle their bodies."

He yanked his bow off his shoulder.

He reached back and jerked not one, but several arrows, from his quiver.

His eyes narrowed in on Pierre as he skillfully notched an arrow in place, then drew back the bowstring and set the arrow free.

He laughed out loud when he saw the surprise leap into Pierre's eyes as the arrow found its target in his chest.

Sun Hawk's warriors then let out a volley of arrows, until all of the men were downed. They lay on the ground, writhing and clutching at the arrows protruding from their bodies like needles in pincushions.

Sun Hawk smiled, finally feeling some semblance of peace inside his heart over stopping these men before they had the chance to harm anyone else. He flung his bow back over his shoulder, thrust the remaining arrows into his quiver, and stepped out into the open with his warriors.

"You!" Pierre cried out as his eyes locked on Sun Hawk's.

"*Ay-uh*, it is the Ojibwa 'white chief,' as I have known you to call me," Sun Hawk said, now standing directly over Pierre and smiling triumphantly down at him. "At long last, your heartless ways have been stopped. You were a fool not to go far away after the massacre at Summer Hope's village, and at the fort."

"The snow . . . delayed our travel north to Canada," Pierre gulped out, his color fading as blood dripped from his chest wound. "But even then I was not going to join my friends. Not until . . . I made certain that Chief Summer Hope was dead."

"She is very much *bee-mah-dee-zee*, alive," Sun Hawk said, his jaw tightening. "If only she were here to see you writhing in pain."

"Were she here, I would find enough strength to shoot her," Pierre growled, clutching his chest when a sharp pain raced through him.

"You forget that you are surrounded by many warriors?" Sun Hawk asked, bending to one knee so that he could get closer to Pierre's face. As he bent down, he slid Pierre's weapons farther away from the dying man.

"Nothing would stop me," Pierre said, his voice having lost most of its strength. "The squaw chief has been nothing but a thorn in my side since the day I grabbed her for my men's entertainment."

Just the thought of what he meant by "entertainment" made Sun Hawk want to finish him off and finally silence him.

But he could tell that the man had only a short while before he took his last breath. Sun Hawk wanted to see him suffer for as long as possible, for this man had caused so much suffering.

Sun Hawk moved quickly to his feet when he heard dogs barking.

His heart beat wildly when he saw who was approaching.

Summer Hope.

She was on a sleigh dragged by a team of four dogs, and behind her were two other sets of dog teams pulling her escorts.

"Sun Hawk!" Summer Hope cried when she saw him standing there. His eyes filled with uncertainty as he watched her approach. "I could not wait another moment! I had to come and tell you that I was wrong!''

Filled with awe, knowing that Summer Hope still cared, Sun Hawk stood for a moment staring at her.

She continued to wave and smile as she directed her dogs toward him, and his joy became too much for him to stand there and wait for her. He broke into a run, laughing at himself as he felt his feet awkwardly slipping and sliding in the snow, and not caring how it must look to the others.

His woman was still his!

She was willing to work things out so that they could be together.

And she did not want to wait until after the burials and mourning to tell him.

She had not wanted him sitting in his lodge thinking that she no longer cared.

Now he knew.

She still wanted to be his wife.

They would meet in council with both of their bands of Ojibwa and work things out between them.

He had a solution, something that could work for them all. He had not voiced it aloud but had decided to wait to see if she still wanted him before offering a compromise.

And now he knew that his suggestion would become reality.

And soon.

He hoped before the worst of winter set in.

He wanted all of their people to be settled before the cold blasts of wind swept across the land and the deeper, lasting snows fell, which would paralyze travel through the forest.

"My love," Summer Hope cried, stopping her dogs, leaping from the sled. She held her arms out for Sun Hawk as she ran toward him.

When they reached one another, Sun Hawk grabbed her fully into his arms and held her close to his heart.

"I need you so much," she murmured as she gazed into his eyes. "I need you now. My heart is so heavy with sorrow. Please help me, Sun Hawk, to get through the traumatic hours that are ahead of me and my people."

She knew the dangers of being so distraught were she truly with child. She had seen many women lose a child in the early weeks of pregnancy. She wanted her child to have a better chance!

She felt that Sun Hawk's presence was all that she needed to get her through these trying times.

"The man who has caused you so much pain has been downed by one of my arrows," Sun Hawk said, turning so that she could see Pierre lying in the snow, still clinging to life.

"I wish I could have sent the arrow into his chest, myself," Summer Hope said, her voice breaking. "I would have sent more than one. There would have been one with Black Bear's name on it, and also Eagle Wing's."

She hugged Sun Hawk, then gazed into his eyes. "I want to say something to Pierre before he takes his last breath," she said.

Sun Hawk nodded, then took her hand and walked with her toward Pierre. He could see Pierre's eyes darken with hate as he stared up at Summer Hope.

Pierre tried to crawl over to his weapons, but dropped back when he realized that he didn't have the strength to go any further.

When Summer Hope finally reached him, she knelt down beside him. Her knees sank into the snow, yet she did not seem to be aware of its icy coldness.

"You have already caused my people so much pain. You had better use the last moments of your life asking your God for forgiveness for all of the evil you have done in your life. Were you to ask it of me, I could not give it. I would, instead, spit in your face."

Pierre grabbed at his throat.

"If the agony you have caused me makes me lose the child I am carrying inside me, I will find a way to haunt your grave so that you will never rest," she added.

Pierre's eyes became wild as he began choking on blood. It rushed up his throat and from the corners of his mouth. It was obvious that he was trying to say something, but his words were lost.

His body jerked, and then it was still. His eyes stared blankly back at Summer Hope.

"He is finally dead," Summer Hope said, almost choking on a sob of relief.

"Summer Hope, what you said . . . ?" Sun Hawk asked, her words about a child ringing in his ears.

Wiping tears from her eyes, Summer Hope rose and moved away from Pierre.

She smiled softly at Sun Hawk as she turned to him. "I was going to tell you soon, but I wanted to be sure," she said, reaching for his hands, taking them. "I still am not positive. It is too soon, but I have had the sort of sickness that I know comes with child."

He slid his hands free of hers, swept an arm around her waist, and walked her away from everyone.

When they were standing behind a cluster of trees, where no one could see or hear them, Sun Hawk framed Summer Hope's face between his hands.

"I have to know," he said, his voice breaking.

"Whether or not I am with child?" Summer Hope said, puzzled. "Like I said, I cannot be sure."

"No, that is not what I was referring to," Sun Hawk said, searching her eyes. "*Ee-quay*, woman, I have to know what your true reason was for coming after me today. Was it because of your love for me? Or because you might be with child and need the father to marry you?"

Summer Hope was taken aback by the mere suggestion of what he was thinking. "If you think I would only come to you for the child's sake, then you do not know me at all," she said, lowering her eyes.

She stepped away from him and headed back toward the others. She felt an emptiness deep within her soul, and wished that she had not come. The man she loved with all of her heart still did not trust her! She doubted now that he ever would.

"Summer Hope, wait," Sun Hawk cried, hurrying after her.

Again he took her hands and led her behind other thick-trunked trees. "I was wrong," he said huskily. "I should have never said that. It is just that you seemed so ready to let me go earlier. I had almost accepted that you did not care for me enough to make sacrifices to be with me."

"Sacrifices?" she said, raising an eyebrow. "What sort?"

"Being chief," he said, again searching her eyes, hoping she would say the right things. If she didn't, then all would be lost to them both, forever.

Her lips parted in a slight gasp.

Sun Hawk could hardly stand waiting for her response, and the longer she took, the more he doubted she was going to say what he wanted to hear.

"Sun Hawk, I, you, we . . ." she stammered, proving to him that she was still battling her own heart.

43

Squeeze as lover should,
O kiss!
O love me truly!
　　　　—JOHN KEATS

Seeing that Summer Hope was still having so much trouble saying what she had on her mind, Sun Hawk felt that she might be better able to say it if they were somewhere alone, away from this place of death.

"Come with me to my village so that we can talk in privacy," he said, his voice thick with emotion. "My village is the closer of yours and mine."

"But I have duties as chief to see to," Summer Hope said. "I must see that—"

"Your warriors, and mine, can do what has to be done with the downed white men," he said. "Let us each give them instructions, and then you and I will go to my village. I will take you back to yours once we have things worked out between us."

She reached up and gently touched his face. "And I do want to work things out," she murmured, those words alone all that Sun Hawk needed to hear. She must be ready to search for a compromise.

Now that he knew that she was going to be his, he could allow himself to glory over the fact that more than likely she was with child.

His.

He would not allow himself to think any longer that she would marry him only because of the child.

Before, when they had spoken of their future, there was no child to sway her decision.

Their joined hearts had led them into talking of marriage, and only then was there a mention of children to be born of their love for one another.

They walked, hand in hand, through the snow and went to their warriors.

They made arrangements to send their warriors to the British fort with the bodies, and to send a scout tomorrow to the fort upriver to explain about the deaths, so that the white people could take care of their own. Sun Hawk boarded Summer Hope's sleigh and sent the dogs onward in the direction of Enchanted Lake.

When they came to the rocky slope that led down to his village, Sun Hawk and Summer Hope left the sleigh. She watched as he led the dogs into a thick cover of bushes where they would be hidden well enough from any passersby.

"I have my own sleigh and dogs at my village," Sun Hawk said as he held Summer

Hope's arm and led her down the snow-laden steps of rocks. "When the weather requires their use, I have a back way to come and go from my village. I did not use it today with yours because we would have had to waste too much time."

When Summer Hope's feet slid on the snow, Sun Hawk quickly reached out and caught her.

He swept her fully into his arms and carried her the rest of the way, all eyes turning when he took her into his village.

His people stared from their entranceways, but Sun Hawk just smiled at them and went on. He hurried into his own lodge, where warmth and the smells of sage and food cooking over the fire greeted them.

"Let's get you warmed by the fire," Sun Hawk said, taking Summer Hope there, gently placing her on her feet.

He removed her hooded fur cape and gloves, and then bent to his knees and removed her damp moccasins.

After he wrapped a blanket around her shoulders, he took off his own winter gear, and opted to stay barefoot as he sat down beside Summer Hope on a pallet of pelts close to the fire.

Dragging a blanket from behind him, he placed it around his shoulders, then put his feet up close to the fire, welcoming the warmth that soaked into his flesh.

He reached for two wooden bowls and spoons that had been set beside the fire. He ladled some soup into each bowl, then handed one to Summer Hope.

They ate in silence for a while until their bellies were warmed inside and out, then set their empty bowls aside and turned and faced one another.

Sun Hawk took Summer Hope's hands in his. "I know that you have been torn by many things, even more than I, since it is your people who have suffered so many senseless deaths," he began. "But all things can be worked out. Especially between you and I. Our love is strong enough to battle anything. Nothing that has happened should dissuade you from doing what your heart aches to do."

"I know," Summer Hope said, nodding. "That is why I wanted to talk with you. I am so sorry if I behaved as though I did not love you enough. I was just so torn apart by sadness. It made me feel so helpless, unable to reveal things to my people that they would find hard to accept or understand."

"But now you have made it past that?" Sun Hawk asked, his voice tight. "You believe you can now tell them about us, and about our marriage? You are ready to tell them about the possibility of you carrying a child?"

"I must tell them these things, or never achieve the happiness you offer me," Summer Hope said, searching his eyes. "Will you help me? Will you be at my side when I tell them? Will you bring your people into council with mine so that everyone will know at the same moment what is going to change?"

"I will do everything possible to make the transition easier for you," Sun Hawk said. He reached for her, glad when she came into his arms. She settled into his lap, her legs straddling him.

He smoothed locks of her hair back from her face as he looked into her eyes. "My woman, let us bring your people here to my village for the first, full council between our two bands of Ojibwa. It will be the beginning of our people's lives as one."

"We can?" Summer Hope gasped, in awe of Sun Hawk's suggestion. "My people can come and meet in council with yours at your village?"

"Why do you seem so surprised?" Sun Hawk asked. "Surely you knew that when I proposed marriage to you, that I would include your people in my plans . . . that they would be welcome in my village."

"Only now, though, have you actually said as much," Summer Hope replied. "*Mee-gway-chee-wahn-dum*, thank you, thank you," Summer Hope said, flinging her arms around his neck.

Then she leaned away from him, her eyes wavering. "But there are still some things that concern me," she said. "What if our people do not agree to this plan? Will they not feel as though I am abandoning them if I give up my role of chief? There are no more Black Bears or Eagle Wings among my warriors whom I would gladly advise my people to appoint chief. Although all of my warriors are special in their own way, I have not studied them enough to know who has the most qualities of a powerful leader.''

She lowered her eyes. ''And if there is no one who they see as acceptable as next in line after me, how can I give up my title, with no one ready to take my place?''

Sun Hawk placed a finger to her chin and lifted it so that their eyes met. ''My beautiful, thoughtful, caring *ee-quay*, woman,'' he said. ''I have an answer for you that should remove all guilt from your *gee-day*, heart.''

''Tell me what it is,'' Summer Hope said anxiously. ''Please tell me. I want to do what is best for my people. I want them to feel as protected, as revered, as they have under my leadership.''

She swallowed hard and lowered her eyes again. ''How can I say that?'' she said sadly. ''They have lost several warriors under my leadership. Surely they no longer feel protected. Surely they no longer revere me, their chief. Perhaps they feel they were wrong to trust a woman to such a job. If so—''

''Stop battling with yourself like that,'' Sun Hawk said, framing her face between his hands. ''Of course you would feel as though you have let your people down. But you are not being fair to yourself. What happened would have happened under a man's leadership, as well. There was no way to stop the evil deeds of those bush rangers. You had sentries posted. Was there anything else you could have done? No. You did all that you could to protect your warriors."

"I truly did," Summer Hope said, swallowing hard.

"Then please stop feeling guilty."

"But still, when I tell my people that I no longer can be their chief, I am afraid they will say that I have betrayed them. This, and only this, is why I have hesitated making final plans of marriage with you."

"Then you do not have to fret any longer about such things," Sun Hawk said, Summer Hope's eyes widening as she heard his determination. "You do not have to abandon anyone. I have thought long and hard about this. Your people and mine can come together as one and live in one village under one chief. I can be that chief. I would willingly double my load as chief, if that would assure peace and happiness for all of our people."

"Live in one . . . village?" Summer Hope said, taking in the full meaning of his suggestion. "You will be the chief to both bands of Ojibwa?"

"I would proudly invite your people to my village to live," Sun Hawk said. "I would proudly be chief. There are many reasons why this plan would be acceptable to both bands. Let us call a council soon and reveal our plan. Once faced with a decision, I truly believe they will vote favorably for it. They will be made to realize the strength of two bands working together in times of trouble. Together, we will be doubly strong. We will be able to stand up against all white intruders with more power. And my village is more secluded than yours, and therefore safer."

"It sounds wonderful to me," Summer Hope said, suddenly excited. Her eyes lit up. "I shall return home soon. I shall stand before my people and encourage them to come with me to your village for a council between the Enchanted Lake and the Northern Lights bands. I will not tell them why until we are all together in your council house. Only then will I reveal to them my feelings, and the fact that I am all but certain that I am carrying your child."

"How long will your people need before they can be ready for this special council?" Sun Hawk asked softly.

"I will encourage a shorter mourning period. I do not want to wait long, since there is a baby to consider," Summer Hope said, sighing. "I do not want to be showing before we speak our vows."

She hung her head, then slowly looked up at him again. "I am trying hard not to feel like a loose woman, since we made love before being married," she said, her voice breaking. "I hope that in my people's eyes I do not see a quiet accusation."

"You are too revered and loved by your people for them to feel anything but happiness over the news," Sun Hawk reassured. "You are anything but a loose woman and everyone who knows you understands that."

"I have tried to be what my people wished me to be," Summer Hope said.

"It is time now for you to be as you wish to be, and do as you wish to do," Sun Hawk said, drawing her into his arms, hugging her. "You have given your all to your people. Now let them give theirs to you."

"By giving me up as their chief?"

"*Ay-uh*, by giving you up as their chief. You still will be a part of their lives and they soon will have a child in your image to glory over."

"I do hope that I am with child," Summer Hope said, placing a hand on her abdomen. She smiled at Sun Hawk. "Would not it be a miracle? That out of all the recent tragedy there comes something so beautiful?"

"The Great Spirit works in strange ways," Sun Hawk said, slowly sliding the corners of the blanket down from her shoulders.

"What are you doing?" Summer Hope said, smiling as her eyes gleamed.

"I am going to make you forget all sadnesses for at least a little while," he said huskily, now tossing the blanket completely away from her.

His hands went to the fringed hem of her dress and slowly began sliding it up her legs, her thighs. Her bare skin glowed in the fire's light. "It has been too long," she whispered, twining her arms around his neck, bringing his mouth to hers.

She flicked her tongue across his lips, then darted it inside his mouth when he opened it for her.

Their tongues danced together as they kissed. She leaned away from him and finished undressing herself as she watched him peel off each piece of his own clothing.

He reached for her and set her down on his lap, their warmth fusing as she eased herself down onto his sex. The way he filled her so magnificently with his thick, hot shaft, made her heart leap with rapture.

He thrust up into her, his hands on her breasts, his fingers stroking her hard, brown nipples. She held her head back and sighed with pleasure.

He lifted her away from him and gently placed her beneath him. As he kissed her deeply and hotly, he again moved inside her.

Tremors of ecstasy cascaded down her back as his hands stroked her legs. Still moving rhythmically within her, he touched her swollen center in light caresses, awakening even more ecstasy in her.

"My *ee-quay*, my woman," Sun Hawk whispered against her lips, then slid his mouth down the column of her throat to cover a nipple.

His lips sucked.

His fingers caressed.

His body moved rhythmically.

And then he kissed her again, his mouth eager

and urgent, his strokes within her coming faster, his thrusts driving deeper.

She was overwhelmed as she wrapped her legs around his waist and arched toward him. She twined her arms around his neck and clung to him.

Sun Hawk could feel the pleasure mounting inside him.

His breath caught in his throat when she reached down between them, and as he withdrew a fraction from inside her, she ran her hand up and down his throbbing sex, bringing him even closer to that point of no return.

Wanting to cling longer to the bliss of the moment, Sun Hawk pulled away and leaned onto his knees. He bent over her, then dipped low and tasted the sweetness as his tongue swept over her.

"Sun Hawk," Summer Hope moaned as she closed her eyes and allowed herself to enjoy this way of making love.

As he continued caressing her with his tongue, and then his fingers, and then his tongue again, she knew that she was too near to the ultimate rapture for him to continue.

"I want you inside me," she whispered. His eyes were dark with passion as he drew away from her and gazed intensely into her eyes.

He entered her again, and in two strokes their bodies exploded with pleasure.

He held her tightly as his body shook into hers. She clung to him and vibrated against him.

When they eased apart, he rolled away to stretch out on his back on the plush pelts.

His eyes closed with renewed pleasure when Summer Hope reached down and moved her hand on his sex. "I want you again and again," she whispered. "Do you want me as much?"

His eyes opened drunkenly as he smiled up at her. He pulled her atop him and showed her just how much he did want her, as with one movement he was inside her again, his thrusts wild and deep.

She leaned down and kissed him, her lips quivering against his as her head began spinning again, the passion filling her, making her delirious with sensations.

As desire raged and washed over Sun Hawk, he wrapped his arms around Summer Hope, cherishing these moments, when nothing but their love for one another took precedence.

44

To serve with love,
And shed your blood,
Approved may be above,
And here below
'Tis dangerous to be good.
—LORD OXFORD

As though a magic wand had been waved over Sun Hawk's village, the snow had completely vanished into Mother Earth. The slight breeze carried a warmth with it. The sun was high and bright as it cast its golden glow on the Enchanted Lake band's large council house.

Facing both bands of Ojibwa, Sun Hawk sat beside Summer Hope on a bench upon which had been placed soft, thick pelts for their comfort.

Circled around them, the men, women, and children sat on their own pelts and blankets on the floor.

Sitting among them was a man dressed far differently than they—Father Herschel Davidson still wore his black robe, although he was now retired from the ministry. He made his home in a brand-new log cabin which sat beneath cottonwood trees beside Enchanted Lake, his son's wigwam close by.

Today, at both ends of the council house, fires burned low in separate fire pits, the smoke rising up into two smoke holes above them.

Food warmed in pots hanging over the fires, or sent out tantalizing aromas as it baked in the hot coals at the edges of the fire pits.

More food that already had been prepared by the women in each household of Sun Hawk's village sat temptingly on huge wooden platters beside the fire, as did many jugs of various delicious drinks waiting to be poured.

The mourning period finally over for the Northern Lights band of Ojibwa, the council had been called. Summer Hope would announce that she had decided to give up her chieftainship for the role of wife.

Summer Hope glanced over at Sun Hawk as they waited for it to be quiet in the lodge so that she could stand and speak. She had changed her mind about telling them about the possibility of a child. She would never forget how Sun Hawk had thought that she might be marrying him only because of that.

She didn't want her people, or his, jumping to the wrong conclusion, thinking that her love for Sun Hawk was not enough to make her give up her role as chief.

When she gave them the news, Summer Hope wanted everyone to know that she had been honored to be chief to a proud people, but now her love for this man was stronger than her desire to continue being their leader.

The news of the child would come later. It would give them another reason to come together in wondrous celebration.

Their chief, Sun Hawk, would soon be a proud father of a child who could be a powerful chief one day.

One thing was certain. If their first child was a daughter, Summer Hope would not encourage her to work toward chieftainship.

She wanted her daughters to be free to love without guilt. She wanted them to look forward to having their own children.

"It is time," Sun Hawk whispered as he reached over and took Summer Hope's hand. He squeezed it reassuringly. "Everyone has arrived. They have taken their seats. Their eyes and ears are eager to know the true importance of this council, that it is not only to bring two peoples together to become acquainted."

"Yes, it is something far more than that," Summer Hope whispered back, her heart thumping wildly inside her chest. The moment had arrived when her people could turn against her.

Or they could accept that she was a woman with womanly desires and needs.

Then there was something else they would be forced to accept, or refuse. Sun Hawk as their chief, a chief of both bands of Ojibwa, which would bring them together as one in all of their future endeavors.

She had tried not to think about the possibility

of her people turning their back on the idea . . . on Sun Hawk!

If that happened, she would have a serious choice to make.

Could she totally abandon her people by coming to live without them at Sun Hawk's village?

But then again, how could she ever consider not being Sun Hawk's wife, the mother of his children?

If she was forced to make a choice, she knew what it must be. Should she have to say goodbye to her people, she knew that it would be forever, for she would be too hurt by their rejection ever to walk or sit with them again.

She swallowed hard, knowing that if she continued sitting there, her thoughts would become more troubled by the minute. She forced herself to stand before the people whose eyes were glued to her.

"I first want to thank all of you from the Enchanted Lake Ojibwa for inviting me and my people into council with you," she said, her eyes moving slowly over everyone around her.

In her snow-white doeskin dress with its lovely beaded designs, and with her hair loose and flowing sleekly down her back, Summer Hope squared her shoulders and lifted her chin, her eyes proud.

She could hear Sun Hawk's steady breathing beside her, his presence giving her more confidence as she continued with the speech that could change her people's lives.

"Enchanted Lake Ojibwa, I know how you have always protected the location of your village," she said. "That you would open up your hearts to my people touches me deeply. You have our word that we, too, will keep silent about your village."

She looked past the people and through the open double doors and could see the shine of Enchanted Lake a short distance away.

Her breath was momentarily stolen when she saw an eagle sweep down and sit on a limb of a cottonwood tree, and then another and another, until there were many.

A sweetness was in the air, coming from the autumn flowers that had not been killed by the recent snow. Even the trees still had many colorful leaves clinging to them.

It was a paradise, a wonderful place to raise children.

When her people had arrived there, they had marveled over the loveliness of the area and surely would, in time, want to live there.

"It is good to see the people of both the Enchanted Lake and Northern Lights Ojibwa come together beneath one roof, the council having been much anticipated by both bands," she said. Knowing that she was coming to the part of her speech that worried her the most, she clasped her hands together behind her.

"There is always much to bring up in council," Summer Hope said. "But since this is the first time the two bands have come together like this, there is only one important item I wish to bring before you."

She stopped and took a deep breath. She glanced down at Sun Hawk, his smile giving her the courage to continue.

When she turned and looked at the people again, she saw that they were becoming restless. They could sense her apprehension.

And she knew that wasn't good.

She wanted to look strong in their eyes, even though she felt queasy.

Usually her sickness came early in the mornings. But since she was so nervous, it did not seem to matter that it was mid-afternoon.

The child that she was carrying was causing her to feel sick to her stomach again.

She had to will herself not to throw up, not to excuse herself so that she could do it in private.

That would certainly raise many an eyebrow. And she wanted no one to know about the child just yet.

After she and Sun Hawk had spoken their vows, she would feel better about sharing the news of her pregnancy with everyone.

There was a time and a place for everything.

Today there was just one thing that should be said.

"Today, while we hold this council, there is much that I need to say," Summer Hope began again, the queasiness having passed.

She singled out her people as she continued talking. "My people, when I became your chief, after my parents died in the snowslide, it was with much humility and pride that I accepted the honor you bestowed upon me," she said. "And I have carried that pride inside my heart ever since."

Her pulse was racing so quickly, she felt dizzy, yet she forced herself to stand steady, and willed her voice to remain calm.

"But, my people, as you know, there comes a time in one's life when things change," Summer Hope said. "Even in a chief's life comes change, especially if that chief is a woman."

She gave Sun Hawk a quick glance again. His smile of reassurance spurred her onward.

She smiled at her people, then told them the depths of her feelings for Sun Hawk, and the depths of her feelings for them as a people.

She found a way to explain why she wanted to give up her title of chief so that they did not stare disbelievingly at her, but looked at her with understanding and trust.

"As you know, a chief must be chosen before I give up the title completely," she added carefully. "For a year or so I have thought about the need to give up my title to someone else, for I believed with the challenges of whites moving into this area and becoming more of a threat, a man might look stronger in the white's eyes and so might better serve you as chief."

She was aware of the silence that now lay over the crowd. No one even seemed to be breathing as they awaited her next word.

She had reached the moment that she feared the most. If they did not accept Sun Hawk as their chief, and if they could not agree to come together as one entity, she would have no choice but to tell them what she must do.

She knew they would not want to hear that, and prayed that they would see how both bands would be better off if they worked together.

She knew how the white man's treaties were so easily broken.

The treaties that protected this forest land would be broken one day, and then whites would come unchecked to destroy everything in their path, especially the lives of the people whose skin differed from theirs.

"My people, I had seen Black Bear as a good chief, and when he died, I saw Eagle Wing as my next choice," she said, her voice breaking. "They were both taken from us. But there is one among us today who is strong, noble, intelligent, and caring, whom I see as the best choice of all."

Still everyone was quiet.

All eyes were on Summer Hope. She could not tell how they felt. They were too good at guarding their feelings.

She smiled down at Sun Hawk and reached a hand out for him. When he took it and stood up next to her, she could tell that her people already knew what her next words would be.

"My people, I am stepping down from my role as chief to become wife to Chief Sun Hawk," she said softly. She sensed a variety of reactions. In the eyes of the elders she saw anger. In the eyes of the younger warriors and the women, she saw a quiet understanding.

In the eyes of the children she saw some surprise, and much excitement.

In the faces of Sun Hawk's people, she saw happiness and pride for their good leader.

"My people, I see Sun Hawk as chief to both bands," she said, pride in her voice. "He has invited us to live among his people beside Enchanted Lake. This place is a safe haven not only for the Ojibwa, but for all sorts of forest animals and birds, including eagles. Living here would bring two peoples together as one heartbeat, and give strength and safety to us all."

She continued with her explanation, trying not to sound as though she was pleading with them. Sun Hawk followed with his own speech and gave reasons why this would work to benefit them both.

And when it was all said and done, not even those elders who had looked uneasy could deny how right this plan was for their two bands of Ojibwa.

After the verbal vote was taken, and each person had a chance to speak his mind, Sun Hawk became chief to two bands, not one.

Proud, touched, and his heart filled with warmth, Sun Hawk slid an arm around Summer Hope's waist. He spoke of his gratitude and love for the Ojibwa, and his deep, endearing love for Summer Hope.

When he said they would be wed on the morrow, the council house erupted in applause and cheers.

Tears came to Summer Hope's eyes, for she had never envisioned this moment to be so grand.

She and Sun Hawk exchanged joyous smiles, then accepted handshakes and hugs as their people filed past and congratulated them.

When Sun Hawk's father came to him, they embraced for a long time, and for a brief moment Sun Hawk remembered when he had thought that he had seen his father for the last time, dead.

The Great Spirit would not have it that way, he thought thankfully to himself. Just as he would not allow these two bands to be torn apart by hard feelings.

It was now the best of times for Sun Hawk.

He smiled at his wife-to-be.

It was the best of times for Summer Hope, too, and the Ojibwa, as a whole!

Afterward, there was dancing, singing, and feasting.

Summer Hope was on her knees facing Sun Hawk. She giggled as she slid a slice of apple between the lips of her soon-to-be husband. "I did not envision such a moment as this," she said. "I truly did not believe my people would so readily accept my proposal."

"Have you not always led them wisely as chief?" Sun Hawk asked, chewing the apple, its juices sweet as they rolled down the back of his throat.

"I hope they think so," Summer Hope said, glancing over her shoulder to watch her people joined with Sun Hawk's, enjoying the togetherness.

"Do you not know that even though you are not acting chief, your leadership will still affect their lives?" Sun Hawk said, drawing her eyes quickly back to him.

"How can that be?" she asked, raising an eyebrow.

"Because I will not only be their chief, but their retired chief's husband, and does not a woman truly affect a man's decisions more often than not?" he said, his eyes twinkling.

"Are you saying that you will listen to my suggestions and be persuaded by them?" Summer Hope asked.

"Well, only if I . . ." he began, then laughed hoarsely when she hit him playfully on his arm with a fist.

"Only if," she said, laughing. She flung herself into his arms and hugged him. "I promise to be a good wife, in all respects."

Suddenly she was aware of how quiet he had become.

He placed his hands on her shoulders and held her slightly away from him, his eyes no longer filled with laughter. She gave him a questioning stare.

"There is something that I am puzzled about," he said slowly.

"What?" she asked. "Did I say something in council that troubles you?"

"Not exactly," he said, searching her eyes.

"What are you referring to?" she asked, reaching a hand to touch his cheek.

"You said nothing about our child," he said, taking her hand from his face, kissing her palm. "Why did you not share that happy news with our people?"

"Surely you know why," Summer Hope said softly.

"No, not really," Sun Hawk said.

"I did not want our people to think that the only reason I was marrying you was for the child," she murmured. "And then there is one other thing, one other person, I considered."

"Who? What?" Sun Hawk asked, uncertain.

"Your father," Summer Hope replied, looking over at Father Davidson, who was sitting with several children around him, attentively listening as he told them stories.

"Oh, yes, my father," Sun Hawk said, now looking at his father himself.

"The wedding is tomorrow, and I will not be showing for a while yet. Would not it be better if your father, being so religious, thought the child was conceived after our vows, not before?" she asked.

"I cannot deceive my father in such a way,"

Sun Hawk said. "I will talk to him. He will understand."

"He will understand better if you tell him while he is holding his grandchild in his arms, marveling over his legacy, do you not think?"

Sun Hawk looked into her eyes. He laughed softly. "Yes, I see what you mean," he said. "While holding his grandchild, so proud of being a grandfather, at that time it will not matter when the child was conceived. Yes, that is best, my woman. You are right to want to hold back possible hurt, when later the hurt will be outweighed by pride."

He drew her into his arms and held her, but could not help but slide a hand down to her stomach. "A *ah-bee-no-gee*," he said throatily. "Our child, Summer Hope."

"And there will be more and more," she promised.

Ignoring how many people might see them, Sun Hawk gave Summer Hope a slow, long, deep kiss, their tears of joy tasting like sweet pollen on their lips.

45

Let me feel that warm breath here and there,
To spread rapture—

—JOHN KEATS

Several autumns had come and gone.

The combined band of Ojibwa was content and remained undisturbed at the Enchanted Lake village.

Fort William stood unoccupied on the shores of Lake Superior.

Sun Hawk's father had died peacefully in his sleep one moon ago. He was buried high on a hill overlooking Enchanted Lake. The bell, inscribed with his family's names, hung on a sturdy post over the grave.

Sometimes the wind would make the bell sway, its peals reaching the Ojibwa's village like a soft angel's song.

Sun Hawk and Summer Hope were proud parents of two children, an eight-year-old son, Brave Bear, and an eleven-month-old daughter named Plum Leaf.

Much meat was stored for the long winter months ahead. Wild rice had been harvested.

Pelts and blankets had been taken from their storage bags.

Brave Bear had killed his first game on a recent hunt with his father. Today had been the "Feast for the First Kill" for Brave Bear and others his same age who also had been successful at the hunt.

Everyone had come together in the council house. Prior to the actual celebration, Sun Hawk had given a prayer of thanks and had asked the Great Spirit for continued help for his child and the other children on the hunt.

The feast had been an unpretentious one. Everyone present had eaten a small bite of the boys' kills.

The celebration now over, everyone was in their own private lodges. Summer Hope, Sun Hawk, and their two children sat beside the fire in their lodge.

"*Gee-dar-niss*, daughter, come to me," Summer Hope said as she held her arms out for Plum Leaf, who had only recently learned how to walk. She teetered and wobbled as she rose to her feet.

Barefoot, Plum Leaf tested first one step, and then another. In her tiny buckskin dress, with ribbons tied in her dark hair, she reached out her arms and hurried on to Summer Hope.

"She did it again," Sun Hawk said, marveling over his baby daughter, who was the exact image of her mother except for her eye color. Their facial features were almost the same. A tiny nose, round face, and perfectly shaped lips showed that they were mother and daughter.

Brave Bear sat beside his father with his newly carved bow resting on his lap. He smiled proudly at his baby sister, whom he had coaxed to take her first step.

When she had come to him with outstretched arms, smiling broadly, it had been an even prouder moment for him than downing his first deer on the hunt.

"It is time now for your first moccasins," Summer Hope said as she drew her daughter onto her lap. Up until now, while the weather had been warm, moccasins had not been needed.

But with winter so close at hand, a child's tender feet must be protected.

"Mahaasins?" Plum Leaf managed to say, mimicking her mother.

"Yes, and are they not pretty?" Sun Hawk said, admiring his wife's handiwork as she brought the moccasins from a bag for all to see. He was very proud of his wife, who, until their marriage, had not sewn, or cooked, or known how. As a chief, it had all been done for her. She had learned everything very quickly with White Fawn as her teacher.

Sun Hawk looked forward to each evening's meal, for his wife was constantly trying something new, and for the most part, delicious. No food was left in the pot after a meal was finished under this family's roof.

"Plum Leaf, I want you to look closely at your new moccasins," Summer Hope said, holding them out for her to see. "A hole about the size of a blueberry has been cut into the sole of each shoe. If I neglected making the holes, it might cause you to grow up to be lazy."

She smiled at the myth. Told long ago by some mother who had made her child a new pair of moccasins, the story went that if there were no such holes, the child would be so lazy that she would not even wear out the soles of her shoes.

As Summer Hope placed the first moccasin on her daughter's tiny foot, Sun Hawk looked toward the window and listened. The wind carried the sound of the pealing of his father's bell. He smiled as he thought of the names that had been added to those already engraved on the bell. His wife's name, as well as those of his children.

And as each child was born, so would his or her name be placed there. It was a way for his father to be close to them all. Although he was not there in person, he was in spirit.

"See how beautiful she looks in her new moccasins?" Summer Hope said.

He watched his daughter prancing around. Never had he seen such a sight. She was an Ojibwa princess.

He moved over to sit closer to his wife. "*Gee-mee-nwayn-dum*, happy?" he asked, drawing her eyes to his.

"More than I would have ever imagined," she said, her voice breaking with emotion.

Sun Hawk slid his arm around her waist and drew her close. They both watched their son pick up his sister and swing her around playfully, laughter filling their hearts with a joyful pride.

Summer Hope leaned up and kissed his cheek so tenderly that his heart melted with the pure ecstasy of it.

She snuggled back against him, her own contentment more than complete.

Dear Reader:

I hope you enjoyed reading *Sun Hawk*. My next book in my Signet Indian Series that I am writing exclusively for NAL is *Winter Raven*, about the Gros Ventres Indians in Montana. *Winter Raven* is filled with much excitement, emotion, romance, and adventure.

For those of you who are collecting all of the books in my Signet Indian Series and want to hear more about the series and my entire backlist of Indian books, you can send for my latest newsletter, bookmark, and autographed photograph. For a prompt reply, please send a stamped, self-addressed, legal-sized envelope to:

CASSIE EDWARDS
6709 North Country Club Road
Mattoon, IL 61938

I respond, personally, to all letters received. Or visit my website at www.cassieedwards.com for more information.

Thank you for your support of my Indian series. I love researching and writing about our country's beloved Native Americans—our country's first people!

Always,

Cassie Edwards